WIDE HIPS, NARROW SHOULDERS

WIDE HIPS, NARROW SHOULDERS

▼

A Bike Touring Adventure Story

Monte M. Lowrance

Writers Club Press

San Jose New York Lincoln Shanghai

Wide Hips, Narrow Shoulders
A Bike Touring Adventure Story

All Rights Reserved © 2001 by Monte M. Lowrance

Writers Club Press
an imprint of iUniverse.com, Inc.

For information address:
iUniverse.com, Inc.
5220 S 16th, Ste. 200
Lincoln, NE 68512
www.iuniverse.com

ISBN: 0-595-18286-0

Printed in the United States of America

This book is dedicated to my
Loving Parents
Jean and George

Contents

PREFACE

Wide Hips, Narrow Shoulders has several different meanings. First of all, it refers to my body. I've always had wide hips (good for rebounding in basketball) and narrow shoulders (I could never do a rollover on the parallel bars in gym class). Second, the term refers to the body of a long-distance bike rider. The more time you put in on a touring bike, the more your body begins to adapt to the position of riding; your chest begins to atrophy, while your legs accumulate mass. And finally, and most importantly, it refers to the shape of my bike fully loaded (wide hips) and the condition of most of the roads I was riding on (narrow shoulders).

When Lance Armstrong won the Tour de France in 1999 it brought tears to my eyes. Even though I had never met him, I felt a tremendous closeness to the man. We had some things in common that made me feel that bond—we each had cancer, a certain amount of perseverance, an ability to climb in the mountains, and a Trek bicycle. Seeing Lance win the Tour de France a year after I had completed my journey made me realize that we all have the ability to accomplish whatever we set out to do, if we just stick with it. It doesn't usually come easy, but if you set a goal and then accomplish it, there is no better feeling.

So many people along my journey told me they "could never do what I was doing." If the truth were known, almost all of them could. There are only two things required to be able to accomplish a bike adventure like mine; you have to keep breathing and you must keep pedaling—everything else is just mind over matter.

I had asked a few of my close friends if they would consider writing an introduction for this book. Most of them respectfully declined, however, a few brave souls stepped up to the plate and produced some interesting literary works. It was then I realized that I couldn't have readers who didn't even know me starting off thinking I was some kind of saint or super hero. My friend's perceptions of me were way too generous.

My mother says I'm a complex person. Maybe that's true, but when you cut through the complexity I'm a simple man who believes in the love of family and friends—without which, I never would have considered such a journey, let alone finish it.

Enjoy the ride and keep pedaling.

LoRent

ACKNOWLEDGMENTS

From reading the book, you can tell there are more people than I can acknowledge responsible for helping me complete The Journey, but I do have to mention a few of them.

First and foremost, there is my family. My parents, Jean and George, for their never-ending love, blind support and constant encouragement.

Thanks to my sister, Vicky, for the same and for handling my administrative affairs and so much more. I will never be able to repay her. And thanks for taking care of my cat, Adrienne.

Thanks to my sister, Renee, and her family for the above. Janae and Renee were putting together a scrapbook with all of the postcards I sent.

Thanks to my ex-wife, Janet Anne, for believing in me and helping me to believe in myself.

I'd like to thank everyone who gave me energy, encouragement and love along the way. Even though I was alone, I never could have done this by myself.

Last but not least, I have to thank my editors, and you should thank them as well. To read this book in its original draft would be either shocking or funny. I know none of them thought it was funny. Thank you from the bottom of my heart to Janet Anne, Vicky, Helen Hudson and Laura

Wegscheid. And thank you Charles C.A. Taylor for helping me through my technical barriers.

INTRODUCTION

What would make a person, normal by most accounts, give up a relatively comfortable lifestyle to ride a bicycle around America? The answer isn't simple, but then it seldom is. On second thought, the answer is simple— I simplified my life.

I'm a baby boomer who, by society's standards, was successful. I have three college degrees, made good money, had a beautiful wife, traveled all around the world, and owned a lot of "stuff." But I wasn't happy! I knew there was more to life than accumulating, owning and trashing things, but I didn't know what that "more" was.

A series of events changed my life. My wife and I divorced on Valentines Day, 1994. I was downsized from my position as Controller/Director of Environmental Affairs for a ski resort on May 2, 1997. And I purchased 40 acres in Fairplay, Colo., on June 1, 1997, to be closer to Nature—I lived in a one room dwelling with no electricity and no running water.

The summer before I was downsized, three other guys and I rode our bicycles across Colorado. It was just a four-day, 400-mile jaunt and I had been on other bicycle tours, but something about that trip moved me. I had just read the book "Ishmael" by Daniel Quinn, so I had a new perspective on the meaning of life. I guess my new perspective combined with the outdoor experience allowed me to wake up.

After that trip, I would sit in my office watching birds and field mice outside my window and I knew I wasn't supposed to be sitting there. I'd go home at lunch or after work to ride my bike around the lake and even though it would help clear my head, it wasn't enough.

My most peaceful moments of each day were when I was on the bicycle. So why wasn't I spending more time on it? Well, because I had to work to maintain all of my "stuff." Then it came to me, this was all a big lie. The American Dream; go to school, get a job, get married, have kids, and accumulate. "He who has the most toys when he dies wins!"

He who has the most toys when he dies is an idiot! It just means "he" couldn't find what made him happy. I knew what made me happy; it was experiencing the wonders of Nature and riding my bike. So how could I do more of each?

I needed to simplify my life more. The first thing I did was sell my house and pay off all my bills—no debt. So my house was sold, I didn't have a job, and didn't owe anyone a dime. I was almost ready to take a bike trip. I gave my Blazer to my nephew for his 16th birthday, my computer to a local school, and my TV to my father. I spent the next six months tying up loose ends, saying goodbye to friends and family, and riding the bike. I rode 2,000 miles; riding 30, 50, 70 miles a day, five days a week. I was serious about the trip.

There were a couple of different ways to approach the odyssey. I could write to companies asking for sponsorship, I could ride for a cause, or I could finance the trip myself. I wasn't rich, but I had some money saved up for a bike trip in Ireland that I could use for this journey. I decided my freedom was more important than corporate support. I named the bike *B.O.P.*—Bike Of Peace and decided to call my journey "A *B.O.P.* Around America."

I was in shape physically, mentally, spiritually and financially. It was time to start The Journey.

CHAPTER 1

▼

SAYING GOODBYE

"What the HELL was I thinking?" Thus began my journey of biking around America on Thursday, January 15, 1998, at 4 a.m.—a journey that would take me 11,800 miles, over 10 months, through all 48 contiguous states and the District of Columbia.

I hitched a ride in my parent's pickup to Texas. They pull a fifth-wheel trailer down south every winter. Not necessarily to escape the mild winters of Pueblo, Colo., but more to socialize with the "army" of their generation that makes that annual migration. I, on the other hand, went for the heat. It made more sense to be starting in the 80-degree temperature of south Texas, than the 40 degrees in Colorado (In fact, it was 88 degrees the day I left). My mother came up with the idea that I catch a ride down south with them and wanted to know if that would be "cheating." I told her it was my journey and it didn't matter where I started.

So, we were down in the southern tip of Texas on the Rio Grande in the little town of Zapata. It seemed as if the town's sole existence was to cater to the needs of this older generation. This made me think, "What did the people of Zapata do before this new migrating species arrived?" Apparently, farming and the oil business were the two greatest contributors to the economy in the area; with some occasional human imports from across the Rio Grande, which appeared to be still going on.

Anyway, I was happy to be there. It was 80 degrees in January and I was riding my bike every day, though usually only 20 to 30 miles a day. I had been training for six months and this was just the final tune up before The Journey began. I had set aside two to 20 years in which to complete the trip, so I was confident I'd be able to do it if I took my time. But on the day I was scheduled to leave, panic set in. Wide awake at 4 a.m., my eyes the size of silver dollars, I was lying on the couch in my parents' trailer, thinking, "This is CRAZY! NOBODY rides his or her bicycle through ALL 50 states! How can I get out of this?" I was afraid.

Understand I am not the kind of person to do something like this. I was an accountant for many years. And even though I had competed in sports my whole life and had enjoyed outdoor recreation, I also liked the creature comforts of home—very much. But that was all about to change.

My mother decided it was too dangerous for me to be biking through the town of Laredo with all the border traffic, so she, my father and their traveling buddies, the Kettermans, gave me a ride to the northern outskirts of town. Jokingly, I asked my mother what she was going to do when I got to El Paso. I think she actually considered, for a moment, the 10-hour drive up there to get me around the city. The ride from Zapata to Laredo took about an hour and I don't think I said two words the whole way—and if I did, I don't know what they were. As I started loading the bicycle I realized I was shaking and tried to keep moving so no one would notice. I was REALLY afraid.

It was a beautiful sunny day and the Kettermans had brought me a package of cashews (my favorite food), a gesture that would grow over the life of The Journey. I thanked them for their kindness and prayers. I shook my father's hand, told him that I loved him and then hugged my mother. We both started crying. I told her I loved her and asked her to remember,

"Life is just a state of mind."—something we learned from watching the Peter Sellers' movie, "*Being There.*" I threw them all the peace sign and took off—The Journey had begun!

That first mile was one of the most difficult of the entire trip. Not just because there were 110 pounds of "stuff" loaded on a 14-year-old touring bike but because there were so many tears in my eyes I couldn't see where I was going.

The bike, a Trek 420, was made exactly for this, but I'm pretty sure the load exceeded the manufacturer's suggested packing weight. The frame was the largest available for a touring bike (26 ½"), to accommodate a large person (I'm 6'4" and 205 lbs.), so it was a bit unstable to begin with. But when the gear I thought was necessary for a two-year bicycle trip was added, it was out of control. There was an unbelievable wobble, a torque so bad I could only imagine when the frame would snap in two. Fortunately, I was on a lonely highway with wide shoulders, which allowed me the time and space to figure out how to maneuver my new vehicle. Understand this was only the second time I had ridden the bike fully loaded. All of those miles of training didn't mean a thing. This was something totally new. What the hell had I been thinking? I had read several books about bike touring and in fact had criticized the authors for not training properly before they left. They "rode" themselves into shape. Now, here I was in an unfamiliar situation, realizing I was no better prepared for all my pedaling. I was in shape, but I was not in control—or if I was, it was shaky at best. To add to my unsteadiness, there was a head wind. Soon after that, there were hills and it all started adding up to be possibly more than I could handle.

Sometime during lunch, I discovered I had been reading the map wrong. My first night's destination was Carrizo Springs, 43 miles from Laredo—in my dreams. It was 43 miles from Highway 44. I missed reading the 20 miles from Laredo to Highway 44. Not only was I trying to handle more than I might be capable of, now I had an additional 20 miles to pedal. The three things I had going for me were a good road (wide shoulders, no traffic), the shining sun, and my good physical shape. When I arrived in Carrizo Springs I saw a sign that read "American Motel $21.00." I decided then and there not to camp out. I had been through more than expected for my first day of bike touring, so I was paying for a motel room—even if it did make me feel a bit guilty.

At the motel there was a young Mexican kid working in the office with the door locked—something I would encounter frequently during The Journey, staying in "budget" accommodations. I had never encountered a locked motel door before, but then I wasn't used to being in this part of town. He unlocked the door and stared at my bicycle and me. I was wearing my biking apparel: shorts, jersey, gloves and touring shoes. The bike, as previously mentioned, was loaded with two years' worth of "stuff"— including: a tent, sleeping bag, stove and miscellaneous camping gear. The first thing he wanted to know was if I was in the Olympics. I told him I was trying to cycle through all 50 states. He started checking me in and then got a big smile on his face. He said, "Oooooh, you're trying to set a world record!" I grinned and nodded. I was way too tired to disagree or explain. For all I knew, I WAS setting a world record and even if I wasn't, it was something I had never heard of anyone else doing.

Wow! What a day! Once in the room, I immediately started looking for the cashews. I had some junk food for dinner and then called the Kettermans' answering service to let my folks know I had arrived OK. It was at that moment I fully realized everything I had gone through that day and briefly recognized what lay ahead. I started crying uncontrollably. In fact, I cannot describe on this page how badly the message came out. It turned out to be a very soul cleansing moment for me, but it was a heartbreaking moment for my mother.

CHAPTER 2

▼

WEST TEXAS

The second day was another beautiful sunny day in West Texas. I woke up early, around 6 a.m., feeling surprisingly well. All of my training did pay off. I had some junk food for breakfast (a trend that would later come back to haunt me) and was off for Eagle Pass, Texas, 43 miles away.

The ride was nondescript, as was the town. I saw a couple of guys on bicycles and went over to see if they might know of a place to camp. They were Mormon missionaries and wanted me to accept a book from them. I explained that my bike was already overloaded and I just needed a place to crash. They didn't offer and I realized we both had failed on mission objectives; them to convert a lost soul and me to secure housing. I observed Maslow's Needs Hierarchy at work; even though we talked a bit about religion and life, my only real interest was food, clothing and shelter.

The next day in Del Rio I found a place to camp in a trailer park at the edge of town for $3, basically a small common area surrounded by mobile homes. I had my own restroom with a shower and when I found a snail in the sink, I knew the place hadn't been used much, let alone cleaned—but

I was happy. The weather was great, I felt good, and the bicycle was holding up. Three days under my belt and how many more to go? It was a question I would struggle with numerous times over the first half of The Journey.

When I rode through Del Rio, I noticed a place advertising an all-you-can-eat buffet. I put the tent up, took a shower, and headed back to town. The buffet was everything I could have hoped for; pasta, pizza, Pepsi and pie.

After dinner I called my friend in Denver, Lupe'. He was having a get-together that night with a few of our mutual friends. They had given me a 500-minute calling card (the perfect gift, lightweight and useful) at a going away party, so I thought I'd try it out. I enjoyed talking with everyone, but I hung up with mixed emotions. I was happy to have talked with my friends, but sad not to be there.

Lupe' and I met over 20 years ago in Summit County, Colo. We did a lot of things together; softball, basketball, skiing, etc. But there was more, there was a fierce competition and a loyal camaraderie between us. We stood up in each other's weddings and he was the closest thing I had to a brother. We had done some bike touring together in the past and he said he was hoping to join me somewhere along the trip.

The following day on my way to Langtry, I met my first cross-country bicyclists, a couple from Iowa. They were traveling from California to Florida on a tandem, with another couple riding one bicycle and driving a sag wagon (support vehicle). They were farmers who had crossed America a couple of year's earlier on touring bikes. I expressed my admiration for their strong marriage that enabled them to do this on a tandem. They smiled and said, "It's the only way to go." I envied their companionship, but treasured my freedom. However, it was reassuring and some sort of relief to see other people out touring on bicycles.

Langtry is the home of the Judge Roy Bean Saloon and Museum. I generally avoided tourist attractions because of the traffic, but there was little worry here. Only one place of business was open, a little restaurant, and it was getting ready to close. I ordered dinner and asked if there might be a place to camp. The owner, a second generation Langtry native, told me I could "free camp" behind the Community Center Building. There was no shower, but the price was right. There was a port-a-john in the back, so I was set.

When I arrived in Sanderson, Texas, the following afternoon, there was only one thing on my mind, a shower. Two days of biking and a night of camping, without a shower, had the ability to turn a person into a slob. Even if you're polite, you're just a polite slob. Sanderson is the home of "good folks and funny cactus"—so the welcome sign says as you enter town. So I followed the tourist information signs to the center of town in search of those good folks, only to find a room full of information, but no people. Just as I walked out of the building, a cowboy in a Cadillac pulled up and said, "Yaw'll stay right there and I'll be right back." He went across the street into a shop and returned with a beautiful Mexican woman. He told me he needed some pictures for their summer brochure and asked if I would mind posing with my bike and the woman.

"I don't mind," I said, "but I haven't had a shower for two days."

"That's aw right," he said, "the camera don't know that."

"I was thinking about the pretty lady," I replied.

Aw shucks," he said, "jist stand downwind from er!"

When we finished with the pictures he asked me how he could help me. I told him I was interested in a shower and a place to camp. He said, "Shit howdy, yaw'll can take a shower at my place and camp in the front yard." In the meantime, the lady who ran the RV camp arrived. Unfortunately, there was no tent camping available because they did not have public restrooms. However, she told me I could take a shower in her trailer and set up my tent in the back of the campgrounds for $2. Not wanting to take business away from a local entrepreneur, the cowboy suggested I stay at the campground. Wow, there really were good folks in Sanderson, but I have no idea what that funny cactus was all about.

At breakfast in The Country Café, I asked an ol' timer if he had heard a weather report. He said, "We don't pay much attention to that stuff around here. We just take it as it comes." I thought that was a pretty good philosophy and that I might try to apply it to The Journey.

That day, a vision came to me that the Denver Broncos would win the Super Bowl over the Green Bay Packers the following week. Somehow it just popped into my head while I was riding. I would have numerous visions that would become crystal clear as I continued to eliminate the distractions from my life; work, computers, television, phones, etc.

I made it to Marathon and then to Marfa. I had been on the road a week and some things were starting to fall into place. I knew that everyone's life had a rhythm, whether they recognized it or not. I was starting to recognize the rhythm of my new life. Part of that rhythm was that every day would be a little different. Yeah, I would be riding a bicycle most days, but I would also be meeting new people all the time and staying in different places every night. Some of the more prominent beats of that rhythm wouldn't be recognized until later, down the road. But for now, I was digging it. I didn't answer to anyone. I was free; professionally, socially and personally.

There was also a recurring theme in my dreams every night of being in charge, a true reflection of my independence on The Journey. The only other constant was Oyler, a friend from Frasier, Colo., who was in every dream. Like Lupe', Oyler and I played ball and skied together for 20 years. But why would he be manifesting in my dreams EVERY night? Then it hit me, it wasn't because he was a good softball player or the "King of Crud" on the slopes or even because he was fun to be around, it was because he was a rebel. A hippie from the 1960s, Oyler never let go of those ideals, or the look for that matter. In my recent transformation (accountant to bike rider) I began to re-acquire that look. I also was regaining the ideals I had before joining corporate America. Wow! What a liberating thought. In my dreams, I would be in a situation where either someone was trying to change the way I was thinking or acting or they were threatening me. Oyler showed up every night to let me know I was thinking and acting OK.

Every day I could feel my mind opening up to look at situations in a new light. Not what is right for this political party or that religion or this person, but what is RIGHT! It was then I realized, out on desolate Highway 90 in West Texas, that I was about to change. I now had the time to rethink my entire value system, my life's beliefs, and challenge them to find out what *is* RIGHT! I knew this task wouldn't be easy and it wouldn't happen overnight, but I also knew that it was something I needed to do.

Over the next few days I paid extra attention to the sun, the moon, the birds, in fact, all of Nature. My entire being was feeling different; physically, mentally, emotionally and spiritually. I was 44 years old and in the best shape of my life. My thinking was clearer than ever before. I was sensitive not only to my needs, but others as well. My mind was being flooded with thoughts of Buddha, Christ, Lao-tzu, God, etc. and I could meditate for hours while riding the bike. About that time I decided I could quit The Journey. I had been on the road for over a week. I had experienced everything about bike touring. Continuing to ride would be redundant. What would it prove? I had "discovered" myself. I proved I could ride my bicycle every day, with a load. I was a cross-country bike rider! Isn't it funny how ignorant we are sometimes? I was at the height of my bike touring ignorance at that moment. But, ignorance is bliss. So I kept pedaling and decided I would re-evaluate my plans when I arrived at El Paso in a couple of days.

I stayed at the KOA Campground in Van Horn, Texas. My first shock at how expensive it is to camp in America, it was $16 dollars to sleep on the ground. But it was clean, the people were nice, and they were having a buffet dinner for $3.50—just what I needed. After setting up my camp and showering, I returned to the common area for dinner. I walked in and noticed only one table still open, so I filled my plate and sat down. Soon after, an older couple came in, filled their plates and began looking for a place to sit. Since I had three extra chairs at my table, I motioned for them to join me.

Well, Ruthette was just like my mother. She sat down and immediately began talking like we had known each other forever. Paul, her husband, on the other hand, was quite distant. However, after some time, she and I hit on a topic that drew him into the conversation. Three hours later, we were the only ones left in the room. We had talked about everything; politics, religion, people and traveling. As we were preparing to leave, Paul pointed his finger at me and said, "I want to tell you something young man. I didn't want to sit at this table. I have a real prejudice against men with long hair. But you are a sharp young man. And when you finish your journey you should run for office in your little mountain community in Colorado." I thanked him for the compliment and told him I would think about it. As I lay in my tent that night, I couldn't stop thinking about the couple from Michigan, the conversation, and the parting comments. I recalled that first day, as I was about to embark on The Journey, my mother had questioned my need to look the way I did (long hair and a beard). I told her I didn't know why, it was just part of The Journey. Now I knew! I realized the next time this man from Michigan met a man with long hair, he wouldn't automatically assume he was some dope-smoking worthless bum. I felt good about the evening, and more importantly, I felt good about myself.

It was 28 degrees the next morning at sunrise. While I was breaking camp, I took the time to take a picture of the ice clinging to the outdoor faucet. Cool weather and sunshine is a pleasant combination for a cyclist. Two more days to El Paso...

I stopped for lunch at a little Mexican café in Sierra Blanca. While I was eating, a young couple came in and approached the table. They inquired if that was my bike outside. I said it was and the young man told me how much he liked the way it was set up. I invited them to join me and we sat down together. Danny and Kale had traveled to Texas to protest the proposed burial of nuclear waste in the region. Some group, I don't know whom, provided them with a per diem if they would participate in the protest. They also were musicians and performed at night to help support themselves. They were young, early 20s and had an abundance of energy. We talked mostly about biking and the environment. When I was ready to leave, I shook their hands and thanked them for trying to help save the Earth. As I was shaking Kale's hand, she thanked me for doing the same. I told her I was just riding a bicycle. She held onto my hand, looked me in the eye with the clearest blue eyes I have ever seen, and said, "Oh, you're doing more than just riding a bike!" I had a big ol' smile on my face all afternoon and I couldn't get her eyes or what she said out of my mind. Not long after that I noticed my journey would end up meaning different things to different people.

El Paso! I made it! I'd been on the road ten straight days for six hundred miles. I was so proud of myself. I thought I could do it, but subconsciously I wasn't sure. Now, all I had to do was navigate the city and find the youth hostel downtown.

My friend, Betty had bought me a HI membership—Hostel International—American Youth Hostels. Hostels were started over in Europe about 60 years ago to try and encourage young people to travel and learn. There are approximately 600 hostels in America, but most Americans remain ignorant about them. In fact, most of the people you meet in a hostel are from another country. My ex-wife, Jan, and I first discovered them when we lived in New Zealand and later when we traveled around Europe. I met Betty when I was traveling through India (we both had an audience with His Holiness The Dalai Lama), and we became lifelong friends. I often tell people that Betty is my Guardian Angel, because she is always looking after me. The membership to the hostel was a classic example. Most of the hostels would prove to be a real haven for me; a bed to sleep in, a shower, laundry facilities and a kitchen.

The HI-El Paso Hostel was in an old downtown hotel. Lucky for me it was Saturday, so there was very little traffic to contend with. I arrived at the hostel and Randolf checked me in. He was from New Orleans, an interesting guy and very hospitable toward me. We had good conversations about music, food and the weather.

The unique aspect of staying at a hostel is that you are exposed to a variety of people. It is usually up to you how much you interact with them. For example, while I was downstairs fixing my dinner, a man came over and introduced himself as Richard. Over dinner, I discovered Richard had been living in El Paso with his parents, but recently was kicked out of the house for biking into Mexico illegally. He was 40 years old, no job and no prospects. He had been a heroin addict and used to sell cocaine in Colorado. He also had a drinking problem. By the way, most hostels do NOT allow alcohol on the premises. Anyway, Richard asked me if I would be interested in joining him the next day to watch the Super Bowl at a friend's bar. Number one, I had quit drinking seven months ago, so I really didn't need to be in a bar to watch the game. And number two, Richard wasn't the kind of person I needed to be hanging out with. My decision was being smart, not judgmental. Over the next 10 months I would meet many people and be in different situations where I had to rely on my instincts and intuition, they would serve me well.

Sunday, January 25, 1998, was my first day off the bike in a week and a half. Another beautiful sunny day, so I decided to take a little hike before the Super Bowl. (I found out later it would be imperative that I periodically do something other than ride the bike—cross training if you will. Because two days after I left El Paso, I could barely walk from having used the different muscles on the hike.) I walked through an upper-class neighborhood (gathering my share of glances) to a lookout where the Franklin Range of the Rocky Mountains ends. This was my first twinge of being homesick—the Rocky Mountains and Denver playing in the Super Bowl.

I watched the Super Bowl in the TV room of the hostel, which was in the basement. For the most part I was alone. A college student from Germany showed up during the second half and kept asking me questions about American football. The game was tied at the time, so I was in no mood to be explaining why we have a huddle after every play, what the flags were for, etc. Then a young man from North Carolina showed up rooting for the Packers right as Elway threw an interception. I was wishing I was alone. Fortunately, Denver held on and The Broncos were the Super Bowl Champions. Again, I had mixed emotions. I was happy they won, but I knew I was missing out on the celebration in Colorado. I called my sister, Vicky, and asked her to buy me some souvenirs. I also called Lupe' and asked him to save the newspaper. The next day I bought a USA Today and read all about my Denver Broncos being world champions.

I had a smile on my face all day riding to Las Cruces, N.M. I arrived in the early afternoon, so I went to the NMSU campus and ate my lunch while watching the kids go to class. College looked different from when I was biking around campus 27 years ago. For one thing, I was practically the only one with long hair, and when did college kids become so young?

Probably the toughest part of the initial stage of The Journey was spending so much time alone. Jan had told me, "If you are having a hard time being alone, maybe it's the company you're keeping." I knew this was a prominent part of my trip and I would have to adjust to it. But of all the places to start a solitary journey, West Texas just seemed to compound the loneliness. There were days I would ride from one town in the morning to another at night and not see anything. No houses, animals or side-roads, just an occasional car, and once in a while some Mexicans that had come across the Rio Grande—oh yeah, and the Border Patrol. The weather through West Texas had been great. There were a couple of nights below freezing, but that didn't bother me and they were always followed by sunny days. The roads in Texas were good (they would end up being some of the best). Now it was off to the Southwest, some of the most interesting and beautiful landscape in the world.

CHAPTER 3

▼

MY PICK CITY IS...

Texas was behind me and I was still filled with enthusiasm about The Journey. Ten days of sun, wide shoulders, and the most courteous truck drivers in America had put me in a very optimistic mood. But the initial innocence of The Journey was about to wear off and the shroud of ignorance would soon be replaced by the harsh reality of life on the road. I had been lucky and blessed that first week and a half, but over the next few months I would experience my limits physically, mentally, emotionally and spiritually.

The first thing I noticed was the beginning of some physical problems. My knees ached from the first day, but now I had two new symptoms; I was losing the feeling in the last two fingers on both hands and I had a sharp pain in my ribs. The numbness in the fingers was part of long-distance bike riding. Even with padded gloves and tri-athlete handlebars, the constant pressure on the hands from holding onto the bike was deadening the nerves. The pain in the ribs was a result of a 44-year-old man sleeping on the ground every night.

Make no mistake about it; this was the hardest thing I had ever done in my life, physically and mentally. I played in weekend basketball tournaments that required a great deal of energy output. I went on weeklong backpacking trips and I climbed 14,000-foot mountains. But all of those events had an end. When they were over, I got to go home. I couldn't see the end of The Journey. I set aside two to 20 years in which to complete my ride, so at the moment there was no end in sight. I also was burning between 4,000 and 8,000 calories a day and I was doing it alone—day after day after day. The solitary journey was my decision and I still think it is the best way to go, but I really missed my family and friends.

I soon discovered, however, my enemy was not pain or loneliness, but the wind. The wind had the ability to affect my journey like nothing else, good and bad. There was nothing better than hauling ass with a strong tail wind pushing you along. When I would spit out to the side and it landed next to me or in front of me, I knew it was a stiff tail wind. I would ride as long as I could to take advantage of it. But if it were not a tail wind, I would have my work cut out for me. Not only was it going to take longer to get somewhere, but also it was going to hurt more. The constant struggle to balance the load made every joint hurt by the end of the day. And it wasn't just physical. The mental anguish caused by riding in the wind was indescribable. I even checked with some other riders at a hostel in Montana and everyone agreed, there was nothing worse than riding into the wind. One person said, "When you have to pedal going downhill, you know it's going to be a bad day." When I read Barbara Savage's book "*Miles From Nowhere*," I couldn't understand why she went on and on about the wind in South Dakota. I thought, "OK the wind is blowing, get over it." I would get plenty of chances over the next 10 months to "get over it."

There was no wind the day I took off for Silver City, N.M., so it was not a bad day. In fact, it was like almost every other day that you get in the Southwest, lots of sun and no humidity. I was in a good mood, even though I experienced my first flat tire that morning leaving Deming,

N.M. I rode about 20 miles and pulled into a very nice roadside rest stop. It was landscaped and very clean, and there was a full-time attendant living there in a trailer. We chatted for a bit and he made a comment about how lucky I was there wasn't any wind that day. If only he had kept quiet. Not long after leaving the rest stop, I encountered the worst wind of the trip so far. I couldn't help but think about the amount of energy I was using to battle the wind and that, under normal conditions, I would already have reached my destination. I tried to think about the positive aspect associated with riding into the wind. The only thing that came to mind was it made my legs stronger. I didn't need stronger legs. I just needed to be there!

I struggled into the town of Bayard around 2:30 p.m. Even though I only had 14 miles to go, I began thinking about stopping for the day—I was beat. Instead, I took a break, had something to eat, filled my water bottles, and took a nap on the sidewalk next to the convenience store.

Refreshed, I made it into Silver City several hours later. As soon as I rode into town I knew things were going to be OK because the first street I saw was Monte St. Then I spotted a bicycle shop. I have to take a moment to thank most of the little bike shops around the country. The majority of them were very friendly and most helpful. This was one of them. Hal, the owner, was 74 years old. I told him he was my hero and I meant it. He was still biking and was in great shape. He had a sign over the counter that read, "Old bicycle riders never die, they just get a little behind." After helping me, Hal told me there had been another cross-country bike rider in the shop about 15 minutes earlier. I thanked him for his help and took off for the hostel on the other side of town. A block from the hostel, I saw the other biker talking to some people down a side street. We met up at the hostel, introduced ourselves, and checked out each other's ride.

The other rider was Perry Shokat from Berkeley, Calif. He was 55 years old, married, with two boys. He was riding his bike, an Italian racing bike, from Florida to California and was pulling a *B.O.B.* (Beast Of Burden)

Trailer. The trailer is what I was really checking out. I noticed after checking into the hostel that he unhooked the trailer and was free to ride his bicycle to the store. I, on the other hand, had to spend about 20 minutes unloading my bike. Perry asked me if I would be interested in joining him for dinner. My first response, in order to save money, was no. But after a hot shower, I decided to reward myself for having fought the wind all afternoon. We went out to get Mexican food, but it didn't compare to the chili rellenos from the Mill Stop back in Pueblo, Colo. More important than the food was the fact I was hanging out with another cross-country bike rider. We talked about biking and (of course) the wind. The next night, Perry fixed a pasta dinner for the entire hostel, including the owner and a guest from the B&B upstairs—what a feast.

I spent an extra day in Silver City doing my laundry and writing postcards. I really liked the town. It was small, with pine trees, cactus, and mountains nearby. The people were friendly and active. There was a nice feel to it. As The Journey progressed, I noticed I almost immediately developed a feel for the places I rode into, again, relying on my intuition. I was also very comfortable at this hostel. It would be one of the nicer ones I would stay at on the entire trip. They kept it very clean, but more importantly they gave you a key to get in and out during the day. Most hostels "kick" you out around 10 a.m. and don't let you back in until 5 p.m. I probably should have stayed longer, but I had people to see in Arizona.

I decided to select a town from each state I visited where I would live if I moved to that state. In Texas it would be Alpine, where the sign welcoming you to town read, "The Alps of Texas—4,481'." In New Mexico it would be Silver City.

CHAPTER 4

▼

FRIENDS

I was on Highway 90 from Silver City to Lordsburg, my first highway with NO shoulder. I crossed the Continental Divide and headed to Lordsburg on a 10-mile downhill stretch—Yahoo! I would cross the Continental Divide several times on this trip and it eventually would become a large focus in my life towards the end of The Journey.

I had thoughts of going on from Lordsburg that day. It was still early, but as I rode into town it started raining. My friend, Chuey, had given me a card before I left that read, "Don't bother riding in the rain." In fact, I had asked all of my friends and family members to give me 3x5 cards with sayings or quotes on them. The cards could be inspirational, humorous, spiritual, or just relate an old story. Chuey had given me two cards. One recalled incidents we had experienced together and the other one had sayings related to biking.

Chuey was the closest thing I had to a mentor. He was an accountant and, in fact, was my boss at one time. He was the original coach of our softball team, a task he later passed on to me. We did extensive traveling together, including two trips to Africa—and he rode bikes. Chuey was the first one, in the group of guys that ran around together in Summit County, to start touring on a bicycle. We all called Chuey "Dad" because he was 10-12 years older than the rest of us. But like Lupe', he was very much like a brother to me. Anyway, I remembered the card and decided to heed the advice. As the storm blew through that afternoon, I was very happy with myself for getting a motel room and thankful for the good advice from my friend.

I planned to be in Duncan, Ariz., by noon the next day, but arrived at 10:30 a.m. I hauled ass all morning with the aid of a stiff tail wind. I rewarded myself with a big breakfast for making such good time and for entering state #3, Arizona—47 more to go. I was hoping the roads in Arizona would improve. For the most part, the roads in New Mexico sucked. They either didn't have a shoulder or the asphalt was torn up from years of use and abuse.

After breakfast, I was preparing to leave when two young boys (eight years old) came over and began asking me questions about what I was doing. One kid was dribbling a basketball and wasn't paying much attention. But the other kid was on a bike and was really interested in what I was doing, as well as what was on my bike. As I was leaving, the kid with the basketball asked where my home was. Before I could say anything, the kid with the bike said emphatically, "His home is a different place EVERY night." He looked at me with a huge grin on his face and I nodded at him. I knew right then that kid would take a journey of his own someday. I rode all afternoon with a smile on my face thinking about his enthusiasm.

I still had the tailwind, so I made Safford in record time. It was my best day of biking so far. I was jazzed about what I was doing. I felt like I could do this forever. Life was good!

About 3 a.m. the next morning I woke up to a sound that was familiar, but one I couldn't identify. Finally, I recognized it was the sound of the heater turning on in the RV I was camped next to, something I had heard numerous times in my parents' RV. This was my first clue it was cold outside. I developed a routine in the mornings at the campgrounds. I would get up and take a hot shower, cook some oatmeal with raisins and a banana, and pack the bike. But this morning would be different, as it was a cold 22 degrees. I took a hot shower, loaded the bike, and headed into town to find a restaurant where I could eat breakfast real slow and let the sun do its thing.

Just outside of Wilcox, Ariz., I experienced something totally different with the bike. There was a broken spoke on the rear wheel, drive-side (the chain side). I could replace a spoke on the opposite side, but lacked the tools to remove the gears on the drive-side. It not only required a special tool, but some heavy torque to remove the free-wheel as well. I limped into town and found a cheap motel room so I could work on *B.O.P.* I trued the wheel as best I could, but there was a huge knot in my stomach. There was not a bicycle shop in town and the closest one was in Benson, 30 miles away.

I wasn't exactly sure what to do. I tried to call Duane and Jeanette Flory, friends of my parents from Pueblo, who were in Tucson. Like my parents, the Florys also headed south each winter. I met them when I moved to Pueblo the previous September to take care of my sister, Vicky, who had blown out her ACL riding horses. I took care of her horses, dogs, cats and equipment. I also cooked, cleaned and painted. It was during this time I began training with Duane. He was in his mid-sixties, but had recently competed in the Senior Olympics in biking and placed in several categories. He was an animal with unbelievable leg strength. In fact, I couldn't keep up with him on the hills or riding into the wind, even though I was 20 years his junior. But at this particular moment, all I wanted was a lift in their pickup. Unfortunately, I couldn't get in touch with them. It is bad enough riding a bicycle with a broken spoke, but add 110 pounds of "stuff" and it can quickly become tragic. I finally decided I would head for Benson the next morning on I-10, and would hitch a ride if the bike broke down.

At a rest stop the next day, a lady offered me a soft drink and a truck driver came over to talk with me. I mentioned to him how courteous the truckers had been and how much room they allowed me when passing. He let me know that it wasn't necessarily kindness as much as "they didn't want to suck me under their rig and have to fill out all the damn paper work."

I arrived in Benson only to find the bicycle shop closed, so I decided to spend the night and have the bike repaired in the morning. I rode out to the KOA campground, where they wanted $22 for a campsite. I refused to pay that much money to sleep on the ground, and the sites weren't even that nice. Not sure what to do, I tried the Florys again. This time they answered and I explained my predicament. Duane offered to pick me up and then have the bike serviced in Tucson—it was music to my ears.

While waiting for them outside the Safeway grocery store, I recognized someone I knew. It was Roger and Kathy Samuels from Pueblo. They belong to the same church my parents and sister attend in Pueblo and Mr. Samuels was my gym teacher almost 40 years ago. We talked for a bit and then my ride showed up.

I spent the next couple of days with the Florys. What a treat for me; we climbed Wasson Peak (the highest point in Tucson), went to an old Spanish Mission, and attended a presentation on how to live to be 100 years old (eat right and exercise). I even got to sit out a huge storm that blew through the area in the warmth and comfort of their trailer. When I was ready to leave, Duane and Jeanette gave me a ride to the north end of town. I couldn't help but think they were acting just like my parents, and I loved it. I thanked them for taking care of me, threw them the peace sign, and I was on the road again.

While in Tucson, I had replaced all the spokes on the back wheel, as some of them were 14 years old. That gave me a new air of confidence in the bike as I headed for Phoenix. I had a flat soon after leaving Tucson but it was no big deal. It was a beautiful day and I could unload the bike and change a tube in 20 minutes. Besides, I had friends in Phoenix I would be visiting, so my mood was light.

I was in Phoenix for two weeks. The first couple of days I stayed with Dan Waldo and M.L. Bernasek. Dan and M.L. were divorced, but had moved back in with each other, which was a bit uncomfortable for me. Dan had hired me at Keystone 14 years ago. He also taught me how to play golf several years ago and I considered him a good friend. Unfortunately, unknown to him, M.L. was the first woman I dated after Jan and I divorced. She was the perfect woman for me at that moment. She was intelligent, attractive, and she liked to have fun. We enjoyed each other mentally and physically. To make matters worse, Dan was working and M.L. had some time off, so we were hanging out together. Out of respect for Dan, nothing happened. They still loved each other, and even though I didn't see them staying together, I didn't want to interfere with their attempt to reconcile.

I spent the next 10 days with the Goffs; Bruce, Kathy, Benn, and Stephanie. I later realized how important it was for me to occasionally spend time with families. In fact, The Journey would evolve around seeing families in America. The Goff family was one of the best. I had worked and played with Bruce in Summit County. We skied, played ball and partied together. Bruce was an average skier, a good ball player, and one hell of a partier. He was the first guy on the team to get married. He married this cute, innocent, young girl who was well endowed. Kathy was an instant hit with the rest of the team, but we couldn't figure out why she was with Bruce. Benn and Stephanie are two of the best kids I've ever met. They are very active and very respectful toward their parents and other adults. Bruce and Kathy had just returned from the Super Bowl, so we got to reminisce about that. But there was an added bonus. The Dalls happened to be in Phoenix at the same time.

Fran and Mad Dog are two of my oldest and dearest friends from Summit County. Fran is a sweetheart and, in fact, people tell her she is a "saint" for being able to put up with Mad Dog. I could write a book about

Mad Dog's exploits and maybe someone will one day. But suffice it to say, there are very few people in this world who have made me laugh more than he has. The mini-reunion was special for me.

After the Goff's, I moved to the Metcalf House Hostel in downtown Phoenix. On the way to the hostel, some guy threw a soft drink on me from his car. People had thrown insults at me, but this was the first time someone actually hit me with something. I have a difficult time understanding the mentality of someone who would do something so juvenile. I was stunned, but I could only forgive someone that shallow.

The hostel was bizarre. An English woman, Sue, who had purple hair, ran it. There were people living there, which most hostels do not allow. In fact, most hostels have a limit on the number of days you can stay. It was located in one of the poorer neighborhoods in Phoenix. This is the case with several hostels because of the low rent. That shouldn't have bothered me, seeing as how my nickname is LoRent—a moniker Bruce gave me many years ago. Actually, I was more worried about my bike than anything else because they didn't allow me to bring it indoors. *B.O.P.* was locked to a bunch of old rusty bicycles in a rack out back. The next morning, one of the residents told me how one rider's bike was sawed in two when some would-be-thieves discovered they couldn't steal it. Thank God he didn't tell me that the night before, I wouldn't have been able to sleep.

One of the benefits of staying at a hostel is meeting interesting people. That night in Phoenix there was a young man, Bart Baggett, who had written a book, *"The Secrets of Making Love Happen."* The "Secrets," it turns out, are in your handwriting. He was a handwriting analyst and was preparing for a conference in India. What he was doing at the hostel, I have no idea. But I decided to take advantage of the situation and presented my journal to him. Reluctantly, he told me: I was still feeling the pain from a past relationship (true), I have anger towards women (true), I'm afraid of an intimate relationship (true), I'm introverted in new situations (true), and I'm on a spiritual/philosophical quest (true). Of course, I realized those attributes could pertain to almost anyone. But he analyzed the writings of other people and they said he was right on, as well. I have no idea if their traits were as general as mine, so I accepted the attributes for what they were—things I saw in myself that I might be able to improve. I think it is funny how we meet people, and in fact, one of my philosophies is that things happen for a reason. Which is why I imposed on this man who appeared to have money, yet was spending the night in a hostel.

I spent one more night in Phoenix at the home of Bob and Audrey Muench. Bob worked with my Dad in Pueblo and our families had grown up together. They took me out to an all-you-can-eat buffet, which was heaven, and we drove up to a lookout where we could see the lights of the city. The next day was Sunday and we just hung out reading the paper and watching golf and car races on television. My stay with them was quite relaxing and I appreciated their hospitality. For some reason, it still seemed important for me to occasionally experience everyday life, like reading the paper and watching TV—simple things that didn't exist in life on the road.

I was about to make some decisions that would significantly affect the nature of The Journey. But for the moment, I was content.

While in Phoenix, I learned that my best friend's mother passed away. Shud and I have known each other since we were three years old. We have experienced life together. Shud is the kindest, funniest person I have ever known and also the best skier I have ever known. If you ever want to learn to ski, go to Breckenridge, Colo., and ask for Jim Banks, a.k.a. Shud, a.k.a. Bomber—he is The Best! His mother, Shirley, was like a mother to me and I felt a tremendous void for not being there for my friend. I knew he would understand, but it bothered me. God bless her soul.

CHAPTER 5

▼

SNOW, SNOW, AND MORE SNOW

The Muenches lived on the west side of town, so it was easy to catch Highway 60 to Wickenburg, my first decision point. I would have to decide whether to go north into Colorado and Utah or head to southern California to kill some time. I was covering territory quicker than originally planned, which meant I was heading north sooner than intended. It was only mid-February and I was close to biking into states noted for their ski areas. On the other hand, I didn't like the ramifications of putting extra miles on the bike or my body. What to do?

The weather was beautiful when I left that morning and I felt good due to two weeks off with some good camaraderie. Having ridden 1,000 miles, the break gave me some needed time to heal both mentally and physically.

While riding through Sun City, I noticed a biker in my mirror gaining on me—not hard to do since I was so loaded down. He pulled up next to me on an eight-foot wide shoulder and asked me where I was headed. His name was Harvey and he was 74 years old. He was riding a Trek 5500 and had already pedaled 30 miles that morning. We rode together for a few miles and I told him he was my hero—and again, I meant it. I love to see older people taking care of themselves. It is so easy to just lie around and complain about all of the little aches and pains we acquire as we grow older. And I know how I feel in my 40s, so I can only imagine what it is like when you are 60 or 70. Like the bumper sticker says, "*Growing old is not for sissies.*"

As we neared where we would part, Harvey pulled out into the road to make a left hand turn and didn't see the car that was coming. The driver locked up his brakes, smoked his tires, and stopped about two feet away from Harvey. It absolutely scared the hell out of me and I was surprised Harvey didn't have the "big one" right there. Later that day a puppy ran across the road toward me in front of oncoming traffic. He was OK, but by the time I got to Wickenburg my nerves were shot from the close calls.

There were storms all around, so I stayed in a motel room that night. Actually, it was two rooms, a bedroom and a kitchen. It felt like a little house so I went to the store and bought food to cook in the kitchen.

I thought long and hard that night and decided to head for Flagstaff to spend some time there, maybe even look for a job. I watched the weather on TV and it didn't look promising. The next morning looked even worse. It wasn't raining, but it was very dark outside. I debated for a while and finally decided to head out for Prescott. I had ridden about 16 miles and was surprised I was only being sprinkled on occasionally. I continued to survey the skies, but it was almost as if I was in the eye of the storm. I could not have been more prophetic. Just outside of Congress, Ariz., the wind picked up and it began to rain. Ignoring my friend Chuey's advice, I stopped to put on my rain gear and at least try to make it to Yarnell, only nine miles away. What I didn't know was that Yarnell was at the top of a 3,000-foot pass. As I continued, the conditions worsened. The wind was blowing so hard I was riding on the flats in first gear (usually reserved for going up steep hills). The rain was coming down with such force I could only look straight down to see where I was on the road. A question came to mind, "Is this a test from God to see what I am made of *or* is He trying to tell me to stop?" Well, I never should have considered it a challenge. As soon as I did, I knew I'd have to show God what I was made of—that was my first mistake.

My second mistake came just moments later when a man in a pickup pulled up next to me and asked if I was all right. I said I was, and in some sort of perverse way I was actually enjoying my challenge of tackling the elements. He then asked if I wanted a ride and in one of the dumber moments of The Journey I said, "No, thanks for asking." It wasn't too long after that I was reminded what happens to rain as you gain altitude—I was riding in the snow. Chuey's card didn't say anything about riding in snow. Unfortunately, the higher I went the more the snow was sticking to the pavement. Until eventually, I had to get off the bike and push it through the snow. But before I started pushing, I took a picture of *B.O.P.* I think I was in shock, I couldn't believe I was this stupid and wanted to document my stupidity. I pushed *B.O.P.* and 100 pounds of gear for two miles through three inches of snow (I had sent 10 pounds of "stuff" home with the Florys) to the top of the pass. Thank God someone was smart enough to put a little town up there!

I found a motel and took the last room available! I would have paid anything for that room but, fortunately, he was only charging $20—and looking at me like I was really whacked. As I was unlocking the door, I looked over at the bike. I couldn't believe the predicament I had put us in and was thankful that we had survived. I was beginning to think of *B.O.P.* in personal terms and was actually carrying on conversations with the bike. It didn't bother me. I just knew it was a little weird (especially when someone overheard me). I actually loved my bike and knew it was responsible for carrying me around America. The wheels had snow packed in the spokes, so I took a picture of it, The Road Warrior! The bike had received its name *B.O.P.*, when I had christened The Journey "A Bike Of Peace Around America." But on a day like this it was The Road Warrior!

I was shaking and didn't know if it was from the cold or because I realized how dangerous it was for me to have been out sharing the highway with cars in an area that normally didn't have snow. The room was freezing so I cranked the thermostat up to 90, took a long hot shower, and went over to the café while the room heated up. The room was tiny. I had to hop over the bed to get around the room once the bike was inside. But I was not complaining. In fact, I was in a pretty good mood considering everything I had just been through. One reason may have been the snow. I had been living at 9,000 feet the last 22 years and skiing was my passion. So in the past, whenever it snowed, I was happy—POWDER! Like Pavlov's dog, I was conditioned to enjoy it.

I received a bit of a shock when I turned the shower on. It was a half-inch pipe sticking out of the wall. Again, I was not complaining—I had stayed in worse places. It was just different. I took a shower, put on all the winter clothes I had and headed for the café. It snowed the rest of the day and I sat in the motel room reading and listening as snowplows continued to roar by.

The next morning was beautiful with a big bright orange sun rising in the dark blue sky with 10 inches of virgin white snow covering the ground. The snowplows had done an excellent job of clearing the roads and I knew with all that sunshine I might have a good chance of making Prescott that day. Again, I went over to the café for some food and to kill some time. I asked some locals about the road from Yarnell to Prescott and they let me know I would be losing altitude, but that it was too cold to be riding a bicycle. I told them the cold wasn't the problem because I was generating my own heat. I was just concerned about the snow, ice and slush on the road.

About 11:30 a.m. I took off. What a fantastic ride; majestic pines and rolling hills, ravens scavenging, and hawks hunting. My biggest concern was being able to get far enough over to the right when cars passed me because of all the snow still on the shoulder. But the traffic was sparse and everyone was courteous. I had a great ride until just outside of Prescott when a spoke popped on the rear wheel, drive-side. They were brand new spokes! I couldn't believe one already popped. It was a bit disheartening to say the least. I found the Ironclad Bicycle Shop as soon as I reached town. While they were fixing the wheel, they suggested I might look into getting a 40-spoke wheel in Flagstaff to handle the extra weight I was packing. It was something to think about. In the meantime, I rented a motel room that afternoon and took some time to ride around town. I liked Prescott and, in fact, would move there if I were going to live in Arizona. It was clean and a college town. I almost always like college towns because they have such good energy. I like the combination of smart people doing active things. Next to Colorado, I love Arizona. Having lived in the mountains for so long, maybe it's the contrast in terrain or maybe it's just because it's warmer. The landscape of Arizona is unlike anything else in the world. And Prescott has a nice combination of being in the mountains and being close to the desert.

The next day would be my longest ride so far, 91 miles to Flagstaff. It was another beautiful day in the Southwest, so I got an early start. I went about 20 miles when I came to some "hills," as one local referred to them, surrounding Sedona. Ten miles later I was at the top of the "hills." I'd been up mountain passes that were shorter! Fortunately, there was a rest area there because I had to completely change my clothes, which were soaked with perspiration. It was only 40 degrees outside, but it was a hell of a workout. I had lunch in the little town of Jerome, an old mining town hanging on the side of a hill. There was a 12-mile downhill run to get out of the hills—Yahoo! At the bottom I had very tired hands from braking and something in my eye. At a convenience store, I stopped to wash out my eye and rest. While sitting there, a man came over to talk with me about bike touring. Paul owned a couple of restaurants in Prescott and had done some bicycle touring on the West Coast from Canada to Mexico. He would ride his bike everyday and his wife would take their mobile home to the next designated campground. What a way to travel! He would get his exercise everyday and had the comforts of home every night. He was concerned about my traveling on the next stretch of road to Sedona and wanted to know if I would like a ride. I didn't even hesitate.

Sedona is a very different kind of place, beautiful scenery with a very new age attitude. Giant red rock formations take on different shapes depending on the location of the sun. Also, there are formations that always look the same, like Camel Rock. Outside of town there are vortexes, electrical and magnetic. Jan and I had hiked into one of the vortexes years ago when we were visiting the area. There is no mistaking when you get to the vortex—it is like a shrine. Shaped much like a 20-foot diameter stone wagon wheel, people have taken to leaving personal effects at the hub of the vortex. For example, if you desire help with your golf game, you would leave a golf ball at the vortex. You also are supposed to be able to feel the energy at and around the vortex. Be that as it may, there are numerous hiking and biking trails around the area. Unfortunately, the town has essentially turned into one money-grubbing hoard, with everyone trying to impress everyone else with what they are doing, wearing and driving—Arizona's Aspen, if you will. I think it is a very spiritual place that has been tarnished by people with too much money, just like Aspen and a lot of other spiritual places around the world.

The ride from Sedona to Flagstaff was tough; highway 89A winds through a beautiful valley until it gets to the hills surrounding the northern boundary of Sedona. There is no shoulder and the climb seems to go forever. Some young man from town on a bicycle caught up with me halfway up the canyon and rode along side until it began to snow. By the time I arrived in Flagstaff, the sun was down and I was tired and cold. I called the hostel, received directions, and thanked God (and Paul) I had arrived safely. I wound up spending eight days in "The Flag" as it snowed six straight days. I used that time to evaluate The Journey-so-far and consider The Journey-to-be.

I checked into the DuBeau International Hostel and the staff was extremely accommodating to me. They even tried to give me a room to myself so I might fit the bike inside. Roommates were inevitable because of the number of people checking in, but the effort was appreciated and I was still able to squeeze B.O.P. into the room. The hostel was the old

DuBeau Motel, which at one time was a nice place to stay in Flagstaff, but was a bit run down now. I wasn't complaining, however, because I received the room for $8 because I had a passport. They catered to international travelers, so if guests had a passport they received a 20 percent discount, and I was always looking for a bargain. The next day I did check out the other hostel in town, but they would not let me keep my bike inside and that was unacceptable. So I decided to make do at the DuBeau and, besides, they had coffee, juice and bagels every morning.

That first night I went around the corner to the Macy Café, a European style restaurant. They had some good vegetarian dishes and the place was hopping; people playing chess, reading books, hanging out, and there was a band playing in the other room that sounded interesting. The place seemed like a mix of Rick's Café in "*Casablanca*" and the bar in "*Star Wars.*" There were travelers, locals, hippies, businessmen and freaks all doing their thing. After dinner I went in the other room to watch and listen to the band. One guy was playing a bass guitar with lead strings tuned to sound like a sitar. Another guy was playing a didgeridoo and two guys were playing rhythm instruments. The band was called Moments of Clarity and they were from Coeur d' Alene, Idaho. Their music was very different and just what I needed. I would later adopt their name to identify my visions while biking.

I spent the next eight days hanging out at the public library and the library at Northern Arizona University. Between library visits I met some interesting people.

The first person was Peter Deane from Australia. As it turned out, Peter was not only the most intelligent person I met on the trip, he was the most intelligent person I have EVER met. We had some unbelievably stimulating conversations about everything. Peter helped me more with aligning my perspective on The Journey than anyone or anything. I was trying to come up with a workable definition of what is "Natural." Peter suggested rather than trying to define what "Natural" is, why didn't I just experience it since I was out in Nature all day. He also taught me that things are not always as they seem and led me to quit trying to label or define everything. When he left, he told me he was taking something from our encounter; freedom, relaxation and pushing the envelope. I have since heard from Peter and he is, in fact, starting his own journey. It's not on a bicycle, but it will be an adventure none the less.

The second person was Rob, my roommate for a couple of days. Rob said he once lived with Indians in South America and in the Grand Canyon. He most recently was a cook in Breckenridge, Colo., and was trying to get back to the Grand Canyon. Weather had stopped both of us in Flagstaff. I couldn't help but question some of Rob's stories. He was at least 10 years younger than I was, but he looked awful. He drank too much and smoked. And even though he appeared to be in good shape, his eyes were always puffed up and his face was very wrinkled. His camping gear looked like stuff from a drug store and his coat was heavy corduroy that he tried to waterproof with Scotch Guard. It didn't look like the equipment of someone who had lived in the wilderness with Native Americans.

Then there was Mike who worked at the hostel. Mike was the most intelligent person he had ever met. He knew something about everything and wanted to make sure everyone else knew that. In fact, if you didn't pay attention to him as he rambled on, he would make some sort of remark about your lack of interest reflecting on your lack of intelligence. He was a smart guy, but he was a brick shy of having a full load.

Finally, there was Mary, a young activist from Oregon. Mary was into biking for ecological reasons and gave me a publication called Auto-Free Times about people who get around without automobiles. Mary was young and a bit idealistic, but she was doing what she thought was right—trying to save the Earth. She was struggling, however, with the paradox of being different and poor, or joining society and partaking in the plenty. Coincidentally, Mary was a friend of Kale and Danny, the activists I met in Sierra Blanca, Texas. They had done some tree sitting together in the Great Northwest to protect the old growth forests.

Once again, I discovered that my trip meant different things to different people; freedom to Peter, I was a crusader to Mary, and I was just an idiot to Mike.

When the weather finally broke, I was ready to leave Flagstaff. My experiences at the hostel were wearing thin. Other people's situations were getting old and I had come down with a severe case of bed bug bites. This would be something I would experience at several other hostels along the way and at the moment I was thoroughly disgusted with the thought of having slept in a bed full of bugs. My thoughts about The Journey had changed dramatically while hanging out in Flagstaff. I no longer considered getting a job. I was going to bike around America, through all 48 contiguous states and maybe look for a sponsor to get to Alaska and Hawaii. I decided to spend some extra time with friends and family for the next couple of months, with the idea of arriving in Seattle by June. I also looked into a 40-spoke wheel while I was in Flagstaff, but it would cost almost $400 for a completely new set-up, so I decided to make do with what I had.

On March 1 I took off from Flagstaff. The sky was crystal clear and the air was cold. It was so cold I was riding with my ski gloves and hat on and the water in my bottles was freezing into ice crystals. But I loved it. I loved being back on the road and away from other people's problems. I had lost some enthusiasm for the trip hanging out in Flagstaff and even started to dread getting back on "the beast."

But once I started pedaling, I began to see life in a new light. One advantage of a solitary bicycle tour is having a lot of time to think about anything and everything. My mind felt as clear as the sky, so I decided to take the time to do a self-analysis. Why not? I had the time and *B.O.P.* wasn't going to complain about hearing everything from my past. My thought was to bring up every incident that occasionally crept into my psyche, address the issue, and dismiss it forever.

I delved back to my earliest memories and began the process. Of course, self-analysis is very personal, but I have to admit it was very therapeutic. I was forgiving myself for hurting certain people, apologizing to those people, and forgiving people for hurting me. The session was powerful and best of all it was free. Not only did I feel fresh and energized, but the miles flew by also. I was standing on a corner in Winslow, Ariz., before I knew it and just like the band, The Eagles, "I was looking for a girl in a flatbed Ford, slowing down to take a look at me." I only received a few waves from some Native Americans, but George, who owned a small motel on the edge of town, gave me an AARP discount for the night— Yahoo!

CHAPTER 6

▼

THE DEAFENING SILENCE

The ride through northern Arizona was cool but pleasant. There was snow next to the road the entire way, but the asphalt was dry. I was on my way to Farmington, N.M., to see my old friends, Mark and Mayre Lou Blanchfield. I had known Mark since Heaton Junior High School, but hadn't really become friends until both our families moved to the country. We ended up at Pueblo County High School and became good friends as a result. Mark graduated third in the class, but actually was the most intelligent person in the entire school, including the faculty. I say that because he accomplished all of his academic honors without studying. But that was not why I hung out with him. I liked being around Mark because he had an unbelievable sense of humor; very dry but very good. Oh yeah, he was also the first one in class to receive his drivers license and he had a cool '57 Dodge that had to occasionally be started under the hood with a pair of pliers, so that complemented his sense of humor. He met Mayre Lou after we graduated and the three of us laughed our way through several years of the 70s. In 1977, Mark and I rode our motorcycles to the Grand

Canyon over the 4th of July holiday. I've never told anyone this before, but that was one of the best vacations I ever experienced. We had so much fun and it was so cool being on a motorcycle trip with Mark. He had talked me into buying my first motorcycle and the trip really had an "Easy Rider" feel to it, plus the freedom of traveling on a motorcycle. Unfortunately, as happens in life, we lost contact with each other over the years. In fact, I had never met their kids, Ashley who was in high school, and Steven who was in junior high. I was anxious to meet them and see Mark and Mayre Lou again.

My ride from Flagstaff, Ariz., to Gallop, N.M., was a kick because I had a tail wind everyday. I averaged 15 miles per hour, which is unheard of on a bicycle that loaded down. The day I flew into Gallup, I averaged 17 mph. I had a flat just outside of town and while I was fixing it, decided to find a room for the night to seek shelter from the wind.

I found a room on the edge of town for $14. That would be the least expensive room the entire trip. The motel was owned and operated by Indians from India. As I would discover on The Journey, Eastern Indians are taking over the mom and pop motel industry. Probably Eastern Indians were running 90 percent of the motels I stayed in over the 10-month journey. Of those, this was the dirtiest—it was filthy. For example, there was a cocoon hanging in the shower. A better example, when I touched the drapes to let some light in, they almost fell apart. Later that evening, I was covered with fleabites. I was so disgusted, I refused to sleep on the bed, so I retrieved my pad and sleeping bag and slept on the floor. The next morning, someone knocked on my door at 8 a.m. and wanted to know when I was checking out. I told her 10 a.m., but she wanted to know if she could come in to clean the room while I was still there. I said, "No!" Then she wanted to know if she could have the laundry. Finally after being pestered a couple more times, I left around 9 a.m. I should have just camped in the wind!

There wasn't an easy way to get to Farmington from Gallup on a bicycle. So I decided to forego Highway 666 and head to Thoreau on Route

66, then up Highway 371. Other than Crown Point, there isn't anything between Thoreau and Farmington, so I knew I would be free camping somewhere. At Crown Point, a small Native American town out in the middle of nowhere, I stopped and had something to eat. I was on a reservation and would spend the next month in and around reservations. As a result, I would have some deep thoughts about Native Americans. Especially, how they had responded to their treatment by the white man. I was looking forward to sharing those thoughts with some Native Americans if the opportunity presented itself.

As I was leaving Crown Point, there was a sign that read, "Farmington 77 miles." Two miles down the road there was another sign that read, "Farmington 68 miles." I went three more miles and the sign read, "Farmington 62 miles." A revelation came to me that if I kept riding I would eventually get to Farmington in half the time I was planning on. Unfortunately, I also didn't know if I was 62, 65, or 72 miles from Farmington. At any rate, the sun was setting and I needed a place to camp. Out of nowhere, a dirt road appeared. I dismounted, pushed *B.O.P.* down the road, and up and over a sand dune.

I sat there awhile to make sure that no one could see me from the road. Looking around, I noticed what a beautiful place this was; a lot of rolling hills with jagged white rock cliffs in the distance. I wasn't far from the Chaco Cultural National Historical Park. After camp was set up, I realized my biggest concern was the distance I would have to travel in the morning before I came to some water. Because of that, I enjoyed some cashews and a Snickers' for dinner, instead of cooking pasta. In the three hours before I went to bed, there were only a couple of cars that came down the road, so I felt pretty secure with my campsite. I was in Nature and I felt good. I didn't know if it was funny or sad that human beings have evolved incorrectly for so long that we have reached the point where most people are afraid to be out in Nature. In fact, we are more comfortable; watching Nature on TV, walking around malls instead of forests, listening to stereos instead of birds, smelling perfume instead of flowers, wasting time on computers instead of watching a sunset. And I can't for the life of me figure out why!

I woke up that night at 1 a.m. I am very lucky in that I have always been able to get a good night's sleep, whether in a strange bed or on the ground. I was sound asleep that night, when something caused me to wake up. From years of camping in Colorado, I knew it was important to identify what it was. One would react differently to a bear than a field mouse, so I remained motionless to see if I could identify the intruder. After a few minutes I identified it as the most deafening silence I had ever heard. There was nothing stirring outside my tent that would cause me to wake up, there was nothing. No wind, no crickets, no cars, no airplanes—nothing. My current existence was void of noise. My first thought was that I was wearing my earplugs. I wore them in the hostels and while biking on the interstate, but not while camping. Finally, I moved my foot just to hear something and make sure I wasn't deaf.

As I lay there, I couldn't help but wonder how many people on the planet had ever experienced such a moment. Not being used to total silence, it woke me up. It was almost as if someone had been standing outside the tent yelling at the top of his or her lungs—the true awkwardness of silence. I treasured the experience and, because our world continues to shrink with technology, I realized it would be difficult ever to be in that situation again. A very spiritual moment for me, I felt blessed to have heard "The Deafening Silence."

The next morning I came across an outpost about 15 miles from where I camped. I filled my water bottles and bought something to eat. While sitting outside eating my mid-morning snack, a man came over and started talking to me about bicycles. He appeared to be around my age, but he was missing some teeth and his English wasn't all that good. Standing there in his dirty coveralls and gumboots, he didn't look like someone who would be into biking. But he knew bicycles and had a desire to be doing what I was doing. As we talked and looked over the bike, I noticed something out of place on the back rim. Upon closer examination, I discovered the rim was worn out, literally. Over 14 years of service the brake had worn through the side of the rim. I immediately got a sinking feeling in my chest. This man, however, not only assured me I could make it to Farmington as long as I didn't use my rear brake, he also gave me detailed directions on how to get to the best bike shop in town. I didn't ask his name, but I have to thank him for the conversation and information and wish him the best on his dream of bike touring.

Later, I could see the city from where I was standing. I stopped to take a picture of the snow-covered mountains north of town and it was then that I noticed the downhill run into Farmington. In fact, it was a 9 percent grade and I was a little bit more than concerned. I'm used to the mountain passes in Colorado that are 6 to 7 percent grades, and I'm on an old touring bike with 100 pounds of "stuff" and no rear brake. Using only the front brake going downhill on a normal bike is tricky, but on a loaded touring bike it is insane. There was no way I could keep my speed down, so I let her rip and held on for dear life hoping for a run-out at the bottom. It wasn't a straight shot either. There were probably two miles of winding downhill. I was going way too fast for the circumstances, so my main concern was to steady the bike as much as possible and keep it upright. Fortunately, there was very little traffic, but I'm sure whoever saw me thought I was crazy. I realized I *was* crazy when I got to the bottom and looked at my cycle computer—43 m.p.h. Wow! I had more than just a little bit of adrenaline racing through my body. Warp speed, on a crippled Enterprise, through uncharted territory—it wasn't something I wanted to try again soon.

At the bike shop, they didn't have what I needed and suggested a bike shop in Durango, Colo., about 50 miles away, another decision point. What to do? I decided to find the Blanchfield's house and deal with the bike later.

The reunion with the Blanchfields was good, but certainly nothing like the old days. They have a family now and I no longer partied like we did in the past. During my training, I figured out it didn't make much sense to be riding a bicycle everyday and then putting crap in my body every night. I gave all of my old drug paraphernalia to a neighbor and quit drinking alcohol. I didn't think I had a drinking problem, I just didn't see the need for it at the moment.

Mark and Mayre Lou treated me great while I was there. Mark let me borrow his truck so I could take *B.O.P.* to Durango and Mayre Lou made some great vegetarian dishes that allowed me to gain seven needed pounds. My weight was down to 179 lbs., the lightest I had been in 27 years, since high school. I ended up spending more time there than planned because I had to order a whole new wheel. Since I was doing that, I decided to upgrade the bike to metric. The bike was originally equipped with a 27-inch wheel, but finding a quality replacement was becoming more difficult as all the new bikes were metric. Plus, I knew there would be long distances between cities coming up on The Journey and my choices for bike shops and parts would be limited as a result. I needed to give myself all the help I could.

CHAPTER 7

FAITH

After leaving the Blanchfields, I spent the weekend at the HI-Durango Hostel. It was a very nice place run by a New Jersey refugee, David. David was a cool old hippie, but he still had some of the East in him. He was very uptight about things being done in a particular way and had signs all over the hostel to remind guests just how he wanted them accomplished. But the place was clean and safe, so what more could I ask for? I would recommend David's hostel to anyone, as long as they follow his rules.

I rode around the area Saturday and Sunday. Durango is a beautiful part of Colorado that was supported by mining in the past, but now is sustained by tourism and skiing. On Monday, I took the bike in for one final adjustment at the Mountain Bike Specialist Shop. I hated taking my touring bike into a mountain bike shop, but that was what was available. The "techies" who had worked on the bike both made snide remarks about the load it was carrying. I tried to brush them off, but as I was climbing the 10-mile pass leaving Durango on Highway 160, I felt something was wrong. I couldn't put my finger on it, but I had an innate feeling something wasn't quite right. I assured myself it was their negative comments causing me to worry needlessly.

Not long after that, I had a flat tire and it began snowing. I was ready to quit. I wasn't in a good mood, it was freezing cold, and the bike wasn't working. Shit! I fixed the flat and made it down the pass to Mancos, Colo., while the snow turned to rain. There was a gazebo in town where I took refuge. I waited there watching and listening to the lightning and thunder, eating peanuts, and noticing the temperature on the bank's neon sign as it continued to drop—45, 44, 43,…I needed to make a decision, so I rode over to the local motel to get a room, but the lady at the front desk wouldn't give me a deal. Actually, she wanted to, but her husband said no. I finally bit the bullet and took off in the rain toward Cortez, two hours away.

I rented a room at the Econo Lodge from the prettiest woman I have ever met in my life. I was standing there with my mouth agape, just staring at her. I couldn't figure out why the most beautiful woman in the world would be in Cortez, Colo. Not that it's a bad place, it's just not the place I would expect to find a woman who looked like that. Of course, maybe I was just lonely!

The next morning I had another decision point; should I ride toward the town of Monticello, Utah, where there would be amenities or head out into the Arizona desert and free camp? Because of my recent encounters with the weather I decided to head toward Monticello. I don't know if I was being paranoid or just prudent. It turned out to be a good decision for a couple of reasons; the ride from Cortez to Monticello was some of the most scenic cycling I had ever done and it snowed the next day. I made the right choice. I was so glad I wasn't camping in the desert when I woke up the next morning and saw it snowing.

The ride to Utah was spectacular. Not just the snow covered prairie surrounded by mountains, but I was lucky enough to see three eagles that day, one Bald and two Golden. One was on a telephone pole about 10 yards off the road before it took off. It seemed larger than life as it flew overhead and is a sight I always will treasure.

The only thing really bothering me was that I was on Highway 666, the same one I avoided in New Mexico. Some people use 666 as a sign for the devil. And even though I don't believe in the devil, I'd just as soon avoid tempting fate. After all, who really knows how accurate our beliefs are? We all have a belief system that essentially guides our individual actions, but when it comes right down to it, what are those beliefs based on? Usually it's faith. And if that faith is attached to a religion, then there are usually restrictions and fears associated with it—not only a fear of the devil, but a fear of God, as well. The Bible tells us to "fear God." On a day like this, I had a faith that some greater power created that panorama and some Supreme Being or Universal Energy created those magnificent eagles. But I didn't fear it and I certainly didn't want to restrict it. I have the most difficult time with religions that preach that their way is the only way. That day, it seemed so clear to me that there were an infinite number of ways to access God. I dated a couple of women who later quit dating me when they found I was not of the same religion. I couldn't understand why anyone would want to limit herself that way. I felt the Presence all around me. In fact, the Spirit was in me and I was a part of God—just as a raindrop becomes part of the ocean. I may have been a small part, but I was still a piece of the bigger picture. So I continued on Highway 666 with no worries.

A few years earlier, Neale Donald Walsch wrote *"Conversations With God."* I now understood that everyone has conversations with God, every day. Unfortunately, those conversations are usually either one way or we are too distracted to recognize the incoming message. Somehow Walsch was able to receive and recognize the message. My solitary time on the bicycle allowed me to do the same; maybe not as profoundly and certainly not as eloquently. But for the time being, there was no mistaking my place or purpose in the Universe.

CHAPTER 8

▼

NATIVE AMERICANS

I spent the entire day in the motel room at Monticello, while it snowed outside. I was happy for the break because I did not feel good. I had a headache, which was rare for me. That night while lying in bed, I could feel my heartbeat in my breath and my resting pulse was 72 (it was normally 54). I also noticed that it seemed like I had to force myself to breathe, almost like I was unconsciously holding my breath. I knew something was wrong and I suspected my diet. I looked awful; like an AIDS patient and I knew my diet had to change. I was a vegetarian, but I realized in order to continue The Journey I was going to have to eat meat, which would provide more protein and calories. I was worried that I was getting so skinny and that I might be affecting my muscle mass. There was no fat on my body, and that coming from the man who at one time was the President of "The Fat Boys Club" at Keystone Resort in Colorado. The FBC was a group of guys who met every Saturday morning to go skiing and we had strict guidelines as to what we could eat and drink and the minimum percentage of body fat we had. Needless to say, I would be heavily fined for my current condition.

The next day I took off south on Highway 191 toward Bluff, Utah. I had driven this road several times when we used to go to Lake Powell every fall for vacation, but this was the first time I had biked it. The morning air was clear and crisp and I was enjoying the ride. It was March 19 and it dawned on me that I had been riding with snow on the ground for a solid month, ever since I left Flagstaff.

Because of my health, I checked out a couple of motels when I arrived at Bluff, but wasn't pleased with the prices. South of town I camped along the San Juan River. What an unbelievable setting. I had the river on one side and was surrounded on the other side by huge red rock cliffs, with petroglyphs. Unfortunately, even the spiritual surroundings couldn't make me feel better. I was getting worse by the minute. I now had flu-like symptoms, a fever, and was extremely nauseated. I couldn't even think of eating, but I was concerned about replenishing my body from all the energy I had burned that day. Finally, that evening I was able to gag down three cinnamon rolls, but I was awake most of the night with a terrible burning in my stomach and a constant feeling of having to vomit. I even put a bag next to my head so I wouldn't make a mess all over the tent.

I arose the next morning to the sound of birds singing and the feel of frost all around. I felt better and everything seemed right with the world. I couldn't imagine being in a more peaceful place. After breakfast, I loaded up the bike and took off for Kayenta, Ariz., 70 miles away. Utah was state #5 and the sign read "Still the right place." I would spend the next several days crossing over the Arizona/Utah state line on the way to Nevada.

I stopped for lunch in Mexican Hat, Ariz., a spot in the road in the vast desert of northern Arizona. I needed to start eating meat, but every time the opportunity came, I passed. For lunch I ordered a grilled cheese sandwich and fries. When the waitress brought the order out, it was ham and cheese. I started to call her back but then remembered that things happen for a reason. I ate the sandwich and again changed the dynamics of The

Journey. I knew there were two things that were essential for this trip to continue; my health and the bike's health. I also wanted to minimize the number of the things I worried about. From that moment on I would not only eat meat, I pledged to eat as much as I could, whenever I could. I didn't need to be agonizing over consuming enough protein or calories. Besides, if you are burning 4,000 to 8,000 calories a day, you really don't have to worry about your waistline.

I struggled the last 20 miles riding into Kayenta. I had no energy and no strength. I was battling a head wind and EVERY joint in my body ached. I paid for a motel room and stood in the hot shower forever. In the middle of the night I woke up and was drenched from head to toe in a cold sweat. My first thought was "the fever broke."—and after drying off I wondered how long I had been sick and with what. I was impressed I had pedaled 70 miles that day, into the wind, being that sick. But mostly, I was happy that I had a motel room.

It was 105 miles to Page, Ariz. Because of my shaky health, I decided to break it up into two days and free camp in the desert one night. There were no towns between Kayenta and Page and I was feeling OK, so I wasn't too worried. Two Native Americans came over to talk with me when I stopped for a snack at a convenience store. It wasn't 10 a.m. yet but they were drunk, very drunk. Their speech was slurred and their eyes had a permanent glaze over them. I knew that talk with Native Americans about their plight would have to wait. From history I knew they received a raw deal at one time. But having biked through their land the past month, I felt some connection to the Spirit that used to be so prevalent in their society. I wanted to hear how Native Americans felt but, unfortunately, these two were more interested in getting money from me to buy some beer. They also let me know it was dangerous to camp in the desert because there were bands of "young Indians" that go around killing people. I accepted their advice for what it was, the ramblings of a couple of drunks.

I thought about the two men a lot that day. They appeared to be my age, maybe younger. I was sad, but didn't know if it was from what the white man had done to the Indians to cause these two to be in that kind of shape so early in the morning, or if it was because the Indians had not taken charge of their lives after all these years. My observation of the Indians, having ridden my bike through several reservations was this: They no longer acted like Native Americans; they wore cowboy boots and hats, they drove nice pickups, yet still lived in shacks and hogans, and they drank too much. I knew this was a generalization, but it was what I observed from my limited contact. I couldn't help but think that Indians needed to return to being Native Americans. Quit trying to live the white man's lie of more is better. Get back to the Native American way of living; simplify their life and get in touch with the Powers of the Universe that guided their ancestors.

That afternoon I pulled 100 yards off the road and set up camp behind some pinon pines trees on the edge of an arroyo. It felt like a setting straight out of a Carlos Castaneda book. I half expected to see Don Juan walking down the gully. I was sitting there eating peanuts and it dawned on me this was what The Journey was all about. It was so peaceful and I had a grand view of the valley that stretched out before me. I decided to take some pictures of my camp and as I walked past the tree behind my tent, something brushed my hand. I looked down and there were two Anasazi pottery shards sitting in the red dirt. WOW! I couldn't believe it. Here I was camping on the very ground where the "Ancient Ones" used to live. There was a reason they lived here and I had to think it was their connection with Nature. I felt privileged to spend the evening in a place with so much energy.

At dusk, while sitting by the tent, I heard some heavy breathing coming down the gully. It was a pack of wild dogs and they stopped right below me, 40 yards away. They couldn't see me through the brush except for one pup that had run out into an opening. He was looking right at me so I attempted to remain motionless. I could tell he was confused. He knew I wasn't supposed to be there, but he lacked the confidence to alert the others, so he just let out a couple of weak yelps. As the other dogs took off down the gully, he quickly joined them. I was a bit concerned about their possible return, so I secured everything in the tent or in the tree. As I sat there that evening taking in the view and feeling the peacefulness of the moment and the area, I thought, "If I were a Native American, I would live in a teepee right here!"

I awoke to another beautiful Southwest morning and felt good despite waking up in the middle of the night in a cold sweat again. I wrote it off as the remnants of being sick. I loaded up the bike and set out for Page, Ariz. While riding through the pine-treed hills I spotted someone on the road ahead. As I drew closer, I could see it was a Native American hitch-hiking in the opposite direction. As I went past him, I threw the peace sign and asked if he needed some water. He said he did, so I turned around. When I pulled up next to him, it was obvious that he was drunk. I handed him a water bottle without conversation. As he squirted the water into his mouth, he gagged and spit up all over the bottle. I didn't say anything, but I was upset. Here I was out in the middle of nowhere trying to do a good deed and I get spit on, literally. Fortunately, I came upon an outpost down the road where I cleaned up the bottle and got some fresh water.

I made it into Page that afternoon before the Lake Powell Int'l Hostel opened for check-in. I rode over to the park and ate some peanuts while resting in the shade. After a while, a Native American came over and sat down next to me. He told me he was a Navajo. He looked to be 50 years old and was very drunk. I'm not so sure that he didn't approach me for some money, but when he sat down and saw I was living on a bicycle, it seemed to dissuade him. He asked me where I was staying and when I told him I camped along the road, he invited me to his hogan. Under any other circumstance I would have accepted his invitation, but I wasn't even sure he knew where his hogan was. Sure enough, before I left the park I observed his buddies throwing him into the back of their pickup. Again I felt sadness for what I had observed that day, but couldn't identify the real culprit. No denying those bad things happened in the past, but we all have to move on. Everyone has the ability to make his or her realities a heaven or a hell.

CHAPTER 9

▼

TIME TO QUIT!?

I spent several nights at the hostel in Page. It was a nice enough place run by an attractive English woman, Kate. There was quite an eclectic mix of people staying there, including; Lea, a psychic, Don, who was an actor from Korea, a graduate student from Stanford named Martina, some Germans and Aussies. One night after dinner, I treated myself to a banana split in my new effort to eat as much as I could whenever I could, while we all sat around talking about our experiences in life. I always enjoyed those exchanges' and especially with foreign people; they have a tendency to view the world, and sometimes life, differently than most Americans.

The morning I took off for Kanab, Utah, was like most of the other mornings I had experienced in the Southwest, pleasant. I even stopped at the Glen Canyon Dam to take some pictures. It wasn't long after that I was riding in the worst wind of the trip. After a couple of hours it occurred to me that I wasn't going to make it to Kanab before sundown, so I began looking for a place to pull off the road. The place I found wasn't perfect, but it had a great view. I was on shale rock and a bit of a slope. I wasn't completely out of sight from the road, so I decided to hang out behind some pinon pine trees and put up my tent after dark. I used the time to listen to the tapes I had from the first two months of The Journey. My mother bought me a voice-activated recorder before I left. Another great gift because the last thing I wanted to do after a long day of riding was to write in a journal, although I did use both methods to document The Journey. Listening to the tapes made the trip seem more depressing than rewarding. One thing that really stuck out was how bad my diet had been. I then proceeded to have some junk food for dinner because I had 40 miles to go the next day and couldn't afford to use any water for cooking. One of the drawbacks to free camping in the desert is water, or the lack of it.

Other than the wind and a flat tire, I had a productive day. Along the road, I found a brand new bungee cord, a pair of sunglasses, and a ski cap. While I was sitting there waiting for the sun to go down, I thought about The Journey and if I was going to be able to make it around America. I needed to start relaxing and quit worrying about things that didn't make a difference in my life. I knew how important it was to live in the moment, but even that can be a challenge. At the particular moment I was, again, covered with bug bites (probably from the hostel) and I was low on food and water. To make matters worse, my thigh began to cramp. That had never happened before and it frightened me to get a cramp in such a large muscle. I massaged it for a while and it seemed OK. The bottom line; I was in a beautiful place, I was relatively healthy, and the bike was working. Not a whole lot to complain about. What did Joe Walsh say? "I can't complain, but sometimes I still do." I was actually looking forward to getting to the hostel in Kanab; it advertised itself as the "best breakfast in the West" and I loved breakfast—my favorite meal of the day.

The next day, the wind was already blowing at 8 a.m. and I only had one bottle of water for 40 miles, so I was a bit concerned. I rode three hours and only covered 18 miles. The wind was brutal. At times, I could only pedal 4 mph. I felt like a salmon swimming upstream. Then, as if that wasn't bad enough, a spoke popped on the rear wheel, drive-side. Taking shelter from the wind behind a pinon pine tree, I trued the wheel as best I could, had some trail mix, a splash of water, and resumed my battle with the wind. As I rationed my water, my thirst became paramount. My concern escalated to worry. With the wind, it would still take three hours to get to Kanab and I had less than half a bottle of water left. Just as I was preparing to move from worry to panic, I spotted a car on the shoulder ahead. There was a young man walking around the car and I asked him if he needed any help. He said they had run out of gas and one of the guys had already hitched a ride to town. They were students from Utah University on spring break. We talked a while and I kept noticing their water bottles. I asked if they might have some extra water and they responded by filling up both of my bottles. How ironic their misfortune was my salvation.

I made it to Kanab an hour before the Canyonland Int'l Hostel opened, so I went to the post office and boxed up anything I hadn't touched in the last month and sent it home. I was desperate to take some stress off the bike. There wasn't a bike shop in town, so I'd have to replace the spokes somewhere down the road.

An Eastern Indian, Errol, ran the hostel. It was close to being the dirtiest place I stayed, second only to the motel in Gallup. The filth was one thing, but when Errol offered to give me a massage, I seriously considered finding a motel.

The next morning at the "Best Breakfast in the West," I almost threw up. There was a variety to choose from, but it was offensive. Everything was in plastic containers that were visibly grungy. There were years of crud on the side of the bowls. I went back to the room, loaded up the bike, and took off in the rain. There was no way I was going to spend another minute in that place.

I was disillusioned with the whole trip at that point and considered quitting. I missed my family and friends and was becoming depressed. I rode 40 miles in the pouring rain to the town of Colorado City, Ariz., a town of polygamists. Someone at the hostel told me that a faction of the Mormons had split off a few years earlier and had started this town in order to practice their beliefs in polygamy. I wasn't too interested in their beliefs at the moment, I was more interested in finding shelter from the storm—I was soaked!

While I was in town, I popped another spoke on the rear wheel and felt like crying. I found a room, got cleaned up, and had a nice dinner. I was contemplating hitching a ride the next day to St. George, Utah, to have the bike repaired. However, the ladies waiting on me at dinner told me there was a bicycle shop in Colorado City and gave me the phone number.

The next day it was still raining, but I rode my bike to All Sports hoping for some new spokes. Unfortunately, the store was exactly what the name said, "all sports," and did not specialize in bicycles. My heart began to pound. Then I noticed the kid waiting on me was about 13 years old. I asked him if he was sure he could help me and he said, "I think so." When I asked if he would mind me coming back to help him, he said, "Fine." He was having a hard time removing the free wheel; which, as I mentioned before, was why I used bike shops when the broken spoke was on the rear wheel, drive-side. About an hour had passed when his brother, who owned the shop, arrived. The kid said, "Alright, here comes the pro." I felt a bit of relief, feeling anyone would know more than this kid. But when I saw "the pro" with a mallet in his hand, I panicked. I yelled at him to "STOP" and told him to put the bike back together. About then, their older brother, Edward, appeared. Edward was the oldest of 18 kids. He appeared to be about my age. He wanted to know what the problem was and his brothers tried to explain it to him. I explained my version and he offered to give me a ride to the bicycle shop in St. George. I think he was concerned I might sue them. On the drive over he explained a little about the history of Colorado City and their "religion" to me. Before we left the shop I saw his father who looked to be about 60 years old and what I assumed were two wives. One looked to be the same age as the father, but one appeared to be in her 20s and had an infant in her arms. I found out later that the ladies who had waited on me at dinner were both wives of the chef. One looked older than I did and the other one was just out of school.

The houses in this town were incredible. Most of them had the appearance of small motels. I couldn't make sense of it all, but I was glad to be out of that town and especially out of that shop. My stomach was in a knot. At one point in the shop I saw The Journey coming to an end. Because I didn't know enough to help myself, I had a 13-year-old boy messing with my bike. I had no one to blame for my predicament but me.

Edward took me to Bicycles Unlimited and they were great. James not only fixed my rear wheel and tuned up the bike, he also reassured me the bike was sound and had many more miles in it. He also sold me a kevlar spoke that I could put on the rear wheel, drive-side, until I made it to a bike shop. Wow! This was just what I needed, some positive feedback and a useful tool—completely different from the shop in Durango. James was excited about his upcoming wedding and he was excited about bicycles. I thanked him for all his help and wished him the best.

I spent three days in St. George waiting out the weather (El Nino was starting to flex his muscles) and trying to build up my psyche. I was extremely fragile at the moment, mentally. I couldn't appreciate The Journey if the bike was going to break down every 60 miles. But three days later I was rested, the bike was tuned up, and the weather was perfect—so I took off for Nevada.

As I rode through Mesquite, Nev. (state #6), I came across someone else on a bicycle. Charles was a retired doctor from Colorado, who traveled around with his family in a motor home. I talked with him about what I was doing and specifically about my diet. He told me that my furnace was burning white hot and it didn't matter what I put in it..."As long as I was always stoking the fire." He was so positive and reinforced me on everything I was doing. He was a helpful person and turned me onto a $20 room at a nearby casino. I not only rested up for the big push into Las Vegas the next day, but also was able to watch the NCAA Basketball Finals that night.

Unfortunately, Utah gave the game away. They had it won and stopped playing too soon. I took that as a sign for The Journey. I could quit right now, or I could continue until the final buzzer.

Taking Charles' advice, I loaded up at the breakfast buffet the next morning. Everything was fine the first 50 miles, and then I popped a spoke—shit! I trued the wheel and went another 10 miles before I popped another spoke. I couldn't believe it. What the hell was going on? I began cursing at no one in particular. The wind was howling and I couldn't true the wheel enough to ride, plus I had forgotten about the kevlar spoke I had, so I stuck out my thumb to hitchhike. The first thing I noticed was a lack of pickup trucks going by and also how much I looked like a bum. I wouldn't even pick myself up. Finally, two Mexicans in a brand new truck stopped. They could barely speak English and didn't know where a bike shop was, but they were giving me a ride—God bless them!

How ironic that Mexicans would be helping me out. I grew up in southern Colorado where I was a minority and frequently was harassed at school by Hispanic kids. Because of this, I've rarely hid my prejudice. This judgmental part of my character was something I have worked to soften over the years and rightly so, for now in my hour of need were two Mexicans helping me out of a jam. When they dropped me off I offered to pay them, but they refused to take any money. The young man on the passenger side threw me the peace sign and said, "God bless you." With a tear in my eye I replied, "And, God bless you."

Once again the bike was repaired and I found the Las Vegas Backpackers Resort Hostel downtown. I knew something was going to have to change, because I could not go on this way. There were going to be stretches on this trip without major cities and bike shops and I was requiring repairs every other day.

But for now, I was at the hostel and they offered dinner for $3, plus, tonight was "Party Night" so beer was free all night. The dinner was OK and I was debating whether I should allow myself the luxury of a beer for all I had been through, when this young lady from Sweden, Anna, came over and asked me if I would like to have a beer. To this day, I don't know why a beautiful young Swedish girl, with her choice of a hostel full of young guys would hang out with some old biking hippie. But we had a couple of beers and enjoyed the evening together. We even decided to tour Las Vegas together the next day. Wow! Earlier that day was about as low as I could go and now I was flying high.

The next day I had breakfast in the common area and was hanging out waiting for Anna, when this young man came in and asked if anyone was interested in a ride up north. At first I didn't pay any attention to him, but then I realized I was trying to make it to Fallen, Nev., and there was nothing but snow in the forecast. We began talking and the next thing I knew I was loading my gear in Rob's vehicle. Anna seemed a bit shocked when she came down and found out I was leaving and I was a bit shocked as well that I would be leaving her, but this seemed like another situation of something happening for a reason.

Rob was a Canadian who had been riding his mountain bike in Mexico. He obtained this car through a service that matches up drivers with vehicles to get the cars from point A to point B in a specified time. He was a cool guy, a very cool guy. He was good looking, had a sense of humor, a sense of adventure, and seemed quite intelligent. We talked about various subjects, but really made a connection on the book "*Ishmael*" by Daniel Quinn, the best book I have ever read. That book was responsible for my being on this journey. He told me about a book club in Ontario that met every week specifically to discuss "Ishmael." I was jazzed; he was the first person I'd met that was affected as much as I was by that book. The miles flew by and we arrived in Fallen by nightfall. I called my friends, the Hegerles, gave Rob $20, and wished him well.

Kevin Hegerle and I used to work together in Summit County. We had won softball and basketball championships together and we received MBAs from the University of Denver together. Kevin was the best athlete I ever played with; an unbelievable talent and a very mellow demeanor. He also was extremely intelligent and very religious. But the thing I always liked about him was that whenever we were together, we found something to laugh about.

Kevin's wife, Elaine, was out of town during my visit, taking care of family matters. Laura, their oldest daughter, was getting a Ph.D. from Dartmouth in mathematics (obviously had some of her Dad's smarts) and Kara, a second daughter, was married and living in Fallen. The youngest two, Brian and Erin, were still living at home attending school. Brian is a jock like his father, although a bit more of a showboat. And Erin is simply The Best! I told Kevin and Elaine I would have children in a minute if I knew they would be like Erin. She was everything you would want in a teenager but rarely get; polite, helpful, understanding—she was the complete package. Like the Goffs, the Hegerles had done an excellent job of raising their family.

I stayed with the Hegerles for a week to let the snowy weather pass, but also because I now had a mental block about getting back on the bike. I didn't want to ride *B.O.P.* anymore. I didn't want The Journey to continue, but I didn't know how to quit. Physically I was OK, so I couldn't use myself as an excuse. Something was always wrong with the bike, but at the moment it was tuned up and ready to go, so I couldn't use the bike as an excuse. So what was my excuse? Money? Camping cost a lot more than I expected, my food budget had doubled, and I was throwing money at the bike in every other town I came to. But money wasn't a big issue in my life anymore. Not since I chose the path to simplify my life.

This simplification began after my divorce from Jan. I dated a few women, but never felt a connection. I decided to eliminate the stress of women from my life and soon became celibate. Not long after that, I was downsized from my job at Keystone Resort when Vail bought them out. That was when I sold my house and gave my possessions away. I bought a trailer and moved it on the 40 acres I previously purchased in South Park, Colo. There was no electricity or running water, but it was the best time of my life. I was 44 years old, didn't owe anyone a dime, and was as close to Nature as I could handle at the moment. It didn't take long to realize that money was not what made me happy and I was determined it would not be an issue on The Journey. I wasn't rich, but I wanted to take the trip and pay for it myself, without sponsors—that was part of the freedom of The Journey. The bottom line was, I didn't have a good enough excuse to quit—The Journey continued!

CHAPTER 10

▼

WHAT ABOUT B.O.B.?

On my way to Reno I rode on the "loneliest highway in America," Highway 50. The ride was pleasant enough in the morning; there wasn't a whole lot to see but there was very little traffic to contend with. The ride in the afternoon on Interstate 80 was another story; rumble bumps extended across the entire shoulder and the asphalt was terrible. I stopped a few miles outside of Reno to have a snack and then discovered I was at the Mustang Ranch, the famous Nevada brothel—some other time maybe.

I stayed with Jerry and Carol Mallen in Reno, the parents of Holly Dobson, a former co-worker at Keystone Resort. Holly and I had shared some office space and I was surprised when she gave me her parents' phone number before I left. I was even more surprised when I called and found out that Holly, her husband Don and the kids were visiting on spring break. Don was a charter member of The Fat Boys Club and a helluva skier. We had spent some great days on the slopes together. I had a great visit with them and took off for California the next morning.

Don gave me a ride to the west side of Reno where I jumped on I-80. At the top of the Sierra Nevada's in California (state #7), it began snowing, hard! I quickly found the Soda Springs Ski Lodge and asked the lady behind the desk, Betty, if she had a room. She did and quoted me a price. As my jaw dropped, she asked if I was on a bicycle. Because I was, she gave me the summer rate. She suggested I get cleaned up and then come down to the restaurant for some homemade German potato soup. What a great lady!

Al, the chef, was from Sacramento. We talked about a variety of topics and although he thought what I was doing was honorable, he cautioned me several times about not dropping out of society. In the meantime, Betty came around and gave me another free helping of soup. It was a good stop for me; I missed the snowstorm, ate some delicious soup, and had some stimulating conversation. Al was African-American, as was Charlie, the doctor in Arizona, and Randolf, the hostel clerk in Texas. I hadn't spent much time around black people, but for some reason they kept showing up on The Journey giving me new perspectives on life. In fact, Betty, my guardian angel, was the first black person I had ever hung out with, but that is a story for another time.

The next morning I had breakfast and waited around while the sun did its work. Around 11 a.m. I headed toward Sacramento. I was at 9,000-ft elevation and Sacramento was at 25 ft—Yahoo! I was hauling ass and would cover the 80 miles in no time. All of a sudden I heard from behind me, "Please pull off at the next exit." I pulled off and a state trooper came up next to me. "What the hell do you think you're doing?" he asked, rather excitedly. I told him I was riding to Sacramento, to which he retorted, "Not on I-80 yer not!" I asked him what he proposed I do and he told me I'd have to use the back-roads. His purpose for removing me from the interstate was to keep me from being sucked under a semi. I told him I had been on the interstate in six other states so far and hadn't been sucked under yet. He then informed me that it was illegal for me to have my bicycle on the interstate there. Getting me off the interstate so a semi didn't suck me under turned out to be a joke. Now I was on a back-road with no shoulder with logging trucks roaring by. Plus, not all the back-roads were on the map, so I had to occasionally stop to ask directions. It took me an extra day, but the ride through the countryside was beautiful. It was springtime and there were fields of flowers, huge pine trees, and rolling green hills all the way to Sacramento.

The extra day also gave me some additional time to think about what Al had said. I thought about how there was a group of people who had dropped out of "society." People who didn't pay taxes, didn't obey laws, didn't live their lives by the rules that "society" dictates. Unbeknownst to me, I would soon get to witness these people up-close and personal.

The HI-Sacramento Hostel is a beautiful old restored mansion right downtown. The manager, Becky, was a nice lady with a bubbly personality. I signed up to stay for five nights. I wasn't sure about my route from there and also wanted to check out some trailers. I couldn't continue the way I was going and needed to find a way to relieve some stress off *B.O.P.* I phoned Perry in Burbank, the biker I had met in New Mexico who had a *B.O.B.* (Beast Of Burden) trailer, to see if he might be interested in selling it. He just had been released from the hospital. Apparently, just before he made it back home on his journey, he was struck by a hit and run driver. He had multiple injuries, but he thought the trailer might have saved his life, as it took the brunt of the impact. He was doing OK, but the trailer was history.

As fate would have it there was a couple from Australia staying at the hostel and they were bike touring with a *B.O.B.* trailer. Warren and Kirsten were riding across North America before heading on to Europe. They loved the trailer and Warren let me ride his bike to get a feel for how it handled. I went out and bought a *B.O.B.* trailer the next day.

Warren and Kirsten were great people; not just because they turned me on to the trailer, but we also spent some time together and talked about touring. They were so positive with very high energy, and I tried to absorb it all. We even talked about possibly meeting again later in the year on the East Coast.

My days were spent at the library and at Capital Park. I read Ayn Rand's "*Anthem*," Tobias Wolff's "*Back To Reality*," and hung out with those people who were not playing by the "rules"; street people, homeless people. This was a real eye opener for me. Because of my appearance and the fact I was showing up in the park everyday, I was accepted into their territory. No one hit me up for money or cigarettes and I quickly recognized whose territory was whose. Kenny, my roommate at the hostel, told me that most of the street people were Vietnam War veterans. Like the Native Americans, I didn't know exactly how to feel. These guys had been through a hell that I had not experienced. But I still wondered why they couldn't pick up their lives and move on.

Then it hit me. We all have demons we are battling and our lives are shaped by how we choose to fight those battles. I had never been an Indian and I had never been in a war. Consequently, I could not pass judgment on how these people chose to live their lives. But I did have a certain amount of compassion for them and it made my biking demons seem insignificant at the moment.

It was April 15, the start of my fourth month, and I could make it to Seattle in two weeks. Because of the weather, I didn't want to be there until June. I made a decision to head south and visit my Dad's relatives, the Hoaglands. Lee is my Dad's cousin, and he and his wife, Lorraine, lived in Pueblo with their five kids, years ago. Now they lived south of Yosemite National Park so I rode on Highway 16 out of Sacramento— *B.O.P.*, *B.O.B*, and me.

Once again, the dynamics of The Journey had changed. At the moment, *B.O.B.* was a welcome addition taking the added stress off of *B.O.P.* It was a beautiful ride; rolling green hills, trees with leaves on them, and flowers everywhere. The sun was shining and I felt strong. I had observed that my knees generally started aching every day after about 40 or 50 miles. Biking in these hills, they started aching after 25 or 30 miles.

I spent the night in Jackson, Calif., and the next day was half way to Sonora when a spoke popped on the rear wheel. I couldn't believe it. This shouldn't be happening. I just spent a wallet full of money so this wouldn't be happening. I took a deep breath, unloaded the bike, and put on the kevlar spoke the guys at Bicycles Unlimited in St. George, Utah, had sold me. I had forgotten about it when I had the problems going into Las Vegas, but thankfully remembered now and it worked great. The spoke is made out of kevlar, which is a synthetic material that is flexible yet durable. The perfect fit for when you break a spoke on the rear wheel, drive-side, and can't get the free wheel off. The first statement in the instructions tells you to congratulate yourself for having a kevlar spoke with you. I trued the wheel and rode into Sonora.

I stayed in the dorms at Columbia College. They had a hostel there once, but it was discontinued for some reason. The girl running employee housing was kind enough to rent me a room for $12 since it was spring break and most of the kids were gone—what a deal! What a beautiful campus with views of huge Ponderosa Pines on the hills outside of Sonora. I felt good despite the broken spoke. The past two days had been some tough biking, but the scenery was outstanding, as was the weather. I had no idea that the next day would be the most pivotal day of the entire journey.

I rode into town the next day to the bike shop to have the spoke replaced. Before I left that morning, these words came out of my mouth, "You would think I would have more warning if today is the day I'm going to die." For some reason, I was feeling really weird. I tried to call Jan while they worked on the bike, but wasn't able to reach her. Jan and I had been divorced for four years. After we recovered from the pain and anger of leaving each other, we became best friends. It made sense to me; no one knew me better than Jan and we had a certain comfort level of being able to talk about anything with each other. She is a beautiful woman, but she is a beautiful person as well. She has a strong desire to make herself a better person and had worked hard on her spiritual growth. She is very talented and extremely intelligent. I don't shy from telling anyone that she is my Soul Mate. I was bummed when she didn't answer.

I picked up my rig and headed down Highway 49. At Moccasin, Calif., I stopped to take a layer of clothes off and put on some sunscreen. Two guys about my age were out walking and came over to see what I was doing. One asked me how much weight I had on the bike and what my gear ratios where. I told him there were 90 lbs. on the bike and trailer and that the little gear on my chain ring was a 32. He said there was no way I could pedal up the hills ahead. He said I would have to push my rig because there were 10 percent grades ahead. I told him I had already biked 3,000 miles and had not pushed the bike up a hill yet, except through snow, and that I had been over the Continental Divide and the Sierra Nevada's. He wished me good luck, but his negative energy really irritated me. Not long after our meeting, I began pedaling up the hills.

It was hot and I was working hard, but I felt strong. All of a sudden, my rear wheel torqued out of the frame. Fortunately, no one was coming as I dragged the bike and trailer off to the side. This wasn't the first time this happened. It began after I got the trailer. The trailer was designed to attach to the rear axle of the bicycle. When you buy the trailer, you receive a new quick release with BOBBINS that the trailer hooks over and is then secured with cotter pins. I noticed it wasn't working when they were first outfitting my bicycle for the trailer at REI, the outdoor-equipment retailer. They eventually added some washers that required extra torque on the quick release to hold the wheel in place; more torque than most riders or bike shop mechanics would apply. Apparently, the guy that morning had not tightened the quick release enough to hold the wheel in place with the additional trailer weight. I unloaded the bike, repositioned the wheel, and cranked down on the quick release. I didn't ride too much further when the rear wheel torqued out again. I was on a very steep winding road and I was freaking out. I momentarily considered throwing the bike and trailer over the cliff. I was completely out of my mind. I kept telling myself to calm down and think of what I needed to do. I put the bike back together again and determined that I COULDN'T make it up the hill. I thought of the guy I had met earlier and cursed him. I cursed him for his negative energy and because I COULDN'T make it. I decided to return to Sonora.

As I was coming down the pass I came to a bridge over a river and actually thought about riding off the road into the river. The fact I even had the thought freaked me out, so I stopped and tried to snap myself out of it. I wasn't the type of person that considered suicide as an option for dealing with problems. I couldn't imagine ever sinking lower in life than I was at that moment. I knew it wasn't a good place to be.

I was often asked why I was doing this ride. My response was because I possessed the physical, mental and financial ability to do it. But I was questioning my mental ability at the moment. This was as fragile a mental condition I had ever reached.

But it is true what they say; "It is always darkest just before the dawn." As I was standing there feeling sorry for myself, I looked down and saw the angel on my jersey. I attended the funeral of my friend, Jeff Hobbs, in November. His niece, Summer, gave me the angel and I wore it every day of The Journey to remind myself how lucky I was to be able to do this. It was times like this when I really needed to take a moment and reflect. Jeff had a horrible disease, Ataxia, which slowly attacks the muscles' ability to function. He spent the last years of his life in a wheelchair with 24-hour care. Jeff's mother, Shirley, and his brother, Steve, also died from the disease, as well as his grandmother. I looked at the angel and realized I really didn't have a problem. Or if I did, I should at least be able to deal with it.

A few miles down the road, I came across a couple hitchhiking. Mary Anne was an old hippie, about my age. She had long curly brown hair, a tank top with a flowery skirt, and an unbelievable energy. She was radiating. Her son, Josh, was a young hippie with the same energy. They were from the little town of Groveland and were trying to catch a ride to the big city, San Francisco, for a weekend of fun. They were both so full of love. In fact, when they heard what I had just gone through, they both came over and hugged me, which meant a lot to me. I wished I could have stashed the bike and joined them.

Back in Sonora, I was feeling a bit shell shocked. I went into the store for some groceries and a young man, Scott, came over and started talking about bike touring. He worked at a local watering hole and told me to come in and he would buy me dinner. I noticed how nice everyone was to me since the incident and I almost started crying.

Back at the dorm, I tried to call Jan again. When she answered I did start crying, like I had never cried before. It was a real soul cleansing and I absolutely could not stop. I missed her so much at that moment and I really wanted someone to take me away from The Journey. She didn't take me away, but what she did was let me know I was one of the luckiest people she knew. She told me she loved me, my family loved me and God loved me. She also told me she didn't know anyone else that had as many friends that loved them, as I did. She saved The Journey. I had an incredible calm after we hung up and seemed to be able to think more clearly. I would never forget what I went through and what Jan did for me. That was an unbelievable day in my life.

I rented a car the next day and drove over to visit with Lee and Lorraine. I spent the night and we caught up on 33 years of happenings. It was strange driving a car, but it was a good break and the guy I cursed was right, those hills would have been tough to bike over.

A couple of miles outside of Jackson, Calif., on the best day of the trip (I love biking through a forest when the sun is shining), a spoke popped. I unhooked the trailer, put on the kevlar spoke, and was on my way in 30 minutes. I was well aware that I did not curse and accepted the incident as part of The Journey—I had a new attitude. In town, the owner of the Jackson Bike Shop fixed the bike for free. His wife also took my picture and put it up on the wall with other cross-country bike riders that had stopped in. They were very nice to me and I appreciated the attention and generosity.

Although the broken spoke didn't upset me, it did concern me. Back in Sacramento I went to REI and told them I was still popping spokes even with the trailer. They took my rear wheel off and a bit later informed me that whoever built that wheel had put too much tension on the spokes. As a result, it had fatigued the wheel and the spokes, thus the constant popping. With their help, I upgraded the entire back end; wheel, hub and axle—all the while cursing those butt-heads in Durango.

It was going to take a couple of days to fix the bike, so I checked back into the hostel. This particular hostel had a restriction of staying seven days out of every 30. My two stays would total 10 days, so I asked for some lenience and offered to work around the hostel. They allowed me to stay some extra days, so I spent one day washing the city grime off the hostel exterior. Not a pleasant job, but I felt useful.

One day I tried to visit Ted Kaczynski, The Unabomber. He was in the Sacramento County Main Jail, just a couple blocks from the hostel. I filled out form 0120 (revised 1/98)—

Inmate to be visited:

Name:	Theodore Kaczynski
Xref:	3165854
Floor:	8w
Pod:	3
Cell:	11
Prsn visiting:	Monte M. Lowrance

I had a tremendous fascination with Kaczynski. I viewed him as someone who understood the Laws of Nature and the fact that humans are the only species on this planet that no longer lived by those laws; e.g. killing for no reason. He was an extremely intelligent man who was in touch with Nature at one time. Unfortunately, he couldn't figure out how to deal with his demons, Nature versus Technology, and ended up snapping. I do not condone what he did to resolve his conflicts, but I was interested in his thoughts on Nature. I thought the longer he was incarcerated, the more diluted his thoughts would become. I thought it was important that someone besides an "official" talk with him before he was put away for-ever. I filled out the visitation form and handed it to the desk sergeant. He typed in the information, looked up at me, and said matter of factly,

"He won't see you!"

I asked, "How do you know that without even asking him?"

"Who are you?" he wanted to know.

"I'm just a guy riding a bicycle around America."

"He won't even see his family, so I doubt he'll see you," he informed me.

The sergeant phoned upstairs, "Bob, there is a Lowrance here to see Kaczynski." Over the phone I heard Bob relay the message to Ted by yelling down the hall...then I heard a loud, crazed, "NOOOOOOO!" The desk sergeant looked at me and shrugged his shoulders with a sly smile. I looked back at him and thanked him for trying. I walked out of the jailhouse disappointed and realized my fears about Kaczynski had already manifested. He was gone! Maybe he was gone a long time ago, but whatever was once there was now buried in the "system."

I spent the last couple of days in the park observing the street people. I had been consumed the last couple of years trying to simplify my life. The thinking being was; the less you have to worry about, the happier you are. Then I got to thinking; these people essentially own nothing, but not one of them ever smiles. They spend an inordinate amount of time searching for food. Were they happier than I was? Were they happier than the busi-ness people eating lunch in the park or the protesters over at the capitol building were? I don't know, but I do know I like to laugh every day and I never saw one of them laugh.

The day I rode out of Sacramento was a bizarre day for me. I felt like The Journey was starting all over. I had been through so much physically, mentally, spiritually and financially. I now had a trailer and a new wheel, and I was rested. I was riding out of town on the old Garden Highway Road, when a group of bikers started passing me. Out of nowhere I heard someone yell, "Monte!" I looked over and there were David and Sean from REI. What a great feeling to be recognized so far from home. David dropped out of the pack and rode with me for a while. He told me about his racing career and how much he enjoyed working at REI. Just as he was preparing to leave, we both heard a ping from my bike. He told me to pull over and he would take a look at it. One of the spokes had pulled loose on the new wheel, but didn't break. He trued up the wheel and told me to check it periodically. He showed me how to check the tension of my spokes in tandem, two at a time. What a nice guy and how lucky I was that he was there at that moment. Was it a coincidence, a random occurrence in a chaotic Universe, or was it part of a Grand Design? I couldn't figure it out, but I sure was happy they appeared when they did.

I battled the wind, sun, and loose spokes for the next three days making my way to Redding, Calif. It was April 28, my 45th birthday. I secured a motel room, two cans of Coors, and a can of cashews. I decided to treat myself, so I had found a Motel 6 with a pool and went swimming. The air temperature was 90 degrees, but the pool was not heated. It was still early in the season, so I was the only one in the pool and it felt good to be using different muscles.

The next two days required unbelievable climbs through the Cascade Mountains on Highway 299. On the top of one pass I hopped off the bike and yelled, "I'm King of the World!" I felt strong and the bike was performing well—Life was good! My only real concern was that I was still waking up in the middle of the night in a cold sweat.

Other than being run off the road by a semi, the ride from Sacramento to the Oregon border was absolutely beautiful. It was the first time I had a truck literally run me off the highway. On the back roads I could always hear the trucks before I could see them. But when they were close I kept an eye on them in my mirror, especially if there was traffic coming in the opposite direction. In this particular case, there wasn't any on-coming traffic, but I could see that he was not going to give me any room. I bailed off to the right and thought, "What would have happened if I hadn't reacted?"

If I had to live in California, I'd live in Fall River Mills where the Mexican restaurant serves a short stack with three pancakes for breakfast, instead of the usual two.

CHAPTER 11

▼

FALSE ALARM

I was just outside of Oregon, when I experienced tightness on the lower right side of my abdomen. I called my sister, Vicky, who is a doctor in Colorado and she suggested I have it checked out immediately. I rode into Klamath Falls, Ore., in search of a clinic and stopped at a convenience store to check the phone book for an address. As I was leaving, a police car pulled into the parking area and headed straight toward me. I stopped and waited until the officer bolted from his car. He was young, had his hand on his gun, and looked nervous. He asked me if I had any identification. I didn't want to do anything that would set him off, so I told him I would have to reach into the pocket on the back of my jersey to retrieve my drivers license. He took my license and called into his dispatcher. A minute later, he handed it back to me and started to leave. I asked him if there was a problem. He said, "You match a description," and took off in a hurry. That night on TV, I saw there was a hold up that day and the suspect was 6'2" tall, 180 lbs., with long hair and a beard. I really did match the description, but how did he think I was going to escape on a bicycle pulling a trailer?

I had a complete physical at the clinic, including a cancer checkup. In 1988 I had Nodular Melanoma, a very malignant form of skin cancer and have had an annual checkup since. Besides the blood work, which would take several weeks to receive the results, the doctor told me I was fit as a fiddle and strong as an ox. My white blood cell count was good, so she didn't know what was causing the tightness in my side and she couldn't tell me why I was waking up, almost nightly, in a cold sweat. I know one thing; I will never have a woman doctor check my prostate again. I didn't know if she had it in for men or if she was trying to compensate for having short fingers, but she sure gave me a thorough exam.

I rode in the rain for several days until I arrived at Bend, Ore. What a beautiful, active town. People were out biking, kayaking, playing ball, and it was the first place an older person (a white haired lady) gave me a thumbs-up. I popped a spoke just outside of town, but it was because I hit a rock in the road. I fixed the bike and was going to spend a few days there, but the Bend Cascade Hostel was booked with a school group from Portland, so I left the next day.

I fell in love with Oregon. The next few days were absolutely beautiful. I even had a head wind and it didn't seem to bother me. I remembered the words of Freddie Mercury, "Any way the wind blows, doesn't really matter to me." Some locals advised me to take Highway 197 to Maupin for a scenic ride. There was no shoulder, but there was no traffic either. The panorama was vast high plains prairie surrounded by majestic snow-covered mountains. A red-tailed hawk flew right over my head and I knew it was a special day. Western meadowlarks (Oregon's state bird) serenaded me all day long. How cool to have a state bird that is visible. I have always been so disappointed that Colorado's state bird is a lark bunting; a bird that can only be found in the eastern plains of Colorado and resides in the state only five months of the year.

It was my best day on the bike, no question. I camped along the Deschutes River that night watching a belted kingfisher dive for dinner and a merganser fight the current to get home. I had the same feeling I had camping out in Arizona. This was what The Journey was all about— Life was good!

I had a spiritual routine every day of praying in the morning when I first started riding, meditating during the day, and praying at night in the tent. I quit meditating when I was having so much trouble in Sonora, Calif. I kept praying everyday, but for some reason I couldn't meditate. This was the first day since then that I could. But I didn't know what came first; did I start meditating after I was having a good day or did I start having a good day after I started meditating? My philosophy was that meditation was just learning how to be at peace with oneself—experiencing life at the moment! I experienced life that day and I was at peace with myself.

How can we be so enlightened one day and so common the next? I went from the best day of The Journey to one of the worst, in one day. I left Maupin, Ore., the next day and climbed 5 miles out of the valley. It was a workout, but I was the "King of the World" again when I reached the top. It was later that day when everything went to hell. I crossed over the Columbia River into Washington—state #9, the Evergreen State. It was a bit windy and I even stopped to take a picture of the wind's effects; the tall grass waving, the ravens gliding, and the flag on *B.O.B.* leaning at a 45-degree angle. It took me three hours to go 20 miles. A few days prior I pedaled 46 miles in three hours. It was blowing so hard it actually blew me off the shoulder at times. After a lot of effort and some serious cursing, I made it to Bingen, Wash., and located the hostel there.

CHAPTER 12

▼

HOSTELS, HOSTELS, HOSTELS

The hostel, an old school converted into the Bingen School Inn, was run by John—who had big ideas for it. However, most of his efforts went into the climbing gym next door and wind surfing; as a result, the hostel suffered. It was dirty and a bit run-down, but it turned out to be a safe haven for me. I ended up spending 10 days there to wait out some bad weather and to build up the courage to battle the Columbia Gorge again.

I quickly found out that the area was the wind surfing capital of North America. Everyday the wind was howling and the locals loved it because it meant good wind surfing. It reminded me of when it snowed in Colorado and I would get a big smile on my face because it meant powder skiing. But I thought this weather sucked! And apparently that is exactly what it does. As the interior land warms up during the day and the air rises, it sucks the cool air from the Pacific down the gorge creating ideal wind surfing conditions, but less than ideal biking conditions.

Once again I found hanging out at a hostel for a week exposed me to some interesting people....

First there was my roommate, Mike, who was from New Mexico and had recently relocated to the area because of his job. I'm not sure what he did, but he was living at the hostel until he could find a place to rent. We were in a huge classroom that had been partitioned into two dorm areas. His area of the room was a pit with clothes and food wrappers all over the floor. He was a junk-food junkie and a bit of a slob, but a nice enough guy. He had a nervous little laugh when he talked and had to have the light on at night when he went to bed.

Second was Trudy, an attractive lady who showed up with her nine-year-old daughter, Amelia. Trudy would leave her daughter unattended at the hostel while she went wind surfing. One day I made Amelia lunch and dinner, because the surfing conditions were so good that Trudy didn't return until late. Trudy reminded me a lot of Mary, the young activist in Flagstaff. She seemed to be struggling with acting like someone who didn't care what society thought, while at the same time trying to be recognized as someone who was important. Unfortunately, I think her daughter was the one who suffered because of Trudy's internal conflicts. But Amelia was mature beyond her years and seemed to understand her mother's desires.

Third, Phil was a nurse from Denver in his mid-forties. He had a wife and two kids, but once a year he took off by himself to go windsurfing. He admitted an obsession with the sport. Phil was good looking and in very good shape. He gave me some suggestions on what I could do for the pain in my knees, which I appreciated.

Then there was John Daly, not the golfer (although he had a four handicap), but the poet. John was about my age and from Virginia. He was working as a waiter, playing golf, and thinking about writing a novel. He loved sports, which is how we met—we watched the NBA play-offs together. John didn't live at the hostel, but used the laundry facilities and watched TV there. It was cool to talk again to someone who really understood sports. I never figured out what John's demons were that kept him from developing his writing, maybe fear—fear of succeeding. John recited some of his poetry for me and I would have sworn he was the second coming of Dylan—not only the delivery (quick and flowing), but the context as well. It was very underground, with a lot of societal issues. He was intelligent, talented and waiting…

I spent a lot of time in the library, up the road in the little town of White Salmon, reading books by Merton, Gandhi, Krishnamurti and Rick Reilly. I also read a book about a manatee written by 13 authors from Florida. Besides reading, I mended some clothes and cleaned all of my camping gear. It was a productive stopover for me.

The day I rode into Portland on the Historic Columbia Highway was outstanding. What a beautiful ride along the Columbia River through rain forests and past waterfalls. It actually felt good this time to get back on the bike. I got into town and found the HI-Portland Hostel down on Hawthorne Street. There were numerous coffee shops, pubs and art galleries. Hawthorne was a happening place in Portland.

I checked in and began talking with Lisa, who worked there at night and worked in pediatric cardiology at the hospital during the day. She was unbelievable; intelligent and attractive. She had thick curly dark hair, piercing blue eyes, and a mischievous smile. We played three games of chess that night, partly because she couldn't accept losing to me. She was very competitive and was determined to win a game.

It was raining hard when I woke up, so I stayed another day. There was nowhere I needed to be and it would give me another chance to see Lisa. Thank God I stayed. That night Lisa asked me if I would like to join her and Vicky for dinner. I thought she really liked me because she touched me a lot and she always grabbed my hand when she saw me. Only later that night at a local pub did I discover that she and Vicky were lesbians. Wow! I was shocked! I didn't have a problem with them being gay. I was just shocked because I hadn't noticed it earlier. We had a great time together and I was laughing inside at my earlier thoughts.

The next day also brought rain but now I had no reason to hang around. I was no longer heeding my friend Chuey's advice of not riding in the rain. I realized I would end up spending the rest of my life in the Great Northwest if I waited for the rain to stop—and it rained all day!

Two days later I was back across the Columbia River in Chinook, Wash. I was at the entrance to the Fort Columbia State Park, preparing to ride up to the HI-Fort Columbia Hostel. There was a sign explaining how Lewis and Clark had camped at that site. Next to it was a sign that read, "NO CAMPING." I thought, "Oh yeah, good enough for Lewis and Clark, but not good enough for the general public."

Actually, I had no desire to be camping in that weather. In fact, I was wondering about the logistics of trying to find a dry spot to set up a tent and getting in without soaking everything. Earlier in the day I went into the woods to relieve myself. While I was standing there, I reached over and touched the trunk of the big spruce I was standing under. I noticed a couple of things: One, the trunk was soaked. I also noticed that the ground under this massive tree was wet. In Colorado, this is where you would normally take refuge in a storm. My observation revealed that, because it rained so much there, the branches were saturated. So as a raindrop fell on a branch, it caused another drop to fall off onto the branch below and so on. As a result, to be standing under a big tree in a rainstorm in the Great Northwest, was to be standing in the rainstorm— miserable camping conditions.

The hostel was a cool old barracks building. In fact, it was a cold old barracks building, run by Dave. Dave had been in town having a couple of beers and was a bit juiced when he checked me in. Other than being cold, the hostel was spacious, clean and empty. There was only one other person staying there, an Englishman who was into hiking. The setting was beautiful, nestled in the forest on a lush hillside overlooking the spot where the Columbia River flowed into the Pacific Ocean. Across the way was Oregon.

I was going to miss Oregon. The people were courteous, the scenery was spectacular, and the state was very biker-friendly; good shoulders, good bike paths and good attitudes. If I had to live anywhere other than

Colorado or Arizona, I would live in Oregon. Even Portland, for a big city, had a good feel to it. They were very progressive and open-minded in their thinking, with some of the best recycling programs in the country. The best t-shirt I saw on the entire trip was in Portland. It read, "It's not that life is so short, it's just that death lasts so long." It was a new mantra for The Journey.

One of the best things I saw on America's highways, as it related to bicycles, were the tunnels in Washington. As I approached a tunnel there was a button to push that started a strobe light to warn drivers there was a bicyclist in the tunnel. I have to thank whoever was responsible for those lights. They provided a bit of comfort in an uncomfortable situation. Poking along through a dark tunnel at 10 mph isn't the safest place to be. And even though there was the inconvenience of having to stop and push the button, the reward out-weighed the cost (spoken like a true accountant).

I was on the infamous Highway 101, riding up the coastline of Washington through a forest in the rain. I came upon a sign that read, "Rough Road." For whatever reason, I said, "Uh oh, rough road." Only I said it like Astro, the dog on the Jetson's, so it came out more like, "Rut roh, rough road." No sooner had the words left my mouth, and I looked through the raindrops on my glasses and saw a road-crew worker looking at me. He had a big smile on his face and nodded at me. I had an embarrassed grin on my face and nodded back. It wouldn't be the last time someone would catch me talking to the bike or myself.

Later that day, I was just outside of South Bend, Wash., when my rear tire went flat. As I was pumping up the spare, the valve stem blew out of the tube. I started over with another tube and as I was pumping up the tire, the valve stem blew out of the tube, again. I only had one tube left and I was extremely paranoid about trying to pump it up. I was using a little nine-inch pump that was better suited for pumping up mountain bike tires to 30 pounds of pressure, instead of the 100 pounds of pressure my road bike tires required. I could see the town from where I was and decided I'd take the rear wheel into town and pump up the tire there. I stashed the bike and trailer behind a county road maintenance building and began walking into town. I looked up and there were two riders approaching on bicycles. They were from Boulder, Colo., and they were riding down Highway 101 to San Francisco, a very popular ride. They stopped to see if I needed some help, so I tried his pump. It worked fine, so I knew I needed to upgrade mine as soon as possible. What a nice treat that they came along when they did.

My ride up Highway 101 was uneventful and, unfortunately, wasn't very scenic either. Between the fog in the morning, the rain in the after-noon, and the dense forests, I couldn't see much. I did see various species of birds, though. I saw more ospreys than I had ever seen because of all the fish, and flocks of robins because of all the worms. They were big worms; some were six inches and big four-inch slugs, as well. The rain could really make things grow up there. One osprey flew directly over my head with a fish still squirming in his talons. One morning I scared up an eagle from along the side of the road. He flew into a tree where a vulture was perched, waiting for the scraps of what the eagle was eating. Seeing them both in the same tree was an odd sight.

I made it to the Gray Harbor Hostel in Elma, Wash., by Memorial Day Weekend. Linda and Jerry ran the hostel out of their house, which was a bit different. However, they had been managing hostels for years, so it was quite comfortable. I planned to spend three days there to stay out of the holiday traffic. I also thought it might quit raining if I took a few days off—yeah, right!

While I was there, Jerry asked me if I was going to write a book about my journey. I told him I hadn't considered it, so he had me read a book about cycling across America that was written by someone who had stayed there years ago. The book was *"Bottoms Up, America,"* written by Bill Fitzpatrick. The first thing I noticed was his decision not to camp out in the waterlogged Northwest. All of a sudden I didn't feel so guilty. I enjoyed the book and could relate to things he had encountered, although he was riding with two other bikers. Plus, they only rode through 13 states and I was planning to bike through 48. But the seed was planted for writing a book and would continue to grow throughout The Journey.

Linda invited me to have a Memorial Day turkey dinner with them. The gesture was nice and the food was excellent, including dessert. I now weighed 181 lbs. I wasn't gaining weight, but more importantly, I wasn't losing any either.

After the weekend, I made it to Olympia where my friend Tobin Booth lived. Tobin had worked for me in the Environmental Department at Keystone and did energy audits on the mountain house at Arapahoe Basin while attending Colorado State University. Tobin was a neat kid, very intelligent and very active. He did a lot of biking, hiking and boarding. The past weekend he and a friend had climbed three volcanoes in the area. That night we had a great salmon dinner and an early evening, as we both were tired.

The next morning I had to wake Tobin up, as he was still exhausted. But I knew he had a big presentation to make at work that morning. After he left, I put on a Neil Young CD and prepared to leave. It was raining sideways outside, but I thought it might calm down by the time I was ready. When I was hooking up the trailer, I noticed a broken spoke on the rear wheel, non-drive side. I unloaded the bike, went back inside, and replaced the spoke; not a big deal, but I had 60 miles to travel in terrible weather. I also had an appointment at 2 p.m. at a clinic south of Seattle to have some more blood drawn in connection with my cancer checkup in Klamath Falls.

As I approached Tacoma on I-5, there was a sign that read, "All bicycles must exit now." I thought real fast about what I was trying to do and decided the only way I would find Highway 99 in time to get to Seattle was to stay on the interstate. There is a reason they don't allow bicycles on the interstate through cities and I was about to find out why. For one thing there is a lot of traffic, which makes the entrance and exit ramps a real challenge, even in the best of conditions. It was raining so hard that the hood on my raincoat was stuck to my head, acting much like a blinder.

My shades and mirror were spotted with rain affecting my vision, but I rationalized that it was early afternoon so the traffic would be light. I was actually doing rather well until my three-lane section merged with a two-lane section to my right, which merged with an entrance ramp to the far right. I glanced over my shoulder and made a split decision that I could cross the two lanes and the ramp and make it to the shoulder safely. The minute I stepped down on the pedal and felt the tire spin out on the wet pavement, I knew I was in trouble. I grabbed for both brake handles and squeezed for all I was worth. Because of all the moisture, I did not have the friction needed to stop the bike in its normal distance. I came to a stop at the pinnacle of the island that separated the lanes of traffic. Cars and trucks were roaring past me on both sides, throwing water and sand all over my "stuff" and me. I literally froze there for a moment, but it seemed like an eternity.

All of a sudden I felt a presence and much like the show, "*Touched by an Angel*," there seemed to be a light around me. Earlier that day, when I was getting ready at Tobin's house, I noticed a St. Michael's medallion hanging in his bathroom. Not being Catholic, I didn't know who St. Michael was but, because my middle name is Michael, I paid attention to it. Tobin later told me that St. Michael was the Angel of Peace and Protection. All I knew was, at that moment, someone or something was watching over me.

It took me 15 minutes to collect myself and walk the bike and trailer over to the shoulder. I immediately got off the interstate and found a Motel 6. I called the clinic and my friend, Hideo, to let them know I wouldn't make it today. I had a rough day and I was glad to be alive. I always tell people that I am a lucky man. A more religious person might say I am blessed. Whatever you want to call it, I was thankful for the Divine Intervention.

On Thursday morning, May 28, I woke up to something really bizarre—the sun. There was a big orange ball of fire lighting up the sky and warming up the earth. I couldn't believe it. It looked good, it felt good and it was good. I remembered when Jan and I would go skiing or hiking, how different our attitudes would be on a sunny day compared to a gray day. Biking was no different. I enjoyed riding into Seattle. What an amazing view, with the snow-covered Mt. Rainer on a clear, cool day.

Like Mark, Hideo graduated at the top of our class in high school. Unlike Mark, Hideo studied all the time. I only know that because we were roommates at Colorado State University. I was also Best Man at his wedding and after that we lost touch with each other. This was the first time I'd seen him in 15 years and physically he hadn't changed a bit. Our conversation at the beach that afternoon, however, showed me he had grown a lot. We talked about life and it was the most enjoyable conversation I'd had since talking with Peter Deane in Flagstaff. Hideo and I traveled different paths over the years, but it was interesting how close we were philosophically. In fact, he turned me onto some interesting books including "*The Hundredth Monkey*" by Ken Keyes, Jr. He also had the book, "*Ishmael*," which impressed me.

Seattle was another good stop for me; I renewed an old friendship, received a care package from home, and had the bike tuned up at REI.

Getting out of Seattle, I took the Burk-Gilman Bike Path for about 20 miles. It was always a treat not having to ride on the city streets, although it was a weekend and the bike path was packed. I passed a couple of women on roller blades and overheard one of them say, "Now there goes the ultimate biking RV." I decided she was right; I was on a bicycle and I was camping around the country. This was the recreational vehicle of biking. Right before I left town, Ben pulled up next to me and told me he had done some bike touring. We rode together for a bit and then he shared a bagel and banana with me. Seattle reminded me of Portland, very progressive and very active. If it wasn't for the weather…

I biked 80 miles that day leaving Seattle. Summer was arriving and every day there was a little more daylight to ride in. I also had more bugs to contend with. One day there was a new hatch of flying black ants that was so thick I had to hold my hand in front of my face when I rode through a swarm of them. They would stick to my hair, my beard and my clothes. It was not a pleasant situation for a person who does not like bugs. My mother has a picture of me as a kid holding a six-foot long snake. Snakes never bothered me, but bugs…

The next day I had Stevens Pass to climb to get back over the Cascade Mountains—16 miles and 3,000 feet of elevation gain from Skykomish, Wash., to the top of the pass. At the summit, I changed my perspiration-soaked clothes and ate lunch. Then I had a 35-mile downhill ride into Leavenworth along the Wenatchee River—Yahoo! I was not only hauling ass, but things were changing; the trees were more like the lodge-pole pine I was familiar with and the ground was dry. I set up camp along the Wenatchee River and watched two beavers gathering willow branches along the far shoreline. The weather was excellent, the bike was tuned, and I felt strong.

There were two different roads to take leaving Wenatchee, Wash., that headed east toward Spokane. While in town, I called a local bike shop and asked them which route they would take with a loaded touring bike. One thing I became very good at was asking questions; and not just asking questions, but asking the right question and asking until they answered the question. So many times, people would want to tell me about what they were interested in rather than what I needed to know. What did Harry Neillson teach us in "*The Point?*" "You hear what you want to hear." I would ask for the easiest way to ride somewhere and they would tell me the scenic route—usually a more difficult route. It taught me to listen and question. Eventually I would end up with the information I needed.

As I was riding through Wenatchee, I popped a spoke on the rear wheel, non-drive side. I put on a new spoke and was on my way in 30 minutes. I was impressed at how much better I was handling broken spokes now compared to the start of The Journey, although there was some concern as to why they were still breaking.

Ten miles out of town, I popped another spoke on the rear wheel, except this time it was on the drive side. The next major town was still halfway across the state, so I put on the kevlar spoke and headed back to

Wenatchee. I asked the techie at the bike shop why I all of a sudden popped two spokes. He said it was because there wasn't enough tension on the spokes. GREAT! First it was too much tension and now it was not enough. Every time I felt like I could do this touring forever, something would happen that would make me question why I was doing it at all.

That night after sunset, an older man on a recumbent, or reclining, bicycle pulled in next to me to camp. His name was Bruce and he was from Colorado. He was attempting to ride his bicycle from Washington to North Carolina and he was 69 years old. He looked to be in good shape, but he was having a little trouble; equal parts physical, mental and his bike. Together it was adding up to be more than he had bargained for. He had only been on the road for eight days, so I wondered if he was going to be able to accomplish his goal. I knew what he was going through, but I didn't know what to say. I had been on the road for five months, so his problems seemed insignificant to me. He could either quit or he could deal with it and continue. I admired him for taking the challenge and told him so, but I also realized how tough long distance touring could be on a solo traveler.

In Davenport, Wash., I was in the grocery store and a lady came over and said she saw me on the road earlier that day. She asked where I was from and where I was going. When I came out of the store, there was a little silver cross on my bike seat that read, "God Loves You." I looked around and the same woman was sitting in a car watching me. I went over and thanked her for the cross. Her name was Autumn and she was about my age, married, with four kids. I could best describe her as a hippie chick; necklaces, bracelets, and long flowing hair that matched her skirt. She said I could spend the night with her family, but they lived 13 miles back the way I had just come. I thanked her for the invitation and the cross, but decided to spend the night in Davenport. She told me her mission in life was to let people know that God loves them. It was nice of her to share that with me.

I made it into Spokane the next day and found the Brown Squirrel Hostel, which was owned by Tom Barker. The hostel was closed when I arrived in the afternoon, so I took a nap in the hammock on the porch. When the hostel opened, Tom invited me in, sat me down and gave me a glass of juice. The next day we took his dogs out for an early morning walk and he told me a little history about the area. I sometimes wondered why people operated hostels and I was wondering about Tom. He was around 70 years old and seemed lonely. I guess the hostel offered exposure to momentary encounters. But I could be wrong. He may just be a caring soul offering a clean, comfortable place for travelers to rest. I spent a couple of days in Spokane and if I had to live in Washington, it would be in Spokane.

It was the start of the second week in June when I took the 30-mile bike path, the Centennial Trail, out of Spokane all the way to Coeur d'Alene, Idaho. This was my occasional treat of not having to contend with automobiles. I made it to Kellogg, Idaho, that night and was beat from fighting a head wind all day. In fact, for the previous five days I had been riding into a head wind. I thought once I left Seattle that the wind was going to blow me all the way to Maine. I thought the wind always blew out of the west. This was really bumming me out. It just wasn't right that I had to battle this wind every day. I had worked so hard to get to a point where I thought I'd have the prevailing trade winds all the way across the country. Funny, how no one seems to notice the direction of the wind unless one's sailing or riding a touring bike.

I went down an exit ramp to relieve myself and look over the bike. While I was standing there, a young man on a motorcycle pulled up and asked me if everything was all right. Todd looked to be in his mid 20s, with long, curly, blonde hair pulled back in a ponytail. I told him I was fine, just taking a break. He had been bike touring in America and overseas, so we traded a few biking stories and enjoyed sharing the tale about the 10-mile downhill run on Highway 90 into Lordsburg, N.M. I told him I had ridden 5,000 miles and he was the first person to pull over when I was stopped along the road to ask if I needed help. He was shocked because people had always stopped to help him. He told me he honestly thought it was because of my beard and not my hair. I had to agree with him. Like I said before, I wouldn't even stop to help me, the way I looked. But I was glad Todd did. He was a neat kid with an abundance of energy and stories, and I enjoyed both. He also told me that the wind generally blew out of the east around there and that I would have to go into Canada to catch a favorable west wind. I had no desire to head north, since I would be going to southern Montana eventually, so I maintained my course.

The next morning I seemed apprehensive about starting out. The weather was a bit iffy, I had a huge pass to climb to get over the Bitterroot Mountains and my knees were killing me. Usually my knees would start hurting every day after 40 to 50 miles, but would be fine by the next morning. I woke up that morning and they still ached and were warm to the touch. The mountains of Washington, Idaho and Montana were trashing my knees and the wind wasn't helping. Years of running up and down a hardwood court playing basketball and severe poundings from skiing the bumps had left me with less than desirable knees to be doing a journey of this magnitude. And the fact that I was not recuperating by morning was bothering me. After Lookout Pass that day, it was downhill all the way to Missoula, so I decided to proceed to the hostel there and see how I felt.

Except for two flat tires, I made it to the Birchwood Hostel without much trouble. The hostel catered to cyclists and even gave them a discount on the nightly rate. When I checked in I was introduced to David Newman from Vancouver, Canada, who was on a 1,200-mile bike trip. I have never met anyone as enthusiastic about bike touring as David. We spent the better part of three days together and talked biking the whole time. David was very supportive about my journey and it was good for me to share his energy.

Some other bikers at the hostel included: Bob, a history teacher from North Carolina, who was biking from Idaho back to North Carolina. Bill, an outdoor sports equipment salesman from Colorado, who was biking from Washington, DC to Oregon. Chris, a young man from California, who was trying to bike from Washington state to Virginia. And Marcus and Elkie from Germany, who had been riding around America for the past nine months. They were the first bikers I met who had been on the road longer than I had, so I talked with them extensively. They were ready for their journey to be over. Nine months is a long time to be living off a bicycle, especially in a foreign country. They visited 15 states and were preparing to go back to Germany. Marcus told me about the problems they had with broken spokes and it helped me in dealing with my continuing saga. I deduced that it had to be because we were carrying much more weight than the average cross-country bike rider, who is generally out for one to three months.

We went out as a group for dinner and a couple of beers and then ended up back at the hostel. We gathered around in the common area and started sharing incidents that had happened to everyone while touring. It was like Christmas, everyone had a new and exciting tale to tell and we all sat around like school kids watching the wrapping being torn off the next story. I received something useful from each of them: David and his enthusiasm supported my mental psyche. Bill was going east to west and had good information about people, roads and dogs where I was heading. Marcus encouraged me to get out of the saddle more when I was going up hills to help my knees (a tip I took to heart that really paid off). The one thing we all agreed on, the worst thing about bike touring was the wind. Everyone had a wind story and almost every story was ugly. There were stories of strong tail winds that blew you *down* the highway, but they were all overshadowed by stories of monster head winds that blew you *off* the highway.

David and I went to Adventure Cycle one day to have our pictures taken and tell our stories. Adventure Cycle is the company who organized the Bi-Centennial Tour back in 1976 to bike across America. They have grown into an organization that promotes biking with a monthly magazine, guided bike tours, and maps for touring. If you are on a tour and stop in, they put your picture on their wall. Because I was on an extended tour, they wanted to know if I could come back the next day with my bike and trailer and give an interview for an article. They were closed the next day but Greg, an employee, was going to meet me there to get a picture of *B.O.P.* and *B.O.B.* and ask me some questions. Unfortunately, Greg never showed up, so there was no article.

Missoula is a great college town; very scenic, very clean and very active. I would move to Missoula in an instant. In fact, I didn't want to leave. The weather was a bit nasty and my knees still ached. But everyone was heading out on Saturday, so I began making arrangements to leave as well. David helped me pick out a more suitable pump for long distance touring. I also repacked all of my panniers, after detecting a foul odor. I had been putting dryer sheets in my panniers to try and keep my stuff smelling fresh. All of the moisture from the Great Northwest, however, had caused those sheets to mold. I decided I really didn't need that freshness.

Originally, Chris was going to ride with me down to Dillon, Mont. However, his knees were in worse shape than mine were. Unlike my knees though, his pain was not from years of abuse. He was still a young man and everyone at the hostel felt as though his seat was not properly adjusted. This was his first attempt at bike touring and I think he was learning a painful lesson.

But then, bike touring *is* a painful lesson. Nothing comes easily, which is probably why more people aren't doing it. I noticed the hard work from my touring was helping me remove the armor from the shield I had been hiding behind the past 22 years in business. I was realizing that simplifying my life and living The Truth was not necessarily easy. Being open and honest with other people begins with being open and honest with oneself, and that wasn't always pleasant. Being human, it is so easy to rationalize our shortcomings. It doesn't make it right, but it allows us to justify less than honorable thinking or actions. I wasn't a practicing Buddhist, but I believed in the four Noble Truths of Buddhism. Part of that was thinking and acting right to eliminate our desires, which caused our sufferings. I had eliminated most of the desires in my life the past couple of years, but was I prepared to think right and act right all the time, honestly?

There was a price to be paid for those "high" moments of the trip; like camping in New Mexico or Arizona, or even hanging out at the hostel with other cyclists. I was going to have ample time to try and sort it all out. The real question was, did I have the insight and fortitude to pay the price?

CHAPTER 13

▼

LEAVING THE ROCKY MOUNTAINS

It was a gray day when we all took off in different directions from the hostel and I had mixed emotions about leaving. I was intimidated sometimes by how much more everyone knew about their bikes than I did, but really enjoyed sharing anecdotes with my fellow two-wheel travelers. This would be my last hostel for 10 states and I knew I would miss the exchange of information, stories and general camaraderie.

Twenty miles south of Missoula on Highway 93 it began to rain, so I pulled over and put on my rain gear. No sooner had I begun pedaling when I heard the sound I dreaded most; a spoke popped on the rear wheel, non-drive side. I was out in the middle of nowhere, so I unloaded the bike and replaced the spoke in the rain. I rode another 10 miles and KABOOM, a blowout on the rear tire. In all my years of riding I had never experienced a blowout. There was a big pine tree about 50 yards off the road, which provided shelter from the rain while I worked on the bike. I put in a new tube and started pumping it up—KABOOM! Another blowout! What the hell? What was causing this to happen? This time it blew out the tube and the tire. I had another tire, but was extremely paranoid. Running my finger completely around the rim didn't detect anything out of the ordinary. My only remaining tube had a hole in it, so I found a puddle of rainwater, located the leak, and patched it. I cautiously pumped the rear tire to below the recommended pressure and rode into town with frayed nerves.

In a depressingly small, dark motel room, I sulked about my misfortunes. Again, I was ready to quit The Journey. What was the point in continuing? I wasn't having fun. I didn't enjoy the constant threat of having to deal with the bike breaking down. Before, it was my health and my diet that were causing me mental aggravation, but now it was the bicycle. Why couldn't I just get on the bike and ride around America? David talked about the "biking gods" when we were in Missoula and I read about the young man who biked around Australia (10,000 miles), who had only two flat tires. He said the "biking gods" had been smiling on him. If there were such things as these "gods," I didn't seem to be on their good side and they certainly weren't smiling on me!

After some soul searching that night, I questioned if I was just a big whiner or if it was time for me to give up. That was my problem—I always gave up. I never finished anything. I loved to begin things, but always lost interest before completion. The start of the trip was so exciting with the support of my friends and family, but now I was just out on the highway every day riding a bike. No one knew how many cars passed me every day, how many trucks and RVs ran me off the road every day, how many revolutions my pedals made every day; the blood, sweat and tears associated with this journey. I knew they cared, but I couldn't seem to make that matter at the moment. Was that the purpose of The Journey, to see if I could do this? Was it a challenge? Who was challenging me? Was I destined to give up? These were questions I needed to answer, and the sooner the better!

Sunday, June 15, 1998, I was starting the sixth month of The Journey. Half-heartedly I went into the bike shop in Hamilton, Mont., to find some new tubes and a tire. An old man, who had opened the store for his friend who was out of town, greeted me. I was apprehensive because he wasn't the "bike tech" I was expecting to see. As it turned out, he really knew his bikes and set me up with a Continental 2000 touring tire and some tubes. He was a good example for me to never judge a book by its cover.

For the next two days I rode in the rain, except on Lost Trail Pass where it was snowing at 7,200 feet. The high temperature every day was 15 to 20 degrees lower than normal. The bizarre weather was being blamed on El Nino.

On Tuesday I took off from Wisdom, Mont., through the Big Hole Valley and over Badger Pass on the way to Dillon. What a beautiful ride. The surrounding mountains were covered with snow and the fields were full of hay, birds and wildlife. I felt reborn. There was no traffic, so I was able to take in the environment; the sights, sounds and smells of western Montana. In 1972 I attended school at Western Montana College in Dillon, so I had a feeling of coming home.

Twenty miles from town Mark pulled up next to me on a new Trek. He was from Austin, Texas, and was riding across America. We rode into town together and I realized it was the first time I had ridden with someone for an extended time since the trip began. He was continuing on toward Yellowstone, while I was spending a few days in Dillon.

I moved to Dillon in 1972 to help my father's friend manage the Elk Horn Hot Springs. Bob had gone to school with my Dad and was starting a new life in Montana. I had been attending Colorado State University, so I transferred to WMC, which was how I became an accountant. WMC is a teachers college and I had no desire to pursue that profession. I had been majoring in engineering at CSU and decided to take accounting classes at WMC, just to be working with numbers. Three years later I was graduating with an accounting degree from USC, but that's another story.

I saw Bob and some old college friends while I was in Dillon. Cindy gave me some cookies for the road and Russ supplied me with some elk jerky and much needed duct tape. Little had changed in Dillon over 27 years. It was still a small college town filled with cowboys and friendly people. I had good memories of Dillon and almost wished I had left it at that. But I caught up with my mail there and my sister, Vicky, had sent some needed bike shorts for my birthday. They were the color of the Colorado state flag, which matched the jersey she gave me at Christmas— I was styling.

It took me a week to get across eastern Montana, which reminded me a lot of western Texas. There were long distances between towns, but at least Montana had nice scenery. It was during these long, lonely stretches that I began to think about what I might do when The Journey was completed. As I watched the Rocky Mountains slowly disappear in my mirror, it came to me; I would hike the Continental Divide from Mexico to Canada! I lived by the Divide most of my life and loved being in the mountains. But more importantly, my current journey was an attempt to get closer to Nature. And even though I was outdoors every day all day long, I also was on asphalt every day. The other thing that appealed to me about the hike was that I wouldn't have the bike to worry about. It would be Nature and me, but that would have to wait. I had other challenges lying before me.

CHAPTER 14

▼

IN SEARCH OF GOOD PAVEMENT

I was in Baker, Mont., and realized I was on the same route as Robert Persig in "*Zen and the Art of Motorcycle Maintenance*," only in reverse. I felt some kinship with the book because of my earlier trials and tribulations with what is "Natural." I would never be so presumptuous as to put myself on the same philosophical plane as Persig, but I couldn't help noticing some parallels with his "Quality" and my "Natural." In fact, I'm sure he influenced me. But then my entire life was a reflection of everything I've read and everyone I've met.

Like Persig, something changed for me in Montana. There was a greater comfort level in dealing with the bike when something went wrong. I don't know if it was "Zen" or if it was just the result of living with the bike the last five months; but as I grew more detached from the problems, they became fewer and fewer. My job, my daily activity, was riding this bicycle everyday. It was my choice and I was finally learning to deal with it. I also noticed that when someone asked about The Journey, my response was, "I *am* biking through all 48 contiguous states," rather than

"I am TRYING to bike..."—plus, I had a short-term goal for riding the next 30 days. My parents were in Green Lake, Wis., doing volunteer work at a Christian camp and my younger sister, Renee, and her family, were going to be there in four weeks for a visit. If I applied myself, I could arrive at the same time.

Coming across Montana, I rode my first century (100 miles in one day) with the bike loaded. In fact, I averaged 90 miles a day for that week. As the weather improved and the days grew longer, the increased mileage didn't seem that difficult. I was completely bushed at the end of each day, but always felt ready to go the next morning. It was amazing how resilient my body was. To soothe my aching knees, I was buying packages of frozen fruit at night, when possible, and putting them on my knees. In the morning the fruit would go in my oatmeal.

By the time I got to Baker it was summer. I was sweating so profusely that everything I wore would be completely soaked by day's end, even my shoes from the sweat running down my legs and drenching my socks. I was obviously drinking more water and stretches like Baker, Mont., to Bowman, N.D. (89 miles with NO towns in between), presented a real challenge. I would buy jugs of water and bunches of fruit for those spans.

I made it to Bowman, N.D., OK and even though I only spent one night, my time there was enjoyable. It was a pleasant town and I met a retired physics professor from Minnesota at the Laundromat. We spent some time discussing Einstein's Theory of Relativity and some lesser-known theories. At one point we were talking about trying to exceed the speed of light. My lame example was that if I had a thought and someone in Florida received that thought as I was having it—that would be faster than the speed of light! Of course, proving that hypothesis was beyond me. His example was to take a pair of scissors; half way down one of the blades was a point that would travel the speed of light when the blades were squeezed together. If that were true, he hypothesized that a point on the tip of the scissors would be traveling faster than the speed of light— like crack the whip! We talked about other enlightening matters but, unfortunately, my clothes were done drying while his were still on the rinse cycle, so our conversation ended. How strange that I would let my laundry dictate how long I would talk with someone, and who would have thought I'd be having that type of conversation at the Laundromat in Bowman, N.D.

That night while I was lying in my tent going over the recent conversation, I realized the flaw in his hypothesis. Light can only travel in a straight line and the points on his scissors were traveling in an arc. Einstein's Theory was still intact. I fell asleep and immediately took off on an astroplane traveling faster than the speed of light—now if only I could prove it!

The highways had been so bad in Montana; "grooved" pavement and old pavement dominated eastern Montana. "Grooved" pavement resulted when a machine was used to scoop up the old pavement, leaving grooves along the base. This was very unstable for 1 ¼-inch tires carrying a load. I was sure the roads had to be better in North Dakota, but they weren't. They were what I called "seamed" highways. About every 10 yards there was a seam in the highway. When you are in a car it makes the noise clunk/clunk, clunk/clunk. When you are on a bicycle, the seams simulate speed bumps; and they not only are hard on the rider, but over time everything loosens up on the bicycle. I was praying to get to South Dakota.

Well, "be careful what you ask for" never had more meaning to me than when I crossed the state line into South Dakota. The road was WORSE! I couldn't believe it. The seams were wider and deeper and the shoulder was almost gravel—loose chunks of asphalt, small stones and patches of sand. I had to ride out in the road, but fortunately there was very little traffic. To give you an idea of just how bad the road was, there was a tail wind and I still only averaged 10 miles an hour. I literally had to brake at the seams to soften the impact. It was a bone-jarring ride for *B.O.P.*, *B.O.B.* and me.

At Buffalo, S.D., I free camped up by the rodeo grounds. No one else was there and I had a rest room with running water—right uptown. It was filthy dirty, but it worked for me. I set the tent up and was getting ready to cook dinner when a storm blew in. With everything secured, I scrambled into the tent to ride the storm out. After a while, I realized I had never been in a tent in a storm this fierce. As the wind kept growing in force, it got to the point where I was actually afraid. It felt like I was being tossed around like Dorothy and Toto and I wasn't so sure I wasn't in a tornado. I'd never been in one before and I couldn't even tell if the tent was still connected to the ground. The rain fly over the tent was flapping so violently in the wind that I couldn't hear myself yell. It sounded like a train was coming right through the middle of the rodeo grounds. The minutes seemed like hours and when it was finally over, I summoned up the courage to survey the damage. I had a picture in my mind of the devastation caused by tornadoes. I could see *B.O.P.* and *B.O.B.* in a pile of twisted metal. I cautiously climbed out of the tent to take inventory. My tent was still staked down, the bike and trailer were still there, and the sky hadn't fallen—and I didn't see the Wizard of Oz. I was glad there was no one else around to witness my "Chicken Little" routine.

Although it was a relatively short ride of 78 miles the next day, there was only one town along the way, Redig, and I wasn't sure what was there. There was already a 25 to 30 mph wind out of the southwest at 8 a.m. and I was heading due south on Highway 85. "How often does the wind lighten up during the day?" I wondered. I wasn't thrilled about what lay ahead.

Twenty-two miles and almost three hours later, I arrived at Redig. There were two burned out buildings, two mobile homes, a bunch of old cars, and a post office/general store. Thank God for small favors! I was never so happy to see a general store. I went inside and met Edgar and Elizabeth Kumley. I bought a couple of candy bars and struck up a conversation—there was no hurry to get back in that wind. I asked them if they had been in Redig long and without ever looking up from sorting the mail Edgar said, "Not really, we moved here in 1929!" I replied with a smile, "Well, I guess in the overall scheme of things, that's not so long."

Elizabeth told me how she had raised 10 kids in their mobile home and that she was anxiously awaiting the arrival of a new trailer any day. She was excited and I was happy for her. I wanted to stay longer and chat, but I still had over 50 miles to go and the wind wasn't letting up.

I was in the Grand River National Grasslands and, as the name implies, there was nothing but grass for as far as the eye could see. I wish I could say it was waving grain, but it was standing at attention at a 45-degree angle. The only time it really waved was when it was knocked to the ground by a microburst. The road curved to the southwest twenty miles south of Redig, which placed me in a 40-mph head wind.

At that point, I had ridden 42 miles in five hours. I was a little more than halfway to my day's destination, with 36 miles to go. I had never experienced anything in my life like what I went through for the next six hours, nor do I ever want to again. It was the bloody wind, the damn wind, the wind from hell, and the wind that almost drove me crazy. Barbara Savage, God bless her soul, I take back everything I said or thought about her complaints in her book on the wind in South Dakota. I have never put out a more sustained effort in one day than I did that day—eleven hours to go 78 miles. It was the worst day of The Journey so far. I was even thinking it was one of the worst days of my life. That was how bad the wind affected my attitude while riding a bicycle. I would have cursed the wind, but I didn't have the energy. No flat tires and no broken spokes—like I said, thank God for small favors!

The next morning I was almost too paranoid to continue. I woke up feeling like I had been in a 15-round prizefight and lost. The wind had beaten the crap out of me, but I hadn't lost. The wind was gone and I could still move, although it appeared to be in slow motion.

The bike and my body were holding up, but there was always room for concern. I was losing the feeling in my fingers again, but it didn't concern me too much. I had been on the bike for almost two weeks without a break and I needed some new biking gloves. I was hoping once I took an extended break the feeling would return and new gel padded biking gloves would help cut down on the constant pressure being applied to the nerves in my hands. The frozen fruit on my knees every night was helping, as was getting out of the saddle occasionally to stand up and pedal. My biggest concern was the cold sweats, but that was bothering me mentally, not physically, and I'm not so sure the problem wasn't psychosomatic.

The bike held up all the way across Montana, through North Dakota, and into South Dakota with no problems. I didn't want to think about it and put a jinx on the good fortune. I still cringed at the abuse *B.O.P.* was taking on a daily basis. Of the 13 states we had been through, the roads in the last three were the worst. I didn't even want to think about the roads to come.

I was packed and took off south out of Belle Fourche on Highway 85. In Spearfish I stopped and asked a local about a good place to eat breakfast. He told me about a place up the canyon on Highway 85s called Cheyenne Crossing where he liked to go, which was perfect since I was heading that direction anyway to get to Wyoming.

I was in the Black Hills National Forest riding along the Spearfish Creek on a crystal clear day—what a difference from the day before. It was a godsend; flowers, birds, butterflies, pine trees, rushing water and NO WIND. I couldn't have asked for a better setting in which to ride. The beautiful surroundings offset the grind of pedaling up a pass, and besides, I felt strong. The contrast in the two days was truly beauty and the beast.

At Cheyenne Crossing, I ate a late breakfast with a bunch of bikers on Harley Davidson motorcycles. They couldn't understand why anyone would do something like this on a bicycle, when you could be doing it on a Harley. Yesterday I wouldn't have argued with them, but today I couldn't imagine doing anything better than what I was doing. Oh, how I wished I could bottle up that feeling, package up that day, because I knew it was the exception. But I couldn't, so I enjoyed it for what it was, another good day to be alive and a great day to be biking.

I sweated over O'Neill Pass, 6,785 feet, and made it into Newcastle, Wyo. Wyoming (state #14), "Like no place else on earth" is what the sign reads that welcomes you to the state. All I knew was that the pavement improved, so I was happy. Bad asphalt was now having as much impact on my moods as the wind but, in addition, bad pavement affected *B.O.P.*; rattling everything loose over time and causing additional stress. The wind didn't have any bad effects on *B.O.P.* and the bike was the controller of my moods. If something went wrong with the bike, the negative floodgates would burst open. I was trying to figure out how I could better deal with these moods, but for now, they were still rising and falling.

The next couple of days I worked my way down to Nebraska, where I noticed three things: Every day was hotter, the humidity was increasing, and the mosquitoes were relentless.

At the state line the sign read, "Nebraska—The Good Life." Right behind that sign was another one that read, "New pavement next 17 miles." It was 18 miles to Chadron—Yahoo. I love Nebraska, state #15.

CHAPTER 15

▼

THE MIDWEST

It was hot and humid and every time I stopped for something I was immediately covered with mosquitoes. But I was on good asphalt and that alone almost made up for the negative aspects. I arrived in Chadron in the early afternoon and began looking for a bike shop. B.O.P. had a taken a beating over the past two weeks and there was an undefined noise coming from the rear derailleur. I found the bike shop; it shared a building with the town barbershop. No kidding, you could bring your bicycle in for a tune-up and have a little taken off the top as well. I was a bit uncomfortable with the set up (not because of my long hair, but because I needed a good bike tech). But the barber's son had been to the bicycle mechanic school in Colorado Springs, which was recognized as one of the best, so I gave him a chance.

Nebraska would end up being the worst state I biked through. The bike worked fine and the weather was OK, but I encountered some rude, angry, ignorant people and the asphalt reached an all time low.

There were some extenuating circumstances that may have contributed to my low opinion of the state. The 4th of July weekend was coming up and I always fell into a depression around the holidays, since the trip began. But that still doesn't explain how some people could be so rude as to stick their head out the car window and yell at me to "DIE"! Or how a kid, no more than 10 years old, could be so angry as to run across a corral in order to curse me for being on the highway that ran by his house. Or how someone could be so ignorant as to throw a firecracker at me. What caused people to act like that? Why were they so insecure that a man on a bicycle brought out such negative emotions and actions? All of a sudden I knew what it felt like to be a minority. People hated me without even knowing anything about me. It was a real wake up call for me to recognize my own prejudices.

That night on local TV they were asking people questions related to the 4th of July. It went something like this:

Q: "Who wrote the Declaration of Independence?"

A: "Congress."

Q: "What was the purpose of the Declaration of Independence?"

A: "To stop the war between the North and South."

Q: "Who has the largest signature on the Declaration of Independence."

A: "Bill Clinton."

I realized the people giving the answers were the same people who were yelling and throwing things at me—totally ignorant. I also knew there were people like that in every state, but this happened to be the state in which I encountered them. I have some close friends from Nebraska and know people, who had good experiences biking through Nebraska, so I wrote it all off as unfortunate close encounters.

My unfortunate encounter with the asphalt came on Highway 20. I was riding on a highway that looked like it had been bombed. There was gravel strewn about and huge divots where I imagined mortars had landed or land mines had exploded. The traffic was light, so I was able to maneuver around most of the disasters. Then I saw a sign I always looked forward to, "New Pavement next 20 miles." Just what I needed...

Well, the new pavement was fresh asphalt that had been packed down by driving over it with heavy equipment. Consequently, there were huge tire tracks embedded in the pavement. It looked to be an uncomfortable ride in a car and was practically impassable on a road bike.

I had some fortunate encounters in Nebraska as well: The truck driver in Rushville who recommended places to camp and things to be on the look out for. There were the kids at the Lone Pine State Park who told me about the upcoming fireworks display in O'Neill. And there was Ernest, who came over and shared stories with me while I devoured my Sunday all-you-can-eat chicken buffet in Orchard.

Then there were the momentary encounters with livestock. I noticed when I went by the cows and horses', they would fixate on the yellow flag that was attached to the trailer. I only knew that because when I would say something to them, their heads would snap to the front of the bike. I also came across some cows and horses that would run along the fence with me, and it would just crack me up. In all my years of biking, I had never witnessed anything quite like that and wondered if it wasn't the trailer that freaked them out. It continued to happen beyond Nebraska and provided momentary comic relief.

Because of all the rain there were battalions of mosquitoes. There also were hundreds of little frogs on the highway every morning. I stopped more than once to pull a turtle off the road and had continuous encounters with the red-winged black birds that lined the willows. As I approached the birds, a sentry would call out. Soon I would have a half dozen birds flying above me squawking and dive-bombing my head. I observed them doing the same thing with a raven that was passing by. The raven turned onto his back in mid-air and grabbed for the black birds. I tried to imitate the raven. I would reach up with one arm toward the birds and startle them, but they were relentless. Actually, if the truth were known, I enjoyed their company.

My last night in Nebraska was spent at the Scenic Park Campground in South Sioux City. I could tell there were some people who had been living in the park for a while. It was very much a low-rent campground, but I didn't care. I set up the tent and walked back into town to do my laundry. My schedule for doing laundry was being accelerated due to the heat and humidity.

While reading a book in the Laundromat, I heard bells and whistles going off. On TV there was a tornado warning for the area. I had never been in a tornado, so I began paying attention. It was totally dark outside at 5 p.m., the wind began rattling the windows, and the rain was dumping—it was a deluge. I felt safe enough in the building, but I was imagining my tent being blown into Iowa. The tornado touched down 11 miles south of town and three hours later I returned to find my life, miraculously, still staked down in the park. Fortunately, I had been smart enough to pitch the tent on a knoll, as the lower ground was completely flooded.

I awoke to a dreary morning and the mosquitoes were already on patrol when I emerged from the tent at 6 a.m. I went to the shower room to prepare to leave but when I opened the door, there was fresh blood all over the place. There was an old man sitting in one of the shower stalls, so I asked him if he was OK. He said he was. I asked him, "What happened here?" He said he didn't know so I bolted. Not only did I not want to get involved, I was scared. I loaded up *B.O.P.* and *B.O.B.* and made it across the Missouri River into Iowa. When I first rode into Nebraska I said I loved it, but now I loved leaving it even more.

Once over the bridge, I hadn't gone three blocks when a distinguished-looking man in a pickup pulled over and jumped out to hand me something. He said he ran a bed and breakfast south of town and that he was a biker. He told me I was welcome to stay at his B&B. I thanked him for the invitation, but I was heading north. All day long, everywhere I stopped, people were asking me about what I was doing and wondering if I was riding in the RAGBRAI (Register's Annual Great Bike Ride Across Iowa). The ride is across Iowa every year with about 25,000 people participating. Two thoughts hit me; how easy just riding across one state sounded to me, and how much I would hate biking with 24,999 other people. But they were proud of their RAGBRAI and they all asked me if I was familiar with it.

I thought about the contrast of my journey compared with a ride like that. Both involved riding a bicycle for an extended period of time, but that's where the similarities ended. They had sag wagons, support teams, medical staffs, and were very structured. I was alone and rarely knew where I was eating or sleeping the next day. The biggest difference, however, was the mental composition of each day. I had the opportunity to get into a "zone" most days that I called my "Moments of Clarity" (after the band from Coeur d'Alene, Idaho, that I saw in Flagstaff, Ariz.). I guess the people in the RAGBRAI might have that opportunity as well, but I think their "zones" centered more on social interactions.

Here's how a "MOC" went for me in Iowa: I was thinking about the Spirit of Christ, which I consider the Spirit of Buddha, the Spirit of Lao-tzu, etc. I was wondering how does one obtain that Spirit? I think everyone has access to it, but how does one actually become The Christ or The Buddha? Jesus was a simple man, who devoted his life to the love of God and became The Christ. Siddhartha renounced power and worldly pleasures and devoted his life to Enlightenment and became The Buddha. They both were able to forego the material world and dwell in the Spiritual World. It seemed so simple to me; give up your material possessions and be open, honest and loving in all thoughts and actions. So why wasn't anyone doing it? Why wasn't I doing it? I knew the answer. I didn't have the fortitude, courage or faith to walk away from everything and let the Universe provide for my well-being. Then I realized, no one else on this planet had it either, that I knew of. We have the ultimate power in front of us, yet no one is willing to obtain it. I have to laugh at people who say it is all right to have material possessions as long as you're not "attached" to them. That seems to be an oxymoron to me. The fact that you own something shows an amount of attachment, and I have to think God feels the same way. Thus, no one currently on this planet has been able to obtain the Spirit, completely. There are people like the homeless who don't own anything, but they do not live entirely for the Love of God. Then there are people like The Pope and The Dalai Lama, who live their lives devoted to The Spirit, but still have possessions. Only when you give up everything, do you gain everything. It is so easy to say, yet so hard to do. And on and on these thoughts would flow.

So many times people would tell me how courageous I was to be on this trip. I never ever thought of myself that way, and in light of the previous MOC, I knew I was lacking. I wondered if I ever would obtain that courage and faith.

At the moment, I was as far from Enlightenment as I could get. I was standing on the shoulder of Highway 60 flipping off a truck driver for running me off the road. It was the first and only time I flipped anyone off on The Journey. As soon as I did, I knew it was a mistake. For one thing, it was the wrong thing to do, but I also was sending a signal to someone with a CB radio who could contact every truck I was going to meet that day. It was the third time I had been run off the road on that highway, which rivaled some of the highways in Nebraska as the worst. Unlike Nebraska, however, there was a lot more traffic on this road.

That evening I was talking to some locals in Sheldon, Iowa, who were telling me about blacktops. Blacktops are tertiary roads used by farmers. They would add miles to the trip, but they would take the traffic out of the equation. The next morning I was riding on blacktops surrounded by corn and an occasional hog farm. I couldn't imagine where all that corn was going. Sometimes I would come up on a rise and for as far as I could see there was corn—a sea of corn.

I was just outside of Thompson, Iowa, when I popped a spoke on the rear wheel, non-drive side. The heat and humidity were in the high 90s and there was nothing around for shade, so I replaced the spoke and decided I would ride into town to true the wheel better. As I approached the town, a car pulled up next to me.

"Where you headed?" The man asked, sitting in the middle of the front seat.

"I'm riding through all 48 lower states," I replied.

"No kidding? Are you going to stop in Thompson?"

"As a matter of fact I am. I have to true this rear wheel."

"Well stop in the general store and tell them that Darryl Morgan is buying you a soda. I'm the Mayor of Thompson and the mailman."

There was a park next to the general store, so I pulled under a tree to work on the bike. Just as I was finishing with the wheel, Darryl came by and took me into the store. He introduced me to the good ol' boys that were hanging around and told me to pick out whatever I wanted. God bless him. Instead of thinking about breaking my first spoke in a month, I was thinking about the really great people in this world; people who don't pre-judge, but do things out of the goodness of their hearts.

I made it to Minnesota that day and tried to camp out in a park at the state line. No one else was there. It had an outhouse and was right on a lake. I soon discovered the real hazard with camping in the Midwest. Before I could get anything unloaded, I was covered with mosquitoes. What I had been calling mosquitoes before were mere bugs. These mosquitoes were dangerous; they were big, brutal and relentless. I loaded up with some bug spray on top of sunscreen and 82 miles of sweat and grime. That just scared off the little ones, the larger ones treated the mixture as a tartar sauce. I then put on sweat pants and a hooded, sweat shirt to protect as much exposed skin as possible. As I sat there in my self-constructed sauna, I watched these beasts land on my clothes and probe incessantly, actually succeeding occasionally with striking their target. Of course, my face immediately became the mother lode. Besides being on the lake, the wet spring season had provided an abundance of breeding grounds for the carnivores. It seemed such a shame not to be able to enjoy the beautiful setting and peaceful evening.

One thing I have to say about Minnesota, besides the large vicious mosquitoes, Minnesotans give a whole new meaning to the phrase "mow the lawn." I couldn't believe how big everyone's yard was and how much time, energy and money were wasted maintaining them. But I must say, most of the farms I passed were immaculate.

The next day I headed for The Old Barn Resort Hostel in Preston, Minn., where I was looking forward to a shower and sleeping in a bed. When I arrived, the hostel was full. It was Friday, summer, and the hostel was on the Root River Trail (a popular bike path in Minnesota). Up until now, I had been traveling in the off-season and wasn't concerned about a reservation. But it was July 10, the heart of summer vacations, and as I continued to head east I was encountering more and more people.

I found a dingy campground in the woods by the bike path, next to the Root River. It was the same scenario as the previous night with the mosquitoes. So I set up my tent, fixed dinner, and sat there in my mixture of sweat, sunscreen and bug spray—two days' worth. I didn't want to take a shower until I was ready to get in the tent, because I would just have to load up on bug spray again. Finally I went to take a shower and then hauled ass back to the tent. I climbed in as quickly as I could and then tried to kill any of the beasts that had followed me in.

The next morning I was up before the sun thinking I might be able to load up the bike and leave before the mosquitoes got bad. I had no such luck. I wore long sleeves and leggings, but still had to spray my entire body.

The next couple of hours on the Root River Trail made up for the camping inconveniences. What a glorious ride in the early morning. It was 7 a.m., so there were just a few people around, but plenty of wildlife. I saw rabbits, herons, songbirds and butterflies. It was all so picturesque and I wanted to capture the tranquility on film, but that was impossible. Some situations are bigger than pictures or words. So I rode at a steady pace and absorbed the peacefulness that surrounded me. One person I did see that morning was Woody Johnson. Woody was a local who had turned me on to the path when I met him in Dexter a couple of days earlier. He was trying to ride a century when I met up with him again. I appreciated the information about the trail. It was 35 miles of the nicest bike path I had been on.

By early afternoon I was at LaCrosse, Wis. My buddy, Chuey, told me I "had to" go to the Old Style Brewery to see the largest six-pack in the world. As I was crossing over the mighty Mississippi River, I stopped to take a picture and two ladies I had passed earlier on bicycles caught up with me. They asked me questions about what I was doing and I suggested we go to the brewery to have a beer and talk.

Susan was from Holland and Svetlana was from Russia. They were in the U.S. on an exchange program working with mentally challenged people. I wasn't so sure I didn't fit into that category, which may be why they related to me so easily. The people in the brewery really treated us well since we were on bicycles. We had a good time, but they had to go shopping at the mall and I had to find shelter. What a good day for me; a bike path all morning, two pretty women to share beers with, and only two days away from being with my family.

I was completing 26 straight days of biking. In that time, I had ridden over 2,000 miles with very few problems with the bike or my body. The bike needed a tune up and some spare spokes. I needed to find some biking gloves, as I was permanently losing the feeling in my fingers and the strength in my left hand. Of more concern, however, was the loss of feeling in my penis. This is common to almost every man who cycles for an extended length of time, but I wasn't experiencing any recovery—it had become a permanent condition. I was talking on the phone with my grandmother, who told me about a program on TV dealing with male cyclists becoming impotent. I told her it might already be too late. I tried to figure out what was more important to me, finishing The Journey or not being impotent. The next day I loaded up the rig and rode 60 miles—I guess I had my answer.

I took off at 7 a.m. on July 13, the day I would make it to Green Lake. It was only a 60-mile ride and I was excited. This distance would only take an hour in a vehicle. In fact, my mother had offered to come pick me up

with their truck, but I wanted to pedal into camp and I think she understood that. I was slowly going down an entrance ramp waiting for a semi
to go by so I could enter Highway 82. Apparently, he was going slower
than I anticipated and as I continued to brake, I eventually fell over. It
seemed to happen in slow motion. Because I was using clip-in pedals, I
had to twist my foot to get out of the pedal, but I waited too long. So
there I was on the bicycle as if I were riding it, only in a horizontal position on the pavement. I bruised my hip and bloodied my knee, but I was
more embarrassed than hurt.

Later that day, just outside of Princeton, Wis., a semi pulled up next to
me and started squeezing me off the road by driving onto the shoulder.
There was no doubt it was intentional. I bailed off the road into the
gravel. Earlier on the trip I would have lost control of the bike, but I was
strong enough now to hold *B.O.P.* and *B.O.B.* upright on a gravel slope. I
only had 10 miles to go, but felt like there was a force trying to keep me
from getting there.

It was unbelievably hot and humid, so I stopped at a convenience store
in Princeton for a snack and something to drink. I was sitting against the
building in the shade when this old-timer came out of the store and asked
about my trip. He told me everyone in town called him Grampa Giz and
he wanted to know if he could contribute a dollar to The Journey. I just
started laughing and said, "Sure." My first sponsor! He told me he would
contribute more if he could and I told him not to worry because he was
the first person to make a monetary donation to the cause. He asked me if
I wanted to come over to his house and have a beer, but I was anxious to
see my family.

As I was preparing to leave, a car pulled up and a man about my age
stepped out. He said his son wanted to know how far I had traveled on the
bike. I told him 6,700 miles so far, which he relayed to the kid in the car.
The kid shot out of the car and introduced himself as Aaron Daullenbach.
He looked to be about 15 and asked me several questions about what I
was doing. As we were talking, some of his friends came out of the store

and started checking out my rig and me. Pretty soon Aaron asked me if he could have my autograph. Again, I started laughing, but I obliged. Usually teenagers didn't pay much attention to me, so I was taken back a bit by their interest. I was smiling when I rode out of town; one stop, two firsts—money and an autograph.

CHAPTER 16

▼

FAMILY

I pulled into the campground and found my parents' trailer, but no one was home. I waited around and pretty soon my mother, sister, and niece arrived. We hugged each other, but it wasn't the reception I was expecting; they were all so solemn. My mother immediately sat down and told me that the doctors had found a spot on my father's lung a couple of weeks earlier. All of a sudden the heat and humidity became stifling. I couldn't breathe and seemed incapable of forming a rational thought. My family had decided not to tell me until I arrived, so I wouldn't be biking and worrying about my father. My parents were in the final stages of packing up and heading back to Colorado for more tests.

Renee, Janae and Sonny, my brother-in-law, were staying in a motel across the lake from the campground. Justin, my nephew, was back in Colorado working at his summer job on a golf course. Vicky, the only Lowrance with a real job, was back in Pueblo working. Mom and Dad sat down with me that night and explained everything that had happened and what was planned. Dad emphasized that he wanted me to continue with

The Journey. He said all I could do if I came back to Colorado was hold his hand, and he had plenty of people to do that. He told me if it turned out to be something serious, I could fly home. We talked about what others would say about him being in the hospital and me out riding a bicycle around America. He didn't care what other people thought because he knew I loved him and just needed my prayers.

The next couple of days were a mixed blessing. We had fun together as a family, but there was a strained atmosphere. We fought through it, however, and I was so happy to be with everyone at that moment. Dusty and Melva Ketterman, my parents' camping buddies, were camped next door and gave me more cashews when I arrived. Melva placed a mothball label on the can to keep Sonny and my Dad away from them. One night we all went to a local restaurant famous for its' all-you-can-eat chicken and had quite a feast.

I had looked numerous times for a reason to quit The Journey and here it was. I felt I should be home with my father, but he made it clear that he wanted The Journey to continue. I was just riding a bicycle, but he seemed proud of that. I know he was disappointed that I didn't participate in high school sports, didn't go into the military, and lived an alternative lifestyle in college. He had been an athlete, a Marine and a conservative Republican. He always told me he was proud of what I had accomplished in life, but maybe it was easier to brag about me riding a bicycle around America then how much money I used to make—I don't know.

We finally decided that I would bike to Chicago and spend a few days with my good friend, Freddie, while the hospital ran the tests on Dad. It would be much easier to fly home from Chicago than to stash my "stuff" somewhere on the road and find a flight from Small-town, U.S.A.

The day we all went our separate ways was difficult. I know my mother felt as though we didn't get to spend enough time together and I was experiencing exactly what they were trying to prevent when they waited to tell me the news about Dad. I could not quit thinking about my father and was struggling to concentrate on riding my bike.

CHAPTER 17

▼

FREDDIE

Before I got to Fred's, I had one more stop to make. Two years ago when I first began thinking about the trip, I wrote a letter to Trek asking them if they would be interested in sponsoring The Journey. I loved the bike. I took it to Europe in 1990, rode all across Colorado and, in fact, had 10,000 miles on it before I started The Journey. A Trek representative wrote back and told me I wasn't really a proven cross-country rider and sent a Trek water bottle, which I assumed was an inference to drink a lot of water.

When I pulled into Waterloo, Wis., the headquarters for Trek, I had ridden 6,800 miles through 18 states for six months. I was thinking that was a good start at "proving" I was a cross-country bike rider. I walked into the lobby with the water bottle, but unfortunately the representative was at a conference in Chicago and I was unable talk with anyone. I was disappointed, but also had a new attitude about The Journey. *B.O.P.* and I had come this far together and I was determined that we would finish together.

To get to Schaumburg, Ill., where my good friend Fred Crivlare lives with his family, I figured two days. Fred and I met over 20 years ago on a ski trip to Michigan when I was living in Chicago. He was a Chicago native, but had attended college in Colorado, so we immediately had something in common. We developed a life-long friendship and stayed in close touch with each other over the years. I flew out to Chicago in 1981 to be in his wedding and he and Robin have made annual pilgrimages to Colorado during spring break to take their three girls skiing. I watched Nicole, Amanda and Jackie grow up and always remind Freddie how lucky he is to have a house full of beautiful women.

Thirteen hours and 108 miles later, I was sitting on Freddie's deck drinking a beer. It was my longest day so far and with the heat, humidity and traffic at all time highs. Once again the dynamics of bike touring had changed. It was a given there would be dense traffic once I was within a certain distance of Chicago and people from Illinois have a reputation for driving fast. Now I got to see the two combined. The last 40 miles were ridden on roads with narrow shoulders and a continuous stream of cars. Not only was there an increased volume of traffic, but it was also moving at an accelerated pace. I was actually impressed that people could pass so close to me at such high rates of speed.

Being at Fred's provided comfort, but I was still distracted by thoughts of my father's health. My relationship with my father could best be categorized as a sports connection. Whenever we talked on the phone or got together, we talked about sports. We looked at things differently politically, spiritually and philosophically, so sports was a safe topic for both of us. When I began playing golf a few years ago our connection became a little tighter. Now, sitting there thinking he could be dying was tearing me up. A couple of days later, my mother called and said the spots on Dad's lungs were bacteria, not a tumor. There was no cancer and no surgery was required, they would fight the bacteria with antibiotics, what a relief for everyone. I talked to my father and he sounded great. He encouraged me, again, to keep pedaling.

The next few days were spent relaxing and doing family things with the Crivlares. Softball games, dance recitals, piano recitals; there was always an activity to attend. On the weekend, we went downtown and saw the "Tall Ships" that had come into the harbor.

On my last night there, Fred barbecued and Nancy Peddle, an old friend from Colorado, joined us. Nancy used to date my buddy, Oyler, and I'd known her almost 15 years. She is an attractive woman with jet-black hair, big brown eyes, and the all-time best laugh. She is thin as a rail and when she really starts laughing, her entire body trembles. It is actually entertaining to watch her laugh. The past few years Nancy had been working with an international organization that helps children in war-torn countries and is currently working on her Ph.D., concentrating on forgiveness. She is a child of God and understands her connection with The Spirit better than most. I hope to be able to spend more time with her someday, because she has an aura of Enlightenment about her—an old soul.

My time with the Crivlares was good. They always treat me better than family and I appreciate it. Fred is truly one of the good people on this planet. God bless him and the ladies.

The Journey was providing a unique arena for me to get together with all these people I had known back in our "rowdy" days and see how they had changed over the years. Everyone had taken their own individual paths, but they all experienced growth. At each stop I found myself extremely proud of what my friends had accomplished.

CHAPTER 18

THE MIDWEST II

It was July 24 and it felt good to be back on the bike. I was riding in an arc around Chicago to reach Indiana. Unfortunately, I couldn't escape the gravitational pull of the city; traffic, people, traffic, people…I was riding through Chicago Heights when some black guys started yelling "whitie" and a hooker whistled at me. Outside of Valparaiso, Ind., some idiot threw a can in my direction as he passed. Fortunately, most people don't understand the relative dynamics of moving objects, so they almost always miss, which he did. But it still always bothered me when something like that happened. I wondered what could possibly be going through their heads.

I was heading up to Grosse Ile, Mich., to see my ex-in-laws and decided to cross into Michigan earlier rather than later to see if the roads might improve. Turning north through South Bend, Ind., I made it onto Highway 12 in southern Michigan. No luck! Not only were the roads just as bad, now there were semi-trucks with 42 wheels roaring past me. I never saw another truck like it in any other state, but there were plenty of them in Michigan on Highway 12.

One thing I noticed in Michigan, that I had only casually noticed thus far on the trip, was how modular homes were taking over the landscape. It was architecture of the 90s, I guess. But if it allows people to live in their own house and not pay rent, more power to them! It's just a little intimidating as a cyclist to have sections of homes passing so closely. I bailed off the road three times that first day in Michigan.

Bad asphalt, 42-wheelers and modular home sections—I was exhausted when I pulled into the Lawcocks on Grosse Ile. Not to mention I rode 102 miles that day in 99 degree temperature and 99 percent humidity. I kept telling myself I needed to quit doing centuries in the middle of summer. But when the bicycle is working and the weather is clear, I just kept pedaling.

Norma and Rex were sitting outside in the shade when I arrived. Rex is retired Navy, retired Ford, and currently successful at playing the stock market. He is a big guy (6' 4"), likes to ride his Harley, and is quite the storyteller. In contrast, Norma is a diminutive 4" 11" with a pleasant face and always seems to be laughing at something. She successfully raised five children, one of whom I married 16 years ago. I felt a bit uncomfortable being there without Jan and told them so. Norma told me, "Jan divorced you; we didn't divorce you."

Grosse Ile was a good stop for me. Norma fattened me up and I was able to visit with some of my former brothers and sisters-in-law, they really made me feel at home. Jan's older brother, "Big Al," had a barbecue at his house. I never have met anyone who tells a funnier story than he does. Her younger brother, Brian, had me over to his house to view his latest art work. He has a tremendous talent that has lain dormant for many years. That type of talent needs to be shared with other people and I hope he figures out how to do it. One of Jan's sisters, Lori, and I hung out together one day and talked about life. She left an inspirational card on my bicycle the morning I left. Little realizing, I'm sure, how thoughtful gestures like that helped me through the tough times. Unfortunately, I didn't get to see her other sister, Jeanne, who was up north.

Energized and ready to head east, I had preconceived notions about the East. I knew it was wrong to pre-judge, but old habits die hard. I tried to tell myself to deal with the East when the time came. It was wasted energy to be worrying now. Besides, I had Toledo to deal with first. I'd only been to Toledo one other time, but it was weird.

Jan and I had been visiting her family and were heading back to Colorado. For some reason, when we got to Toledo, we couldn't access the highway heading west. It was the most bizarre experience, like being in a force field. We were two intelligent adults, but were unable to get on the freeway for a variety of reasons. I swore then never to go back to Toledo and here I was preparing to ride a bicycle right through it.

Thinking ahead, I stopped north of town at a little place to get something to eat. I thought it was a good idea to have my strength before tackling the monster, Toledo. It is funny how our minds can create realities for us. While eating, a young black man came over and asked me if I was training for the Olympics. I told him I was just biking around America and we talked for a bit. He told me he was pretty sure I could beat any of those guys currently riding in the Tour de France. I thanked him for his positive energy and took off into the bowels of Toledo looking for Highway 2 East.

Sure enough, I got lost before ever making it to the Maumee River that cuts right through town. I was stopped at a light looking around, when "the force" hit me. I immediately fell over—bike, trailer and rider all just lying there on the streets of Toledo. Did I bring this on myself with the power of my mind or was there some "force" in Toledo? I got up chuckling, when two guys pulled up next to me in a Cadillac. They were laughing as well and wanted to know if I was all right. I said I was and asked them for directions to Highway 2. They were stumped.

I noticed a delivery truck in a parking lot and figured the driver ought to know how to get there. I pulled up to the truck and asked the young, black driver for directions. He stared at me and wanted to know what I was doing. After I told him, he stood there shaking his head. He said he never heard of anything like that in his entire life, but he did give me good directions to get out of Toledo, thank God.

Heading east on Highway 2, I rode until I came to Lake Erie. The next day brought the welcome relief of a cool breeze off the lake. It would be another 100-mile day to get to the HI-Stanford House Hostel in Peninsula, Ohio, so the cooler weather was a blessing.

I was a mile away from the turn-off to Highway 250, when an Ohio state trooper pulled me over. Turning around, I couldn't believe my eyes. He was the biggest policeman I had ever seen. In fact, he was big and very upset that I was on this highway.

"What in the hell do you think you're doing?" he asked.

When I told him, he let me know that it was illegal to ride a bicycle on a divided highway in Ohio. I told him it wasn't divided when I started that morning, I hadn't seen any "No bicycle" signs, and it wasn't an interstate. He reiterated that I could *not* ride a bicycle on a divided highway in Ohio, period. He allowed me to ride down to the next exit, but he didn't want to hear that I was on another divided highway while I was in Ohio. He seemed more confused than angry and just kept staring at the bike and trailer. Finally, he told me that he had never heard of anyone traveling across the country on a bicycle. I was going to tell him that a lot of people do it, but decided to leave him with the illusion that I was completely nuts. They must not see many people touring on bicycles in this part of Ohio because everyone I talked to was freaking out and people on the two lane highways were struggling to pass me.

I had become aware over the past six states that no one waved at me the way the people had in the West. My interactions with them had been good, but the residents of Minnesota, Wisconsin, Illinois, Indiana, Michigan and now Ohio seemed conservative and somewhat reserved. Many times when I stopped, people would look over my rig but would never say anything. My policy on The Journey was not to initiate the conversation unless it was to ask a question. I didn't want to bore people with what I was doing unless they were interested and asked. Consequently, I had very few conversations in the last six states. So I was pleasantly surprised as I was pedaling down lonely Highway 303 and the driver of a bright yellow and orange car waved at me. As I prepared to wave back, I saw that he was waving with his middle finger and he seemed very upset with me. I had to laugh; here I was waiting for someone to wave to me and I get so excited, only to find out I'm being flipped off.

After riding 100 miles that day, I reached the hills of Ohio. I thought it was some cruel joke having to deal with hills after already biking a century. Twenty miles later I made it to the hostel. One hundred and twenty miles in one day was a record for me on a bicycle—loaded or unloaded. I was tired, but felt good. I felt strong.

The hostel was a beautiful old mansion in the woods. There were deer grazing by an old barn and flocks of birds around a pond. Kate, the manager, was as pleasant as the setting. She went out of her way to give me a private room and hooked me up with a ride to Cleveland the next day to visit the Rock and Roll Hall of Fame. I spent the entire evening talking with Kate about life and the struggles we go through trying to justify living in a peaceful environment without making money or joining the "rat race." I was no longer experiencing that struggle, but I understood her dilemma as a young person and how easy it is to get caught up in the hype and feeling like you are being left behind. We seem to think we are wasting time if we are quiet or that we are missing out on something if we are not involved. Unfortunately, Kate was having those thoughts and nothing I could say or do was going to change her perceptions.

The next day I caught a ride with Delores and Beth Holl to Cleveland. They were a mother/daughter team from Pennsylvania and going to the RRHoF, as well. Delores worked in a hospital and Beth was a college student. They were good people and I couldn't thank them enough for the ride. I coerced Delores into letting me pay for the parking so I didn't feel like a complete mooch.

The Rock and Roll Hall of Fame; few things have influenced my life as much as rock and roll. From the time my best friend, Shud, and I cut out cardboard guitars to play along with the Beatles to the Neil Young concert we went to right before I left, music has been a constant companion in my life. The irony of that was I didn't listen to music while I rode because it was so important to listen to the bike and the traffic.

I can't overstate my disappointment with the RRHoF. It was way over the top for me. My senses were bombarded from every angle. Every theater room had three screens, all showing different scenes at the same time. The display rooms had different music coming from the displays, a screen on the wall, and speakers from the ceiling. It was way too new age and high tech for this old hippie. Plus, most of the groups I used to listen to weren't even inducted. Where were Deep Purple, Uriah Heep, and Lynard Skynard? But what really got to me was sitting in the courtyard in the late afternoon and having to listen to Michael Jackson and Johnny Cash being broadcast outdoors. I'd been on the road for seven months and would have loved to hear some classic rock 'n' roll like Led Zepplin or Pink Floyd, but the music gods weren't smiling on me.

That night I returned to the hostel and was introduced to another cross-country bike rider staying there. Robert was riding his bike from Maine to Washington, state. He was a very strange person: He talked about joining the KKK rally down south, but said he wasn't a racist. He said he always lied to the police when they pulled him over. He mentioned being hit by a car a few years ago while riding through Connecticut and taking the old guy who hit him for a few thousand dollars and a new bicycle. There was a very negative energy emanating from Robert and I didn't like being around him, even if he was a cross-country bike rider.

The next morning was the kind of morning cyclists' love. It was sunny and cool, with no wind. I was heading east on Highway 303 and stopped in the little town of Hudson for breakfast. When I came out of the café, there was a crowd of people around the bike and trailer. They immediately started asking me questions about what I was doing. There also was a 65-year-old man there on a bicycle, and he had done some touring. We talked a bit and I felt really pumped up as I rode out of town.

At noon, I popped a spoke on the rear wheel, non-drive side. Because I hadn't picked up any spares since the break in Iowa, I had to use the kevlar spoke. At 2:30, I popped another spoke and before I could get to Geneva, Ohio, I popped a third one. Wow, talk about putting a damper on a good day. I started the day feeling great and now I was dragging. But it was a valuable lesson. If I had the spare parts, I could have replaced the spokes and continued with no problem. As it was, I was riding a loaded bicycle minus two rear spokes.

I woke up the next morning in a terrible mood. I had to pay $40 for a dumpy little motel room because I was in a resort town. There was no phone in the room and the waterbed was in dire need of some water. Also, the bed was so cold and, as a result, I woke up in the middle of the night with a cramp in my thigh. I unrolled my pad and sleeping bag and slept on the floor. This was the second time I didn't sleep in the bed in a motel run by Eastern Indians.

It was Sunday and I couldn't find a bike shop that was open, so I pedaled 10 miles down the road to Ashtabula to camp out by Lake Erie. As I approached where the campground should have been, I stopped and asked directions from some people who were out in their front yard enjoying the pleasant weekend weather. They didn't have a clue where the campground was, but some guy standing nearby with his bicycle did. At first, I couldn't understand what he was saying. Then as he approached, I realized he was mentally handicapped. He was a big guy and I would guess over 20 years old, but he talked like his tongue was too big for his mouth. We had a connection though; when he was next to me, I noticed he kept staring at *B.O.P.* He was on an old Schwinn and I could tell he was proud of it. Even with his difficulties, he was able to communicate that I needed to go over the bridge to get to the campground. He was proud to be able to help me. He puffed his chest out, pointed the way, and patted his bicycle. I thanked him for his help and told him, "God bless you." He stood there with a big smile on his face and watched me ride off. Only later did I realize that he was another angel guiding me on The Journey.

I camped in a meadow by myself next to Lake Erie. I had all day to ponder the significance of three broken spokes in one day. Of course, as mentioned before, the first lesson was to be prepared and I couldn't blame myself enough for not having spare spokes. But the more important lesson was how I was handling the adversity.

It was so easy to be spiritual when things were going well, but every time something bad happened, the wheels would fall off. I would start cursing and inevitably want to quit. My spiritual development was going nowhere until I could conquer my negative attitude. I compared myself to people who go to church every Sunday and think all is forgiven for their week's indiscretions. Why can't we continue to develop ourselves EVERY day? We always like to think of ourselves as being further along than we really are. The real tests always come during times of adversity. I have never been able to handle stress on an even keel, but I also realized that recognizing my weakness was half the battle. I had plenty of time to work on my stress management and knew many more opportunities would inevitably arise.

I located the bike shop the next morning. It doubled as a picture framing shop. It was a strange combination, and once again I had a sinking feeling in my stomach as I sat there listening to the owner ordering framing supplies on the phone. I tried to remain positive and remind myself I was just riding a bike. This might not be the best bike shop in the world, but it was the best one available and they were providing a service to me that would allow me to continue riding.

The bike was repaired, I had spare spokes, and the owner had given me some good information on getting through western Pennsylvania. He told me to get off Highway 20 and onto Highway 5, a smaller road but with less traffic. It was just the type of information I needed.

CHAPTER 19

▼

WHO ARE THESE PEOPLE?

I began riding late that day because of the bike repairs, so just south of Erie, Pa., I started looking for a place to camp. I was in the suburb of Mill Creek when a van pulled over and the driver jumped out to talk to me.

Warner Bacon was a bike rider and, in fact, had his biking clothes on and his bicycle in the van. He had just completed a ride with his girlfriend and was on his way home. He was interested in *B.O.B.* and asked numerous questions about how it handled, how much it could hold, etc. He knew about these trailers, but he had never actually seen one. As we stood there and talked, we discovered we had Colorado in common. He used to teach skiing at Breckenridge and had worked for my best friend, Jim Banks, a.k.a. Shud. America seemed so big while riding my bicycle around the country, but I realized how small the world really is.

I asked Warner about a good place to camp, but he insisted I come home with him. As I followed his van onto the grounds, I knew this was going to be a bit different from what I was accustomed to. We were on 10 acres where Warner was restoring his deceased grandfather's house. His parents and an aunt and uncle also had homes on the property. The houses were grand, as were the cars and even the trees. It was a magnificent setting and I realized I was around money, more money than I was normally around. I grew up in a steel-mill town on the prairies of Colorado. We weren't poor, but the only time we went to the Country Club was to attend someone's wedding, and I remember it looking something like this place. Warner opened the garage door and the interior looked like a bike shop. There were over a dozen bicycles with every part and tool needed to work on them. A car was parked on the other side of the garage. I can't remember if it was a sports car or an antique, but it was valuable.

I offered to pitch my tent in the yard, but Warner said, "You're going to sleep in a bed tonight!" He also wanted me to have a good meal and called his girlfriend, Jenn, to inform her I would be joining them for dinner. Warner made me feel at home and, being a biker himself, he knew exactly what I needed; a shower, some food to snack on, and some conversation about touring. We sat around and talked like we had known each other forever. We talked about biking and he told me about being hit by a car while riding. He wasn't seriously injured, but he thought the more hours you put on a bike, the more susceptible you are to having an encounter with an automobile. We also talked about skiing, but that made me homesick. He showed me through the house he was renovating and also showed me his gun collection. Warner's business was buying and selling small gauge shotguns.

Warner was a couple of years younger than I was and in incredible shape. He had a good body for biking (small, with powerful legs), but his upper body was much more developed than the average "serious" biker. Most bikers who ride 200+ miles a week eventually notice atrophy in their upper body, unless they do some cross training such as weight lifting. Warner had obviously been doing some. He was very tan and fit.

Jenn was a very attractive lady in her mid 30s, with a young son, Brit. I thought she was special for fixing the dinner, but when she brought out the strawberry shortcake for dessert, I knew she was special. I couldn't believe how at home they both made me feel, like being with old friends. In fact, Jenn thought Warner and I *were* old friends and was shocked when she found out we had just met that day on the side of the road. We had a good laugh about that.

The next morning I thanked Warner for his generous hospitality and told him we would definitely stay in touch. I made it through Erie without too much trouble and stopped at a little roadside café, Christia's. I was the only one inside, except for the young girl waiting on me, and the lady cooking. They began asking me questions about my trip and when I approached the counter to pay, they told me breakfast was on them.

What the heck was going on here? I was back East! This wasn't at all how I expected people in the East to be treating me. I decided not to make any snap judgments. I was going to be in the East for some time, so I'd wait to see how things progressed.

As I was riding through one of the small towns, I saw someone on a bicycle. Rusty was a young man in his 20s who loved his bicycle. He had just finished a four-day trip and had a *B.O.B.* trailer just like mine. He rode his bike everywhere and was pretty impressed that I had been on the road for seven months. We talked almost entirely about biking and he told me about being hit by a car recently. He used the money he received from the settlement to go to Hawaii. Rusty gave me some insight into good camping spots up the road and I thanked him for the information. I told him how much I enjoyed our conversation. I almost always felt better after interacting with another cyclist, especially if they were touring or had been touring. Robert, in Ohio, was the exception.

It was muggy, but the clouds were keeping the heat down to a tolerable level, maybe 90 degrees. A couple of hours down the road I stopped at a peach stand and asked the lady sitting under an umbrella if I could buy just one peach. She said, "Just take one!" Henrietta was an older lady of Polish descent. She wore a big sunbonnet and Onassis-looking sunglasses. No sooner did I finish the peach, than she told me to have another one. And before I could finish that one, she came over to pick out a firm one for the next day. She was killing me with her kindness and I loved it. The peaches were the best I ever ate!

I was about to cross over into New York and realized I hadn't sent my niece, Janae, a postcard from Pennsylvania. Before I left on the trip, Janae had asked me if I would send her a postcard from every state. I was in my 23rd state and hadn't missed yet. But there were no towns along this stretch of highway, so I was going to have to turn off and ride into a town. Before reaching Highway 89 I came upon another peach stand, but this one was a little more substantial with a couple of buildings, so I pulled in on the chance they might have postcards—no such luck. But after seeing the disappointment on my face, the lady started thinking of how she might be able to help me. Seconds later she raised her finger and said she might have a postcard up at the house. She left for a few moments and returned with a postcard of the farm. Westgate Farms had advertised their fruit with postcards over 40 years ago! I told her I couldn't accept something that old, but she said it was OK as long as my niece didn't throw it away. I told her that wouldn't happen as Janae was making a scrapbook with the cards. This great lady even offered to mail it for me, so it would have a PA postmark—unbelievable!

The ride that day reminded me of the trip Jan and I took through France in 1990. For three weeks we rode from Bordeaux to the Atlantic Ocean, through the wine country, and into the Dordogne region. It was such a great way to see the country and the experiences we had in the little villages were priceless. Now, here I was with Lake Erie on my left and vineyards covering the rolling hills to my right. Like France, I could see the church steeples off in the distance announcing a new town, but unlike France, the grapes here were not used for wine. I learned that because they don't receive enough sun, the grapes are used for jelly. At the moment, however, I was sold on their peaches.

As I crossed the state line, I met another biker who had passed me earlier. Walt was also of Polish descent and this was the first time he had been on a bicycle since being hit by a car a year ago, shattering his knee. He looked older than I was, but appeared to be in good shape, except for the swelling in his knee. I told him how nice everyone in western Pennsylvania had been and about staying in Mill Creek with someone who was heavily into biking. He asked me if it was Warner Bacon. I asked, "You know him?" He said Warner was well known in that area for biking, especially for his time trial criterions. I thought, "Wow, I was staying with a hot-shot biker and didn't realize it." I was embarrassed to think of what I might have said about biking in front of him. Walt wished me well and headed back to Erie. I congratulated him on his rehabilitation and began pedaling in New York, the Empire State, #24. I was a little intimidated when I realized that the last four guys I met on bicycles, had all been hit by cars. All of a sudden I became very cautious. But I also realized that the people in western Pennsylvania were the nicest people I had met so far, and to top it off, the asphalt was getting better. Life was good!

CHAPTER 20

▼

THE TRUTH

I headed to Dunkirk, N.Y., along the shore of Lake Erie. From there, I rode east on Highway 39 and eventually linked up with Highway 20. In Forestville I stopped in an old bar for some breakfast. It was a dark, dank place with posters of the Buffalo Bills everywhere. Other than the elderly couple minding the store, I was the only one in there. I had a feeling the majority of their business probably didn't begin until the afternoon. There was no menu, but they cooked me some eggs, sausage and toast for a couple of dollars. I wanted to ask them about their Bills, but considering the Broncos had just won the Super Bowl and given the Bills recent failures, I thought they might think I was bragging. Actually, I was in need of a decent conversation, but I wasn't going to get it there.

Every day there was a threat of rain that made it extremely muggy, but the battleship gray sky kept the temperature down, so I wasn't complaining. I had a sore throat, a new pain in my right elbow, and my rear tire was out of round. But the asphalt was the best I had been on the entire trip, so I just kept pedaling.

I began to notice some subtle changes: The terrain had more hills. The road signs were very confusing about when you actually entered a town. Apparently, for tax purposes, there would be a sign announcing your arrival into a township, but the actual town was still miles off. This could be very disheartening at times, especially when I was ready for a break. And some towns that appeared to be on the highway according to the map were actually a mile or two off the highway. Again unsettling, considering that could represent 20 to 40 additional minutes of pedaling. But the biggest change I noticed was in the make-up of the small towns. In Indiana, Michigan and Ohio, almost every small town had a bait shop and a tire repair shop or auto parts store. They might not have a grocery store or a library or a motel, but by God you could always get some worms or spark plugs. Now, the big attraction in each town was antiques. The farther east I traveled, the older things were and it seemed like most of it was for sale. Maybe the fact that my mother never throws anything away will come back to profit her someday, or at least her grandchildren.

As I was riding through Springville, N.Y., I met Michael, who ran a non-profit store in town. His proceeds went to "Habitat for Humanity." We had a pleasant conversation and he told me about places to camp up the road. There was a little café at the edge of town that served breakfast all day—my kind of place. I ordered some pancakes and when the young kid brought them to me, they were turned upside down. When I turned them over I saw why, they were burnt. I buttered them, drowned them in syrup, and began chowing down. The owner of the place was sitting a couple of tables away and asked if the pancakes were burnt. I said they were, but that it didn't bother me. I told her I rarely complained about food, but she called the kid over to kindly reprimand him and she gave me my meal for a dollar.

Things were going good and my daily "Moment of Clarity" went like this: I am no better or worse than anyone else. If the prophets had the answer, you will never know unless you live their lives—completely, and that requires faith and courage. And what if you go down that path only to find they *didn't* have the answer or worse yet, that you can't access it. What then? I already knew that path requires giving up everything. Jesus didn't say, "Ok, I'm the Son of God, but I'm going to hold onto this house." Buddha didn't attain Enlightenment and say, "But I really want to keep my silk garments." But even then, did those prophets find The Truth? And if they did, then why when Jesus was on the cross did he ask God, "Why hast thou forsaken me?" That tells me that even Jesus, in his moment of truth, was unsure of The Truth. NOBODY really has, does, or will ever know The Truth—and that's The Truth.

CHAPTER 21

▼

THE KILLER HILLS

As I rode into the quiet little town of Avon, N.Y., there were two ladies sitting in their front yard having a rummage sale (what they would call a yard sale in the Midwest). I stopped and asked them if they might know of a place to camp nearby. They went inside and brought out the phone book and a cordless phone. One of the ladies told me that she and her husband used to bicycle tour before they had kids. They also told me about a musician in town who was playing an acoustic guitar that night and about a good bike shop down the road the following day. I still couldn't believe how everyone was so open and friendly. I was impressed and pleased.

My rear tire, along with a lot of my belongings, was rotting away. The sun, rain, wind, and wear and tear of 8,000 miles were having an impact. I was riding on a Continental 2000 touring tire, a tire that a lot of cross-country riders swear by. Usually good for about 5,000 miles, this tire only had 3,000 miles on it and was shot. Understand it had been exposed to the elements for almost 60 straight days with a 300-pound load. El Nino hadn't helped either with a wetter summer than normal, so the tires were constantly treading water. The thing that bothered me was that it wore out before the front tire, a Specialized touring-model I put on in Seattle. It had an additional 1,000 miles on it and was still in good shape. Of course, it wasn't bearing the load the rear tire was so I attributed that to the difference in wear.

As fate would have it, the bike shop was a licensed Continental dealer. As luck would have it, they didn't have any Continental tires in the size I needed. Cross-country riders normally have wider tires for stability, rather than the narrow ones for speed. One observation about bike shops around the country; with the increased popularity of mountain bikes, the inventory for road bike parts has diminished. They did have a Specialized tire in the size I needed, but their warranty covered Continental tires. My rear tire was still covered under warranty because it wore out from weather, not from riding. There was still good tread on it, but the sides were rotting away. After some negotiating, they honored the warranty and gave me the Specialized tire for free—Yahoo!

As always, my good fortune was followed by some not so good fortune. Outside of Geneva, N.Y., I popped a spoke and searched out a bike shop in town. The techs in the shop were pleasant enough and while they were working on the bike, they discovered that the quick release axle was bent. They put on a new one, but now the trailer wouldn't fit on the new axle. Turns out the guys at REI in Sacramento, Calif., had sold me a trailer yolk for a tandem bicycle. That explained all the washers they used to jury-rig my bike so the trailer would fit. I upgraded the yoke and with a thinner wallet than I had anticipated, I pedaled out of town.

August 8, 1998 was a beautiful morning. Two young men on bicycles caught up with me and we rode together for 30 minutes. They were on what they called "The Final Bike Ride." One of the guys was to be married and his buddy was taking him on a four-day "bachelor bike ride." It was a great idea, but the groom-to-be was already having some serious knee problems. I wished him luck on his ride and his marriage.

Just outside of Skaneateles, N.Y., a man on a recumbent bicycle pulled up next to me. The asphalt was excellent with eight-foot wide shoulders, so we rode into town together. John Manring was a professor of Psychology at the University of Syracuse. He was a serious bike rider and had recently switched to riding a recumbent because of back problems. As we rode into town he pointed out several places I could go for a good breakfast and then said, "Or you can come up to my house." He looked to be about my age and I assumed he would probably have a pretty nice bachelor pad. Upon arriving at his house I saw that, like Warner, his garage was full of bicycles and an expensive car. I was surprised to discover he was married and had kids. I felt like I was intruding, but John said, "It's no problem because we already have company, so what's one more body." We went inside and he introduced me to his wife, Peggy, and her sister, Deb. John told them I was riding my bicycle around America looking for the best pancakes. Peggy immediately reached for the skillet. I told her it really wasn't necessary, that toast would be fine, but not with much feeling. She said, "It's no problem," and had Deb pour me a glass of milk and a glass of juice. John and Peggy explained that the flour she was using was ground locally at a mill outside of town and the syrup was from their backyard. It was 10 a.m. and I had already pedaled 20 miles, so I was ravenous. Peggy's pancakes were not only the best I had on the trip, they were The Best Pancakes I have ever had in my life. They were outstanding and so were the Manrings.

After breakfast, Peter and Tom returned from a bike ride. Peter was Deb's husband and Tom was a friend of the Manrings. They told me I had some "killer hills" coming up and Tom showed me an alternate route that would be a bit easier. Wow! What a beautiful morning topped off with some special people.

There was a "Road Closed" sign when I reached the turn-off Tom had told me about. I pulled out the map and began looking at my alternatives. While I was studying the map, a distinguished-looking older man pulled up in his car and asked if he might be able to help me. I told him where I was trying to go and he told me about a paved farm road that would take me to the same place.

The next two hours I experienced not only the most difficult thing I had ever done on a bicycle, but it was the most difficult thing I had ever done in my life. I had never ever ridden on hills comparable to those. They weren't incredibly long, but they went straight up and straight down—one after another. I've ridden over mountain passes out West that climbed for 12 miles, but the road had switchbacks that allowed somewhat of a break. There was no taking a break here. As I reached the top of a hill, I could see the downhill run and the next uphill climb. No turns, no switch-backs, just up and down and up and down and…

I was in the region of upstate New York known as The Finger Lakes. Millions of years ago glaciers carved out the hills and valleys. A few years later, man came along and put in a road. The predominant thinking at that time was, obviously, the shortest distance between two points is a straight line. As a result, there was very little steering needed, just a lot of gas, brake, gas, brake. For a bicyclist, it was 20 minutes of pedaling and two minutes of gliding.

Every time the next hill came into view, I would wonder if I could make it up the grade, usually 10 percent or more. This from a guy who believes in positive thinking, but I couldn't help myself. I had never experienced anything like that. Finally, on one of the longer climbs, I stopped on the side of the road. I was either out of oxygen or my heart was about to explode. While I was standing there trying to let my body functions return to normal, I realized it was the hottest day in two weeks—barely a cloud in the sky. I needed to get out of the sun, but I questioned whether I could start up the hill again. For a moment, I considered pushing the bike and trailer the rest of the way up. Fortunately, there was very little traffic, so I turned around and went downhill to clip my shoes into the pedals. I can't tell you how much I hated giving up even just a few yards of the hill to get going again. I made it up the hill and at 1 p.m. I arrived at Tully, N.Y., for some much needed rest and nourishment.

I was sitting at a table in a fast food joint when a young lady asked if she could join me. Louise was an air traffic controller from Syracuse. She was cute, with curly dark hair, and she was wearing a Colorado t-shirt. She was intrigued about what I was doing. When she told me it was 95 degrees outside, I began wondering what I was doing, as well. I told her about the incredible hills I'd just come over and then sat there and thought, "And this was the "easy" route."

That night I camped off of Highway 20, somewhere between Morrisville and Madison. I wasn't bothered at all by the mosquitoes, or the heat, or anything. There were mosquitoes and it was hot and humid, but I was oblivious to everything. I set up my tent and passed out. The next morning I woke up thinking about those hills. I even told myself that I would never forget the "killer hills" of upstate New York.

Later that day I met a biker on the highway and was asking him about an easy way to get over to Vermont. He asked me where I was coming from and when I told him The Finger Lakes, he almost dropped. He said those were the steepest hills in America and he couldn't believe I pedaled over them with my rig. It didn't make me feel good to hear that, it only made me more exhausted. He told me I'd have fewer hills if I rode down by the Mohawk River.

I made it to the Mohawk River and he was right, thank God! Unfortunately, the weather changed and I was riding in the rain. And if that wasn't enough to dampen my spirits, I discovered that a spoke was pulling out of my rear wheel. In the little town of Scotia, I located a bike shop, however, it didn't have any double-walled rims. Because of the weight I was hauling, it was imperative to have double-walled rims. The owner was preparing to close because he just found out that his brother had died. He had a tandem rim that he claimed was just as strong as a double-walled rim and offered to put it on before closing. I felt bad for him, but the work seemed to relieve his grief momentarily. I was thankful for his time and help.

A couple of days later, I was sitting in the Benson Diner in Eagles Bridge, N.Y., having breakfast and preparing to enter Vermont. It seemed like I had been in New York forever and in the infamous words of the Grateful Dead, "What a long strange trip it's been." The asphalt had been the all time best and the people had been more than I could have hoped for. Even in the diner, people were treating me in such a friendly manner. Mechanical problems with the bike I now expected, the hospitality I was receiving, I didn't expect. I had a preconceived notion there would be so many people in the East that no one would have time for me. Instead, people were very inquisitive and very friendly. I was shocked and pleasantly surprised—so much for being judgmental or forming uninformed conclusions.

CHAPTER 22

▼

NEW ENGLAND

On Highway 9 outside of Bennington, Vt., I was headed to the Greenwood Lodge Hostel at the top of the pass on Prospect Mountain. A 2,000-foot elevation gain at the end of the day seemed like cruel and unusual punishment. Near the top I spotted a couple filling up jugs with spring water. I asked them if I was nearing the hostel and they said I had about a half-mile to go. Then the woman yelled at me, "My brother runs the hostel."

While I was checking into the hostel, the couple from the spring showed up. The man came over and his first question was, "Where are you from?" When I told him I was from Colorado, he yelled into the other room, "Bev, I told you he was from Colorado." He told me his nephew lived in Colorado and was always riding a bike. I asked him who his nephew was and he told me Brian Hager. I worked with Brian at Keystone Resort! This was his uncle, Larry, and we both laughed at the coincidence of meeting on top of this mountain. Bev came in from the other room and told me to get cleaned up because they were going to take me to a play in Dover that night.

I showered, we grabbed something to eat, and went to the play "A City Slicker Comes to Town" which was written and produced by Larry and Bev's niece. They treated me like family and told me all about the history of their families and the surrounding area. That night when they were dropping me off, Larry gave me the address and phone number of his twin brother, Brian's father, who lived in Connecticut. I told him if I found myself in the area, I'd give him a call. I thanked them both for their hospitality.

The next morning was the first time in months that the temperature made it necessary to ride with long sleeves and leggings. There were mountains, pine trees and cool air and I loved every minute of it. Leaves were already changing colors on some of the bushes by the streams, so fall couldn't be far behind. I was looking forward to the cooler weather, fewer bugs and the autumn colors.

I made it across Vermont in one day and into New Hampshire, state #26. The asphalt was still good, so I tried to ignore the sounds coming from my knee and the rear wheel. My right knee had developed a clicking sound while I was training for the trip. My sister, Vicky, had successfully treated it, but with all of the recent climbing, the worrisome clicking had returned. The noise didn't get my attention as much as the pain did. I was going back to placing frozen fruit on my knees at night and taking glucosamine. I needed to stand to pedal, getting out of the saddle more often when climbing hills, but I knew that put more stress on the bicycle. Ironically, the noise coming from the bike also was a clicking sound, in the rear derailleur. At the moment, however, I was more concerned about finding a place to stay.

I remembered a comment my ex-wife made about missing all of the trees back east while we were living in the West. I was beginning to get a firsthand look at what she was talking about. There were so many trees and so much undergrowth it was almost impossible to sneak off the road and free camp. As a result, I ended up paying $22 to sleep on the ground at a campground. Of course, I knew things were going to cost more once I got back east, but this was a long way from the $3 I paid in Del Rio, Texas.

The next day in Rochester, N.H., the guys at the fire station offered me a place to leave my bicycle while I went to find a postcard for my niece. When I returned they were cooking hamburgers on the grill. They asked about The Journey and when they heard about a possible book, they almost insisted I mention them by name. In fact, they started calling out their names. But when they didn't offer me a burger, I decided they could write their own book. Everyday I was meeting more and more people who were giving me directions, encouragement, shelter and food. If I were going to write a book, I'd have to reserve spots in it for special events and people. So to have hamburgers on the grill and not give one to someone riding a bicycle across America—I decided their names would remain in my journal.

Before riding into Maine, I called Barbara Siegert in Durham, N.H., who had ridden across America several times and had written a book about it. Barbara was over 60 years old and still biking, God bless her. We talked for 30 minutes about biking, but she was preparing for an interview, so we weren't able to get together.

In Portland, Maine, I called Rob Lowell. I met Rob, the summer before I left, on a bike path in Summit County. Rob was riding his bicycle across America at the time. I rode with him and John Dorsey, another transcontinental rider, and had lunch with them in Frisco, Colo. We had a great time talking about their trip and my up-coming trip. They gave me some good pointers on what to pack and what to leave at home. I was looking forward to talking with Rob again. Unfortunately, I only connected with his answering machine.

Riding south on US 1 the next day was quite an experience. At times I was moving faster than the cars. There was way too much traffic on the road for me to be biking, but people were being very courteous. I even had a couple of conversations with people in convertibles as we proceeded at the same rate of speed. Because of all the people, I decided to head inland, instead of trying to camp on the beach. My mission was to ride my bicycle through the lower 48 states, not to go sight seeing. If something presented itself along the way, fine; but I wasn't going out of my way to see something beautiful or historic, and the coastline was a zoo!

Riding back into New Hampshire, I found a little campground on Highway 33. Helen was a very interesting, elderly woman who ran the old run-down Liberty Hill Campground on land that been in the family for years. She provided me a campsite for $12 and we sat on her front porch talking about life until the sun went down. We talked extensively about education, something Helen truly believed in. She told me she could tell I was educated the moment I began to speak. Helen had provided a good education for her children and was proud to tell me the colleges they had attended. I was happy for this woman, to see the glow in her eyes as tears flowed down a face that told many stories. She seemed happy and I sure did enjoy the conversation. But I couldn't help feeling that certain people were taking advantage of Helen, including her family. She was a very generous woman, so people were living in the campground for free, as was some of her family. The freeloaders repaid her by trashing out the place. The campground was a mess; there was trash everywhere and the shower room was filthy. I was glad to be on the road the next morning heading to a hostel in northern Massachusetts.

I felt like the born loser that morning. From the time I left Peninsulas, Ohio, until I made it to Maine, I never had a wind out of the west. I kept hoping for at least one day with a westerly wind to give me a boost to the East Coast. That morning, there was finally a wind out of the west and guess what direction I was headed on Highway 33…

I wasn't going to let it bother me though. The previous night in a more positive frame of mind, I realized I only had a couple of thousand miles to go to finish the trip. I decided to get to the hostel and map it out. I was a bit excited at the prospect of being back home by the end of the year. It was the first time I saw an end in sight—the light at the end of the tunnel. In the meantime, I had the heat, humidity and hills of Massachusetts to deal with.

I stopped at a Tastee Freeze for my daily ice cream fix when I entered the state that calls itself "The Spirit of America." The girl working there told me it was 94 degrees outside with 100 percent humidity. She took both of my water bottles and washed them out before filling them with ice water—what a sweetheart. It is very hard to keep water cold when biking a long distance in the summer. Even ice water becomes warm rather quickly in that weather. Usually, I filled my bottles from the sink in a rest room of a convenience store or gas station, so I really appreciated her gesture. For seven months I had been drinking some pretty bad tasting water. This young lady's ice water tasted spiritual. As I was leaving, one of the boys working there asked me if I was on drugs. I looked him right in the eye and said, "You couldn't do this if you were on drugs!" Riding away, I realized how clean my mind and body had become because of The Journey.

With the help of some young mothers out strolling with their babies, I found the Friendly Crossways Hostel outside of Harvard, Mass. The setting was very peaceful. There was an old farmhouse connected to a barn, with no visible neighbors. The hostel was in the old converted barn, but was actually a lot nicer than it might sound. I sat out on the deck shelling peanuts and talking to a few people who were lounging around. After a couple of conversations, I couldn't help but feel like I was in some kind of "B" movie. Everyone was being so dramatic about their situations; how long they had been sitting on a bus, how homesick they were, how tired, hot, lonely, and on and on. As if they were auditioning, each sad story was more tragic than the previous one. I kept stuffing peanuts in my mouth to keep from laughing and eventually had to stand up and walk away. I don't know if I felt like no one was going through anything tougher than I was or if I was just tired, but the whole scene seemed surreal to me.

It started raining the next day before I made it to Worchester. Locating a gazebo in a park next to the cemetery, I sat there snacking on some fruit and trying to decide how I was going to dress for the weather. The forecast that morning was "sticky." So I was already drenched with perspiration and was trying to figure out the logic of putting on rain gear. The longer I stayed there the more the temperature dropped, until I was finally able to put on my raingear and continue.

I rode in the rain all afternoon to the HI-Dudley Home Hostel on a back road outside of Dudley, Mass. Back-roads can be very confusing in the East, so I was asking for directions frequently. I stopped at the Midas shop in Oxford and asked the young man if he could direct me to the hostel. He did and then asked where I was from. When I told him Colorado, he said, "WOW! That's all I can say—wow!" I knew what he meant. Sometimes that was the only word I could come up with to explain what I was experiencing.

When I arrived at the hostel, dripping wet, Chet had me put my rig in the garage and come inside for a cup of tea. Chet and Ann ran the hostel out of their home. Again, it was a farm surrounded by huge trees and rolling farmland. After I got cleaned up, Ann invited me out to the sun porch to join in some conversation. Their neighbor, a young lady from Australia, was visiting as well. We talked for hours and Chet asked me if I would like to join them for dinner. He made spaghetti with meatballs, which is a staple for every biker, but his was different. Chet made his meatballs out of salmon and they were delicious. Something new and different, it was a true taste sensation. Later, Ann gave me a ride into town so I could buy some fresh fruit and we also cured my ice cream craving while we were there.

There was something special about Chet and Ann and something special about their place. They were some of the kindest people I had met and I never felt so at home with strangers before. I was the only one staying there, so I had the entire back room to myself. Plus, they left the door open to their end of the house and even let me use their laundry facilities.

Outside, flowers and more birds than I had ever seen in one place surrounded the property. I could feel this was a spiritual place.

The next morning, the sun was shining on the porch where I joined
Chet and Ann before I left. We were talking about the love of God when
Ann said something I'll never forget. She said, "You can't hoard the love of
God, you have to let it flow through you." I had never thought of it like
that. Until that moment, I had been going around trying to gather as
much of God's Love as possible and hold on to it. I really liked this new
insight—it felt very liberating. In my enlightened state I remembered
what Jan once told me about God's Love, she said, "Pass it on, it's a circle
just like rain and evaporation."

The morning ride was very pleasant; lots of trees and birds through
rolling hills in Rhode Island, state #29. I stopped at the Chelsea Diner in
Harrisville, R.I., in search of breakfast and a postcard. The waitress, Chris,
asked where I had begun my trip. I told her Colorado and she said,

"NO SIR!"

"Yeah."

"NO SIR!"

"Yes sir."

"NO SIR!"

I explained that I was riding my bicycle through the lower 48 states and
only had 19 more to go. She absolutely could not believe that anyone
could ride a bicycle that far. She said she couldn't even ride a bicycle up the
hill going out of town, and she looked to be in pretty good shape.

I asked her if she knew of any place in town where I could get a
postcard. I explained that I needed one before reaching the Connecticut
state line, which was 11 miles away with only one little town in between.
She told me there weren't any postcards in Harrisville and then picked up
the phone to call the little town of Chepachet to see if they had any. They
didn't and I was thinking I might have to make a homemade card. About
that time the owner, Bill, got involved. He said if there was a postcard to
be had, he knew the person that would know. He picked up the phone

and in a few minutes had someone "working on it." In the meantime, I was sitting at the counter with a big smile on my face as other people in the diner were taking an interest in the situation. A minute later the phone rang and after a brief conversation, Bill bolted out the door. He returned in a few minutes with a postcard his wife had found at the City Historical Society Building.

It was lunchtime, the diner was packed, and the owner was taking off to go get me a postcard. These were the coolest people I had met in America. I was a bit ashamed that I wasn't spending more time in their state. But suffice it to say, the people of Rhode Island were well represented by the gang at Chelsea's Diner.

I rode all afternoon going up and down the hills of Connecticut. It was tough biking, but I was feeling good. Between Chet and Ann and the people at Chelsea's, I was on a high. They were such good people, so positive and loving. I rode 90 miles that day in extremely sticky conditions, but I felt strong. I was eating well and drinking gallons of water. I had very little body fat and; other than my aching knees, sore elbow and deadened body parts, I was in great shape. People were being warned not to overly exert themselves in the heat and I was riding 90 miles. I was proud of myself, but at the same time, I needed to be careful.

When I reached the city limits of Hartford, Conn., I called the Mark Twain Hostel for directions. Some man answered who could barely speak English, so I noted as much as I understood and took off. It was around 5 p.m. and the dark sky let loose with everything it had been storing for the day. It was rush hour, very dark and raining. I was tired and not exactly sure where I was going. I stopped to put my lights on. I had a headlight that fit over my head like a miners' lamp and a taillight that could be attached anywhere. While I was stopped, I called the hostel again, but not only did he not help me, he was getting rude. I was wet and tired and didn't need an attitude after experiencing one of the best days of The Journey. I was trying to let the love of God flow through me, but this guy seemed to blocking the flow.

I ended up riding on the interstate for a half-mile to reach the road I needed to be on. Flashes of Tacoma came splashing back to me and it was almost as tragic. The rain was pouring down, people were honking at me, and I was barely visible with all the water spray. Just as I was preparing to exit I hit a pothole and blew out the tire on the trailer. I made it off the interstate, but wasn't sure where I was supposed to be. I was in the poorer section of town and people were gazing at me curiously. I tried the hostel one last time, but his only response was to ask some people around me. There was an old black man sitting there against the wall and he spoke very broken English, but was able to communicate enough to head me in the general area of the hostel. When I was in the vicinity, Steve, a homeless man pushing a grocery cart full of "stuff" took me by the hand and showed me where I needed to go. He was pleasant, smiling and laughing the whole time. He was my age, a Vietnam War vet, and he just took things as they came. His attitude was so different from the other homeless people I had met along the way. I thanked him for his help and kindness. There always seemed to be someone to help me keep everything in perspective.

The hostel was an old mansion in what used to be an affluent part of town. I tried to be open and loving with the man running the hostel, but he was not receptive. He was an older Asian man and unlike Steve, he was not smiling or laughing. He acted like it was a chore for him to check me in and I wondered why he was even working there. Most hostels are very friendly to travelers; providing local information and some interaction. This place gave me the creeps. It felt like the night of the living dead.

I woke up the next morning glad to be alive. The ride through the rainy city the night before had really frightened me. I used maps in the local phone book to figure out how to get through the city, since the hosts were no help. I didn't want to stay at that hostel any longer than necessary. Besides being void of emotions and feelings, it reeked of fish and cat piss. I never knew what I was going to find at the hostels because I couldn't afford to carry around the bulky book describing each hostel. How ironic that the previous day I stayed at the best hostel on The Journey and now I was at one of the worst. The place was a pit and the people were rude. In fact, it was one of the worst evenings of my life on the heels of one of the best days of my life—just to prove that life is a balance, yin and yang.

That evening I arrived in Southbury, Conn., and called Lee Hager, Larry's twin brother and Brian's father. Lee and Norma took me into their home and treated me like family, considering they didn't even know me. Lee showed me the airplane he was building. He seemed to be a very handy person. And Norma stuffed me full of food at dinner. That night we called Brian, who lives in Arizona now. We laughed about the fact I was talking with him from the house he grew up in.

The next morning, Norma fixed me a huge lunch to take with me and I was on the road early. It was very cool out and I really enjoyed that. What I didn't enjoy were the bug bites. I knew they were from the hostel the night before in Hartford. I just hoped I hadn't tracked any into the Hager's home. At lunch I counted over 30 bites. They itched so badly that I'd try to scratch my ankle on every rotation when I was pedaling.

I was approaching New York City and was anxious to see Betty, my Guardian Angel, but dreading the ride. I decided to spend the night in Norwalk, Conn., and attack the "Big Apple" when I was rested. I retrieved the map to find the least intrusive way of getting into Norwalk. If I rode on Interstate 15 for one mile, I could access Highway 719 and avoid a lot of traffic. No sooner did I enter the interstate than a trooper pulled me over.

"What the hell do you think you're doing?" He asked very sternly.

"I'm riding my bike around America."

"What the hell are you doing on this interstate?"

"I'm trying to get to Highway 719."

I knew I wasn't suppose to be bicycling on the interstate because I took note of the sign prohibiting bicycles, pedestrians, etc., but I explained that I was actually causing less trouble than if I had continued on Highway 7. The trooper was not impressed with my reasoning and when I asked him if I could walk my rig the half-mile down the road to the exit I was look-ing for, he replied, "I'll tell you what you can do. You can haul your ass and that bike through those woods, up to that overpass!"—pointing his finger in my face the whole time to make sure I received the message. He had already let me know that he could arrest "my ass" for being on the interstate, so I didn't argue with him. He was a little short man, with a Napoleon Complex, so I didn't need to give him any more of an excuse to show his "power." I had traveled 8,700 miles and this was the first real butt-head I had encountered from the law enforcement. I understand hav-ing to do your job, but I also understand being compassionate, flexible and understanding. He was none of those and I was glad he didn't arrest me. His attitude and karma were in bad need of an adjustment and I thought about him as I made several trips through the woods to haul "my ass" and my "stuff" up to the overpass.

I decided to find a motel room so I'd be rested for The City the next day. I was in a resort town, so I knew it was going to cost big money. The local Chamber of Commerce never likes to reveal the low-rent districts in their town, but I convinced the lady working there to take pity on me. She found a room for $45, a real deal in that area. As I was checking in, the manager said she would give me the room for $42 because it was small. It was small, and dirty, and depressing. They actually rented rooms out by the hour, with a three-hour minimum—not the kind of place the Chamber of Commerce wants to be promoting. But it was a place to sleep, so I did, thinking about New York City as I drifted off.

CHAPTER 23

▼

SOUL IN THE HOLE

I didn't want to be in The City too early because of the traffic. I needed all the breaks I could get. I was going to have to bike the entire length of Manhattan, not to mention the Bronx, to reach Betty's house in Brooklyn.

The sky was overcast when I left Norwalk, but by the time I rode 30 miles to the New York state line, the clouds had burned off and the temperature was rising. Besides the weather, another thing that was very noticeable as I proceeded into the Bronx was the deterioration of the asphalt. The road had severe cracks and major potholes everywhere. I told myself to just slow down and take it easy.

I stopped at a Taco Bell in the Bronx to use the restroom because I wasn't sure what would be available in Manhattan. The Big Apple loomed ahead of me like the Wild West stretched out before the pioneer settlers. I didn't know what to expect. I was excited and afraid at the same time. When I came back outside, *B.O.P.* had a flat rear tire. I pulled everything into the shade and put in a new tube. While I was working on the flat, one of the Taco Bell employees came out and offered me some water. He told me he had a bicycle, but he would never be able to ride it from Colorado to New York.

I went a block and had another flat! Oh man, I really didn't need this. Again, I found some shade and started working on the bike. A young kid came by and asked me a continuous line of questions. He also told me he had a bicycle, but he said his tires were flat. I gave him some patches and a tube of glue to patch his tubes. As he was leaving, a young black man made him come back and say thank you. The man asked me where I was from and when I told him Colorado, he shook my hand and said, "Welcome to the Bronx."

OK, two flat tires, but I had already met some very nice people, so I tried to remain calm. Approaching the Willis Bridge area, I realized I was lost. Not only did I not know where I was, no one around me seemed to speak English. And what English they did speak, I wasn't picking up very well. Finally, a young kid on a bicycle pulled up next to me and rode with me to the bridge. A few minutes later I was in Manhattan.

For the next two hours I watched the entire world pass before me. I rode through communities of Asians, Latinos, blacks and whites—a cornucopia of humanity. I was heading down Second Avenue and it just seemed to go on forever. The traffic was heavy, but I seemed to be doing OK. Mainly because the far right lane was used for parking during the day, which provided me with a bike lane. My biggest concerns at this point were double-parked cars and being "doored," a term bikers use to refer to a bicyclist running into the street-side door of a parked car when it is opened. I was doing better than OK—I was kicking ass. I was moving faster than the flow of traffic and even followed some bike couriers getting around parked delivery vans. At a stoplight, I asked a woman if she would take my picture with my camera. She could have bolted down the side street with my camera and I never would have caught her, but she was very obliging.

I was having fun riding a bicycle and pulling a trailer in the heart of New York City. I was in awe; there were big buildings, lots of traffic, and non-stop movement. At 14th Street I turned right to reach Broadway in order to access the Brooklyn Bridge. It was 5 p.m., downtown Manhattan, and there were more people than I had ever seen in one place. I was about to become overwhelmed when I yelled out to a young man in a three-piece suit,

"Do you know where Broadway is?"

"Yeah, it's right here. You're on Broadway!"

With a laugh I thanked him. He asked me where I was from and when I told him, he said, "Welcome to Manhattan."

I rode across the Brooklyn Bridge at 5:30 in the evening with everyone else who was trying to get home. At the time, I didn't know there was a bicycle/pedestrian path above the traffic lanes and I'm surprised no one yelled or honked at me. In Brooklyn, I had the same experience as in the other boroughs; some black man about my age pulled up next to me and said, "Welcome to Brooklyn." I guess he could tell I wasn't from around there. Hey, where were all those hard-ass New Yorkers I had always heard about? These guys had better watch out or they were going to give New York a bad name—the "Welcome Wagon State." But I truly appreciated the hospitality.

I found Betty's brownstone and was never so happy to be through with a day of riding. I've had tougher days of biking, but all of the new experiences had worn me out. Betty was waiting for me. She had a spacious place and I had the entire basement to myself. After a refreshing shower, Betty fixed me a dinner fit for a king. In fact, I thought maybe a kingdom was coming over for dinner. She had two kinds of chicken, a ham, sweet potatoes, green beans, corn on the cob, collard greens, Brussels sprouts, okra, corn bread, salad—I could have eaten forever.

Betty had a wedding to attend in Maryland that weekend but her son-in-law, Paul, was going to show me around New York. He was temporarily living with Betty while doing some work for the IRS in Manhattan. Paul was a big man, probably 6'6" and 240 pounds, and he was the spitting image of John Thompson, the basketball coach at Georgetown University.

And to add to that image, Paul carried a towel around to wipe away his perspiration, much the way Thompson did during basketball games. While touring Manhattan, I walked behind Paul to observe the people who mistook him for the celebrated coach. We both got a kick out of it.

Saturday after Betty packed up and left for Maryland, Paul and I headed to Manhattan. We watched the semi-finals of the Inner City Basketball Championship; some of the best basketball I've ever seen on an outdoor court. This was a big event. There were referees, a scoreboard, and hundreds of people crowded around the court. The crowd was almost as entertaining as the game. I found out later that people had bet considerable amounts of money on the outcome of the game.

When the game was over, Paul and I went to a park and watched the best street entertainers I have ever seen in my life. They were tumblers from Jamaica who were unbelievable. They were strong, flexible and funny. I had no problem donating money at the end of their show—it was true entertainment.

We started walking around and I was amazed that so many people knew Paul. Here we were in a city of 12 million people and an inordinate number of them seemed to know Paul. I fleetingly noticed it when we were walking around Brooklyn, but didn't think too much about it. Now we were in the middle of Manhattan and people were still calling him by name. There was some sort of security for me knowing he was so well connected.

In fact, Paul was the perfect guide; he knew people and he knew the city. One example was when we were sitting in the subway at a stop when another subway pulled in that would take us where we were going quicker. Paul grabbed my arm and said, "Let's go!" We jumped off the subway we were on and slid into the express subway with no problem. He obviously knew the system. I was impressed and wondered if he would be equally impressed if I took him hiking on a trail in the backwoods of Colorado and didn't get lost. What a strange thought, but this was his comfort zone and I suppose that would be mine. He also knew the best place to get a deal on a hot dog, the cleanest restrooms and where to just hang. He was showing and teaching me about a whole new world.

Back in Brooklyn when we were walking home, I noticed there were a lot of people outside. It was late, but it was too muggy and uncomfortable to be inside without air conditioning. As we headed down the walk, Paul very calmly told me to move to his other side. There was some action up ahead and he wanted to put himself between me, and what was going down in the street. He was really good at looking ahead and spotting trouble. However, one time when we walked around a corner, there was a guy in my face before Paul could react. He wanted to know if I wanted to buy any dope. Paul quickly got me out of there and explained that because I was white and had a ponytail, the brothers figured I must be looking for some dope. Why else would I be in that neighborhood?

Betty had told me that when she first moved there it was a nice neighborhood, but over the years things had changed. In fact, the next morning Paul and I found out that someone was killed where we had been walking the night before. Paul had known something was wrong as soon as we turned the corner and had steered me across the street. I now knew it was important to pay attention to him when we were out and about. His city instincts were focused and accurate.

The next day, Paul took me to the New Hope Church in Brooklyn, where Reverend Marguerite Goodall was preaching. I had met Reverend Goodall when we were both in India and I was excited to see her again. At the end of the service, Reverend Goodall asked me to come to the front of the congregation while she told everyone how we met and about The Journey I was currently on. She asked everyone to stand and raise their arms towards me to send me some positive energy during the final prayer. Afterwards she invited everyone to come hug me and bless my journey. It was one of the most spiritual moments of my life—a powerful experience that I will never forget.

Then we went upstairs for a buffet luncheon. When I first walked into the church, I noticed I was the only white person there. But by the afternoon I had forgotten all about it. Reverend Goodall is such a loving person and she has a way of making everyone feel like they belong, which is probably how I originally found her and Betty in India. I was a lost soul and they both radiate Love!

That afternoon Paul and I had a full agenda. We wanted to get over to Manhattan for the Inner City Finals, then back to Brooklyn to watch his cousin play in the "Soul in the Hole," the Brooklyn outdoor basketball championship.

We saw an outstanding game in Manhattan, and then discovered a whole contingent of people with the same agenda. In fact, we all caught the same subway back to Brooklyn. Paul and I met a high school basketball coach from Queens and we walked together to the court analyzing the game we had just watched. It felt great talking sports with people who understood the intricacies. I hadn't had a good sport fix, since my time with John Daly in Bingen, Wash.

As we approached the court where the game would be played, we could feel the electricity in the air. We came around the corner and I had never seen anything like it. There were 400 to 500 people crowded around an outdoor basketball court. Again, I was the only white person there, but there was a comfort level in that most of the people were there to watch some good basketball. Who knows, maybe the fact that I'm 6'4" tall, with a local basketball coach, and a guy who looks like John Thompson made people think of me in basketball terms; an ex-player, a scout or a coach— maybe. Understand, some of the players had played college ball and still had hopes of making money, playing basketball. So they were always looking to impress anyone that might be able to promote their skills.

Midway through the first half the "local" team was falling behind and by half time they were close to being out of the game. They weren't playing as a team and most of the crowd recognized it. Anyone who has played any street ball has experienced being on a team with ball hogs. They're like a black hole. Once the ball is passed to them, it never comes back. Eventually, no one is passing the ball and shots are being launched from every angle. That was what was happening here. Paul said he was going down by the court to urge them to start playing as a team. I wasn't convinced that would help, as I was pretty sure the other team just had more talent.

Sometime during the second half, things started getting weird. There was a group next to me drinking beer and now they were smoking a joint. That, per se, didn't bother me, but when a huge man charged onto the court going after one of the referees, things became tense. He was one of the largest human beings I have ever seen, maybe close to 400 pounds and moving rather quickly for such a large person. Immediately, the game stopped and several big "security guards" tried to corral the intruder. He was mad. He was real mad and there was no mistaking where his anger was focused. People had been complaining about the refereeing ever since the local team fell behind. As an unbiased observer, I could see bad calls on the court, but they were going both ways. I didn't see the refs helping one team or the other. Apparently, this mountain of a man didn't feel the same way or maybe he thought they should be helping his team a little more. I found out later he had a $25,000 bet on the game, so I understand his intense interest in the outcome. Unfortunately, his demonstration was stirring up the emotions of the crowd and they were becoming very animated. I was beginning to feel a bit uneasy and was considering my options if the situation continued to deteriorate. I looked around for Paul but couldn't see him. Fortunately, order was restored and Paul soon appeared. He had been trying to calm down a few guys he knew who also were upset with the refereeing.

When the game was over the security people rushed the referees into the nearby school building with an escort. Paul told me not to move. Excitedly I asked him, "Where are you going?" He said, "I'm not going anywhere, just make sure you stay close to me." His shadow couldn't have been closer. Like a mime, I followed every move he made. After going down on the court to console his cousin, we made our way back home.

Betty was back from Maryland when we arrived home.

"Where have you guys been?" she asked.

Paul replied, "Soul in the Hole!"

"Soul in the Hole? What the heck is Soul in the Hole?"

"The basketball championship for Brooklyn."

"Where was it played?"

"At Kingston and Second."

"KINGSTON AND SECOND! Paul! You took him to Kingston and Second?" She looked at me with her eyes wide open and said, "I'm black and I wouldn't even go to Kingston and Second!" Paul and I began laughing and Betty just walked around the house saying, "Oh my God!" When she calmed down a bit, she told me my mother had called. She said, "I told her you were out with Paul. And now I'm glad I didn't know where you were."

I asked her how her weekend was and then proceeded to tell her about ours. We sat there and laughed all night about the stories of Paul hauling this white hippie all around New York City. I could never thank him enough because I know I experienced things that few, if any, people from my background would ever get the chance to. I even apologized several times for intruding on his weekend and he always said it was no problem because it was what he was going to be doing anyway. I even sensed that he enjoyed being able to show me how life was in his world. It was a world I had only heard about or observed on TV, and even then, there are some things that can only be experienced in person.

Paul never acted like he was embarrassed or ashamed to be seen with me. He always made a point of introducing me to the people we met and even told them about my journey. I found it interesting to observe how Paul greeted the different people we met on the street. With some people he would exchange a polite handshake. Others would receive a more elaborate handshake, with several movements. But with his "brothers," he would shake their hands while pulling them toward himself and tap them on the back. The day I was leaving, Paul grabbed my hand, pulled me toward him, and tapped on my back. For a brief moment I was a "brother" and realized how special he was for treating me as such.

My last night in Brooklyn, Betty had some friends over for dinner; including her sister Clorese, Gwen, whom I met in India, and several people from the church. It may have been the hottest day of the year, but Betty was in the kitchen with both ovens and all the burners on. We had another tremendous feast and a lot of fun sitting around telling stories. At one point Betty was laughing so hard she had tears running down her face. Betty is quick to laugh and it's too bad more people aren't. She has a certain confidence about who she is that allows her to laugh at herself, the world, indeed the Universe. Betty is the foundation of my spiritual development. Whether it is a question about Christianity, Buddhism, Taoism or any other belief system, she has an answer because she is grounded in the Love of God. And I am so lucky to know her.

CHAPTER 24

▼

THE NEVER ENDING CITIES

I usually tried to ride through bigger cities on weekends to avoid traffic, but it was time to go and it happened to be Wednesday. I was on the Brooklyn Bridge heading back to Manhattan, this time on the bicycle/pedestrian path. The path was full of walkers, joggers and a few cyclists. It was more comfortable than being on the road and much safer.

In Manhattan I rode through the financial district to reach the waterfront, where I caught a ferry to New Jersey. Ninety-nine percent of the commuters had the same blank stare on their faces. They didn't notice me, the weather, the pigeons, or the small trees that were trying to survive in a concrete jungle—they didn't even notice the person standing next to them. The only thing they seemed to notice was the sign that flashed, "Don't Walk...Don't Walk...Don't Walk..."

With the help of some more nice New Yorkers, some people who did notice, I caught the ferry to New Jersey. When I landed across the Hudson River, I called Betty and told her she was no longer responsible for me. I did this because in Seattle, Hideo told me I could call him for help until I crossed over into Idaho. I adopted that policy with everyone I stayed with after that. I could call them for help until I made it into the next state, and no one ever objected.

Heading down a road strewn with broken glass, I was dreading the ride that would take me through Jersey City and Newark, when my front tire went flat. I found some shade and began replacing the tube when a young man came over and began talking with me. After hearing my story, he told me he had never heard of anything like that in his life! He asked me if I was in training for the Olympics. So many people figured I had to either be in the Olympics or setting a world record. I told him I wasn't in the Olympics or setting a world record that I knew of. He wondered if I would remember his name when I became famous—he called himself "T."

Getting through Jersey City and Newark was less than pleasurable on a bicycle; constant traffic, bad asphalt, and nothing to look at but industry. I was exhausted.

The next day was better as I made my way into the countryside headed towards Pennsylvania. I had already biked in there, but I was going to visit my good friend, Richard, in Philadelphia. Richard and I met over 20 years ago in Summit County. We had done all the same things that I'd done with the other guys from Summit County; play ball, ski and drink beer. But Richard and I had another connection. One night in a bar after a game, we somehow were able to determine that we could combine our resources and buy a house. He had enough money for the down payment and I was earning enough for the monthly payment, so we formed a partnership and bought a house. It quickly became "Party Central." We always had someone hanging out or staying over. There were two refrigerators, two decks and two televisions. In fact, the day we moved in we had one TV on top of the other watching the Broncos game and the World Series. Oyler, Mad Dog and a couple of Texans, Rob and Thom, were there to properly christen the house. We had some unforgettable times together in that house and it would be good to see Richard again.

Before leaving New Jersey, I realized I hadn't sent a postcard to Janae. I stopped in the little town of Sergeantville, but no luck. An old man came over and began talking with me. Albert Newcombe was 75 years old, with one arm and a three-day growth on his face. He told me that he tried to push a baby carriage across America when he was younger. He didn't make it, but he admired what I was trying to accomplish. He wanted to know what he could do to help my journey and told me if I got in a pinch to call him and he would wire me $20. He didn't look like he had $20 to spare, but what an incredible gesture. By now I knew the old maxim was true, "You can't judge a book by its cover."

I ended up mailing a homemade postcard from Stockton, N.J., before crossing over the Delaware River into Pennsylvania. The countryside was beautiful with old stone buildings and rolling green hills. The weather was threatening rain, but so far I was only wet from perspiration. It was August 28 and summer was hanging around like unwanted company. I was really tired of this constant heat and humidity and couldn't figure out for the life of me why so many people lived here. The weather was so much nicer out west, but I guess jobs kept people living in the East—it couldn't be the weather.

Upon arriving in North Philadelphia, I phoned Richard. He lived in the southeast section of the city and I needed directions. He wasn't comfortable with the part of town I was in, so he gave me directions and told me to "start riding." As soon as I hung up the phone, a young black man came over and inquired about my rig. I explained the journey to him and asked if there was a good place to eat nearby. He pointed out a little place down the road.

As I entered the restaurant every set of eyes were on me; like a room full of liberals would look at Pat Buchanan showing up at their convention— "What the hell is he doing here?" I was a white man in a black man's neighborhood, but I was on a bicycle and that is the purpose of telling this story. I was accepted into places because I was on a bicycle, and it seemed to break down barriers. The bicycle made me different to minorities. Out

West, the Native Americans, Chicanos, and the homeless related to and accepted my difference. Now I noticed it with the African Americans. And maybe it wasn't acceptance, as much as curiosity, but I was able to go places and do things that I wouldn't have been able to if I were in a car. I *was* a minority, sometimes to the point of being a "first sighting." Some of the people I met had never seen someone traveling cross-country on a bicycle. I thought it odd in this day and age, but I enjoyed opening their eyes to something different.

And that was what it was all about for me. Not being brave, but being different and getting out of the rut. I'm amazed, not that people get in a rut, but that they stay there. Some people actually love their ruts; it provides a comfort level and they prefer to stay there. I had made it out of mine, so it was easier to spot other peoples. But I also was falling into another one, my biking rut. I cooked oatmeal every morning and pasta every evening. I ate peanuts, a banana, an apple and a grapefruit everyday. I stopped every hour to check my spokes and stretch my muscles. I rationalized that I did all of these things for my survival on the road, but I also recognized that it was a rut. Meeting new people everyday, however, was not a rut and I was glad they were accepting me into their hearts.

After lunch I proceeded down Highway 611 into the heart of the city. Again, I noticed how easy it was to ride a bicycle through a major metropolitan area. The outside lanes were converted into parking spots, so I was able to cruise through Philadelphia. Plus, it was brand new asphalt and probably the smoothest ride yet. Philadelphia is loaded with history but, never being a history buff, I just tried to absorb and appreciate Philadelphia's significance to the formation of our country as I pedaled through it—the Liberty Bell, Independence Hall, etc.

Richard was busy both professionally and personally, but I did get to spend two evenings with him and catch up on what was new. We have stayed in close contact over the years, taking annual golf trips in the spring to Puerto Rico, Florida, and elsewhere. One year we rented a van in Florida, along with Oyler, and played golf all the way up the East coast;

from Myrtle Beach to Hilton Head to Pine Hurst—eventually ending up in Philadelphia. It was a fun time.

The changes in our lives were extraordinary. When I first met Richard, he was Richie, a carpenter driving an old jeep. Now he was a successful businessman, driving a nice car, living comfortably. On the other hand, I used to be an accountant with a lot of toys and now I was living on a bicycle. There is nothing wrong with either scenario, as long as you are happy!

At one time after leaving New York, I was concerned with Hurricane Bonnie and thought I might have to spend some extra time in Philadelphia. But she politely headed out to sea, so the sky was clear the day I left. I was making my way toward Washington, D.C., through Baltimore. John Dorsey was the other half of the duo riding cross-country I had met last year on the bike path in Breckenridge. I had talked to him on the phone and received an offer to stay at his place. So even though I didn't know him very well, I was anxious to see him again and trade touring stories.

I had been riding for hours and, other than a brief conversation with Aziba, a beautiful woman from Africa, the scenery never changed. I thought Delaware should be close, but I still hadn't left Philadelphia. Finally, I stopped and asked someone how far it was to Delaware. They said, "You're in Delaware!" In fact, I was just outside of Wilmington. Since Greenwich, Conn., I essentially had been biking in a city, with only a few miles of country riding. Wow! So many people, so much asphalt and concrete, I was really looking forward to getting into some rural areas after Washington, D.C.

Heading through Wilmington, I kept losing my way because someone had gone through town and knocked down the road signs. As I was passing a group of people, this big black man yelled out to no one in particular, "That's the way to do it...he doesn't have to pay any taxes." Since I wasn't exactly sure where I was going, I turned around and asked him if he might be able to give me directions out of town. Big Shakey was big, but he was quick with a smile and more importantly, he gave concise, detailed directions. We talked for a while and after a few photos and exchanging addresses, I was off for Maryland.

In Maryland, I found a place to camp and the next day I headed to the HI-Baltimore Hostel. When I pulled up to the bridge crossing the Susquehanna River, there was the standard "No Bicycles, Pedestrians,…" sign. There were no signs indicating where an alternate route might be, so I dug out my map to find another way across the river. The alternate route was 10 miles to the north, which meant an hour up and an hour back. Did I mention it was hot and humid outside? I didn't need to add another two hours to the ride. The bridge in front of me was three miles long and if I really pedaled hard, it would take me 15 minutes to get across. I was breaking the law, which I didn't like to do, but I also was gambling on my chances of making it across without getting caught.

I was two-thirds of the way over when the lights and siren came on in Officer Cobb's patrol car. He climbed out of his car with a dumb-founded look on his face and asked, "What the hell do you think you're doing?"

"I'm biking around America…through all 48 states."

"You can't ride a bicycle on this bridge."

"I know. I saw the sign, but didn't see an alternative route, so I decided to get across as quickly as possible. I know I'm breaking the law and if you have to fine me or arrest me, I understand."

I think my honesty caught him off guard, to the point where he offered to stay behind me the last mile until I was off the bridge. What a great guy, the complete opposite of the butt-head I encountered in Norwalk, Conn. I remembered at the hostel in Peninsula, Ohio, Robert telling me that he would always lie whenever a cop pulled him over. He would play dumb like he didn't see the sign or he didn't know what highway he was on. I dis-agreed with that philosophy and sure enough, the truth paid off.

Just off the bridge there was a diner, so I stopped in for some pancakes. My waitress, Lisa, couldn't believe I was riding a bicycle around America and asked me for my autograph. I felt a little self-conscious, but proud, also. I didn't set out on this journey looking to be noticed but, when someone took the time to talk about my efforts, I tried to accept their recognition, humbly.

That afternoon I arrived at the hostel in Baltimore. Every hostel had its own energy just like every town and city. The energy at that hostel was dark. The girl working there buzzed the front door to let me in. She never said hello, how are you, or go to hell. She simply took my money and handed me a sheet with the hostel rules on it. I settled into the dorm room and listened to a young man play his guitar while I cleaned myself up.

That evening I sat outside in a 12-foot area between the brick buildings hoping for any kind of breeze to stir the stagnant air. I swore sometimes that I was swimming just to make progress moving around in the thick air. I had on a minimum amount of clothing, but even being naked would be uncomfortable in the stillness—it was stifling. Two young French ladies who were trekking around the Northeast joined me. We talked for a while about the events of traveling and I noticed one of the ladies was covered with bug bites. I inquired about the bites and she said they appeared after staying in a hostel in New York City. I told her she was covered with bed bug or fleabites from the hostel and that it had happened to me several times on my journey. I also told her to get some aloe vera to put on them. When I was in Brooklyn, Betty gave me a leaf from her Aloe plant to use on my bites from the hostel in Hartford, Conn. I broke the leaf open and applied the gel on the bites. The results were amazing; the itching stopped immediately and the bites soon disappeared. I told the French lady that if she couldn't find a plant, she could buy some lotion at a drug store that contained aloe. She probably had 30 bites just on her neck and shoulders and I really felt empathy for her. I knew how much the bites itched and irritated. I usually enjoyed listening to a foreigner's viewpoint on America, but after they kept going on about how Americans talk, how they do everything in excess, how they do this and that, I excused myself and left them with a young Australian who had joined us.

The odometer turned 9,000 miles the next day on the way to Washington, D.C. Maryland was state #33, but I told my niece I was doing Washington, D.C. for extra credit. To make the postcards more interesting, I would ask Janae questions relating to the number of the state I was in. For example: Who wore number 33 for the Los Angeles Lakers and what were his lifetime statistics? What is the seventh Amendment and how does it relate to your life today? What is the 24th element in the Chart of Elements and how does it impact your life? I gave Janae an extra credit question for our nation's capitol—"What states border Washington, D.C.?"

Like Manhattan and Philadelphia, Washington was easy to bike through. I rode straight to the White House and then began touring the Washington Monument, the Lincoln Memorial and the Vietnam Memorial. As I started down the Vietnam Memorial, there was a sign that read, "No bike riding or skate boarding." So I dismounted and began walking along the wall. As soon as I looked over at the names, I began to cry. I didn't know if it was because I was so moved at seeing the names of the people who had died or because I had come so close to being drafted and going to war.

When I was a sophomore at WMC in December 1972, I received a notice from the draft board to take my physical for induction into the Army. I thought my world was falling apart when I read that. It wasn't as if I hadn't been expecting it; the year before I had the second lowest number in my dorm at CSU for the draft lottery. That meant I was a two-time loser; I didn't win the dorm cash pool for the lowest number and I was still going to be drafted. A lot of people were "helping" me with information on how to flunk the draft tests, but I decided to play it straight, even though I didn't agree with our involvement in the war. I couldn't understand what we were doing over there. It was a civil war and who made us directors of the outcome? There were radicals who said North Vietnam was a Communist nation and had to be stopped or Communism would spread throughout the world. Well, guess what? North Vietnam won that war and where is communism today? In the meantime, how many young men and women from the United States lost their lives because of our involvement in that stupid war? I was crying tears of sorrow for the people who had died and tears of rejoice for myself—once again being blessed. In January 1973, Richard Nixon, God bless his soul, "halted" the draft and I was spared that hell.

I finished touring and decided to have the bicycle serviced. John was still at work, but gave me directions to a good bike shop in Georgetown. I rode there and had them replace the chain and cassette. The last few hundred miles the chain had been slipping under stress, so the up-grade was inevitable because I still had the Blue Ridge Mountains and Appalachians to tackle.

John took me out to dinner and showed me around some of the city. He also pointed out a bike path I could take in the morning to get out of Washington and later showed me on a map a path in Virginia as well. When we went for some ice cream, I insisted on paying—$5 for two ice cream cones. Wow! Time to be moving on. However, it was nice spending time again with a fellow biker—someone who also had lived on the road with a bicycle. We shared numerous stories and I felt rejuvenated the next morning when I left.

It was September 1 and all I could think about was autumn. I had seen signs of fall when I was in New England and now I was praying that the cooler weather was not far off. That last night in Washington, D.C., I stayed in John's basement and slept on my pad with no covers. When I woke up in the morning it was cool enough that I grabbed a throw rug to put over my legs and a towel to cover my torso. I was riding and laughing at the image of me lying in that basement covered with a rug and a towel. Then I realized that a lot of people had been putting me up in their basements. I didn't take it personally, though. In fact, I was hoping there would be a few more basements in my future.

CHAPTER 25

▼

COUNTRY ROADS

My ride through northern Virginia wasn't cool, but it was enjoyable as I was on the Washington/Old Dominion bike path almost all day. It was the base of an old railroad track. In fact, a lot of the bike paths I had used since Minnesota were converted from abandoned train tracks. They made great bike paths, especially for touring, because of the gentle grade.

While I was riding along, Ray pulled up next to me on a recumbent and began talking. He worked at a local bike shop while attending college. I asked him how he liked the recumbent and light-heartedly he said, "It sucks." Later when I asked him about school he had the same response, "It sucks," with a smile on his face. I didn't know what to make of him, but he made me laugh. He liked to take riding breaks when he was studying to clear his head and talk to people. Ray said there was no way he could do what I was doing because "I would die of boredom." He had to be able to talk to people. He asked me if I had heard about the stock market and I said I hadn't, realizing I hadn't seen a TV or newspaper in three weeks. He proceeded to tell me the market had fallen over 1,000 points and brought me up-to-date on the Clinton/Lewinsky affair. It was like having a CNN rolling review. I got a kick out of seeing the joy he was receiving in delivering the news. He rode with me for about 10 miles before departing to return to his studies.

The flowers along parts of the path were incredible; pink, purple and yellow. I didn't know if they were wild or planted, but they were a taste sensation for my eyes. I thought about how different The Journey would be if I were always on a bike path. It felt so peaceful not having to battle the traffic and it was so much easier to appreciate the surroundings, especially the natural surroundings; the flowers, the birds, the water.

For miles I rode, not seeing anyone, and then I had the first "Moment of Clarity" I'd had in a month. Thinking back to my rides through the big cities, I realized my praying and meditating had taken on a different aura in all of the congestion; more like a supreme focus on the cars, people, and potholes, rather than enjoying the relaxed rhythm of pedaling. I allowed myself to be in the moment and the next thing I knew I was through the city, or finished riding at the end of a long day; being aware of what was going on around me but not being affected. When I first moved to the mountains, a co-worker, Bill, turned me on to yoga and meditation through the teachings of Baba Ram Dass and his book "Be Here Now." The book had been my bible for the past 22 years and its teachings allowed me to deal with a variety of events on The Journey; the congestion of a big city or the serenity of a deserted bike path.

My "MOC" was centered on the enormity of God and wondering how minute a detail She was concerned with, especially as it related to my thoughts. Because if God was paying attention to every little thought I had, then I'm exposed whenever I'm kidding others, or myself about who I am. So many times I witness people "living the lie" and catch myself, as well, being less than truthful. Mankind has that terrible ability to rationalize, which allows us to justify "living the lie." Even though I had simplified my life, there were still issues that haunted me that I would have to address to right myself with God—even if it's justifying the reason for this journey. My initial thoughts were that there was no purpose to The Journey—it was just a bike ride. When I was in Phoenix, Bruce gave me a new nickname, LoRent Gump, but instead of running around the country I was cycling. In fact, I would tell people there was a Forrest Gump element to The Journey and I believed that. But as The Journey continued, there was obviously more. I may not have set off looking for anything, but I was sure discovering a whole new life along the way. Everything from patience to the meaning of the Universe, and I couldn't ignore what was being put before me if I wanted to be true to myself. I learned earlier from my experiences that nobody knows The Truth, but that was no excuse to stop searching. Most times we ignore the path to The Truth because ignorance is bliss and usually the easier way out. I usually looked for the easier way out because I'm a lazy person. But I had been riding a bicycle for more than 9,000 miles—a long way for a lazy person to be pedaling. Actually, I no longer wanted to ignore my search for The Truth, I just wish I could have recognized that 6,000 miles ago. But all of those miles had allowed me to experience The Truth. In fact, my "Moment of Clarity" was that everything we "experience" in life is The Truth. Once we begin "thinking" or "talking" about The Truth, it then becomes our "perception" of The Truth. Peter Deane told me way back in Flagstaff, to quit trying to define Nature and just "experience" it. I was finally getting the message.

I was heading for the Bear's Den Hostel outside of Bluemont, Va. Some fatigue was setting in as I had been on the bike path for 50 miles and still had 15 miles to go on the highway. I needed to eat something and take a break, but at the moment I was in the forest and knew I'd be eaten alive by mosquitoes if I stopped. Feeling a little light headed, I experienced a strange sensation; the bike seemed to be moving under its own power. I wasn't pedaling, but somehow was maintaining my speed, even though there seemed to be a slight uphill grade. I'm a rational person, so instead of just "experiencing" it, I went about trying to figure out what was going on. The first thing I checked for was a tail wind. There wasn't even a wisp of a breeze. Then I wondered if it might not be some kind of optical illusion. I wasn't familiar with the terrain and I was tired. About that time I came around a bend and spotted another cyclist. Here's where it turned weird. He was pedaling and I passed him, still coasting. He looked at me like he was seeing a ghost and I sheepishly nodded my head. I only reluctantly tell about this event because it sounds like an "alien abduction" story, but it happened and I experienced it. I accepted it as Divine Intervention. I made it into town, had a rest, something to eat, and finished the day on a 10 percent grade hill going up to the hostel.

The hostel was a beautiful stone building built by a doctor years ago for his wife, who was an opera singer. The acoustics in the house were fantastic, just in case anyone felt like singing. Jim, who ran the hostel, was a peaceful soul. He had a very pleasant face and a calm demeanor. After I checked in, he told me about the area, the hostel and the Appalachian Trail. The hostel was just off the trail and was used by many hikers. In fact, the majority of the people staying there were either hiking or doing volunteer work on the trail. Two exceptions were John Rothfield, an 86-year-old German who lived in Florida, and Dick Martin, a retired math teacher from North Carolina.

John liked to take cruises on freighters, something he had done 15 times and he told me about all 15 voyages. He explained that there was none of the pampering that goes with a cruise ship, but it was a way to get on the ocean and was cheaper.

Dick was headed to a BMW motorcycle rally. Like Jim, Dick had a very gentle nature about him and offered me a place to stay when I made it to North Carolina.

The next day I left *B.O.B.* at the hostel and rode *B.O.P.* to Charlestown, W.Va., state #35. Just recently I had discovered that West Virginia's nickname was "The Mountain State." Because of that, I decided not to spend much time riding through there. My knees were in bad enough shape as it was and I still had vivid memories of the 10 percent grades in upstate New York. It was hot and humid, but without the trailer it didn't seem so draining. What was strange was the way the bike was handling. This was the first time riding without any weight for a long time and the bike seemed squirrelly. The asphalt deteriorated once I crossed the state line and there was no shoulder on Highway 340. There was a peach stand, however, and when I stopped they gave me free fruit. Jeff Burnum also gave me a free sermon about the lack of respect in America.

Actually, I steered the conversation that way because I had this omnipresent feeling that things were going to hell in America. I couldn't help but look at the condition of certain people and property around the country and feel that there was a lack of respect. Some people didn't respect themselves, their families, their communities, their country, their planet, and it showed in their appearance and the appearance of their property. I don't mean the way they were dressed or the type of structure they lived in, I mean they were fat or their homes were surrounded by trash. Jeff and I felt that people needed to begin respecting themselves before conditions would change.

Back at the hostel that night, Jim told me that there was someone else staying there from Colorado. He introduced me to Dave Gustoff, who was not only from Colorado, but also from Summit County. What were the odds? Dave was in Virginia visiting Jane Kelly, who lived in Staunton, Va. They had met in Colorado when Jane was visiting her relatives there. We enjoyed a pleasant evening talking and Jane, later, offered me a place to stay if I came through Staunton. Two offers at one hostel, not bad.

That night I had one of the most enjoyable evenings of The Journey. The hostel was deep in the woods on the hills outside of Bluemont. The night air was cool and the woods were alive with a symphony of sounds; like crickets, nighthawks, owls, and toads. I lay on the bed listening with a feeling of contentment.

I left the next morning feeling good about The Journey. The bike was holding up, as was my body. I still was waking up at night in a cold sweat, but I was sure it had to be psychosomatic, because I couldn't imagine being physically ill for that long.

As I was riding through Front Royal, Va., some employees from the Warren Sentinel, a local newspaper, pulled up next to me in a van at a stoplight. Steve wanted to know where I was from and where I was going. They wanted to buy me lunch while they conducted an interview. I followed them to the Fox Diner and had a satisfying lunch with Michele, Steve, Heidi and Drew. Steve took pictures and Michele asked questions while I appreciated the free lunch and the attention. As I was leaving town, the van pulled up alongside of me and Steve took pictures of B.O.P., B.O.B., and me going down the road at 30 m.p.h.

Earlier that day when I was riding over the Shenandoah River, I began singing John Denver's song "Country Roads;" West Virginia, Blue Ridge Mountains, Shenandoah River—it all added up. But as I was singing, I started crying and didn't know if it was from John Denver's recent death or because I really did want those country roads to take me home. I had been feeling so lonely that morning but now, thinking about home, I was riding with a smile on my face. Plus, my first interview had filled me with energy.

When I got to Jane Kelly's house in Staunton, I could tell she was a little uncomfortable with my staying there. After all, she had only just met me. A friend of hers joined us for dinner and an evening performance of the band, Baba Seth, on the courthouse lawn. The band had a contemporary, high-energy sound, much like Rusted Root. So I purchased a CD for a keepsake.

Back at Jane's place, I offered to sleep downstairs on the floor because the next morning she had to leave at 6:30 a.m. to run in a 10k race. I knew I wouldn't be ready to leave that early and asked if she could lock me in the walkout basement, whereupon I would lock the door behind me when I left. Not long after she left the next morning, I had to use the bathroom in the worst way. I went up the stairs and picked the lock with a credit card. When I opened the door, Duke was standing there staring at me. Duke was her Great Dane, but luckily I was good with animals *and* I knew his name. Plus, he didn't know I wasn't supposed to be upstairs. I used the bathroom and when I came back through the kitchen I noticed my street shoes sitting in a chair. It's funny how things work out. I gathered up my shoes, loaded the bike and trailer and left.

It was a holiday weekend, Labor Day, so I was in my holiday depression and feeling blue. Plus, I really didn't want to be out on the highways competing with automobiles for space on the asphalt. One thing I noticed, however, was how courteous the drivers were in Virginia. So if I had to be on the road, this was the state to be in. Later that day, I was on a two-lane highway with a six-inch shoulder when a logging truck approached from behind. Because there was oncoming traffic, he came to a stop behind me. Wow! That hadn't happened in any other state and, in fact, the only other place I ever witnessed that was in France where bicyclists have a supreme right-of-way. Many times in Virginia I had to wave drivers around me. I didn't know if they were being courteous or if they were frightened, but I appreciated the space they allowed me. I knew they had seen cross-country bike riders before because at times I was riding on the Bi-Centennial Bike Route, which was used by a lot of bicyclists. But that event was 22 years ago and this wasn't the easiest cycling in the world, so maybe not many cross-country bike riders used this route anymore. There was a lot of up and down riding, which made touring all that more strenuous.

Beside the strain of the hills, summer had returned so I seemed to be working just a little harder. As I rode through a small town the neon sign on the bank read "99" degrees, and when I reached the other end of town, another bank thermometer read "100" degrees.

I only rode 50 miles that day and felt guilty. It's funny how our perceptions change. When I started The Journey, I thought 60 miles was a long day and now I was trying to apologize for only going 50 miles. Then I thought, "How many of my friends rode their bikes 50 miles today, and especially in this kind of heat or humidity?" I patted myself on the back and went in search of ice cream.

I hate to keep harping on the heat and humidity, but it was a big component of The Journey. Now La Nina, El Nino's sister, was being blamed for the severe summer, and I just wasn't accustomed to that type of weather. Summers in the mountains of Colorado rarely get over 80 degrees with 10 to 30 percent humidity. So not only was I battling the cars, road and miles, I had a daily challenge with the elements. The one thing I did do was drink gallons of water every day. I also stopped every hour to rest, stretch my muscles, and check the tension on the spokes— my rut!

Mapping out the remaining 14 states, I only had a bit more than 2,000 miles to go; a journey for some cyclists, but to me it sounded like a piece of cake. Two more months and I'd be home for Thanksgiving. I was riding with a new purpose and attitude. I felt strong, really strong. In fact, I had never been this strong in my entire life. I didn't have bulky muscles, but what muscles I did have were tight and I had very little body fat. I was much more impressed with my upper body strength than my leg strength. I had expected my legs to be stronger and bigger, but was surprised with the rest of my body. I hadn't considered the isometric exercises associated with bike touring.

It was a good thing I was feeling strong because it took every ounce of strength and energy I had to make it up Bent Mountain outside of Roanoke, Va. Other than upstate New York, Bent Mountain had four of the toughest miles I pedaled. At the top of the climb there was a fruit stand. They didn't give me any free fruit, but they had just what I needed, sweet and juicy peaches.

In southern Virginia, I rode on the Blue Ridge Parkway—a very serene experience. There is very little traffic, as there are no commercial stops. But the scenery is breathtaking. Along the Parkway I came to the HI-Blue Ridge Mountain Hostel run by Alex and Lois, two very pleasant people. The hostel is in a beautiful setting in the woods on top of a hill and upstairs from their living quarters. Good directions are a must, as there is no advertising allowed on the roadway. That night I watched Mark McGuire break Roger Maris' single season homerun record, so I was glad I wasn't camping out.

It was cool when I arose the next morning; cool enough that I had to ride with my leggings and a long sleeved jersey on. Yahoo! It was September 9 and fall had arrived. The next morning was even cooler and I put on a long underwear top to ride in. I was loving life!

I'm not sure exactly where the Bible Belt is, but I had a feeling I was close to the belt buckle. Not only was I seeing more churches, but also there were many houses with religious signs in their yards: "The person you worship is the one who controls you." "If the Devil knocks, let Jesus answer the door." "You need to get more Son, so you don't get burned." "Fervent prayer dispels anxious fear." And my two favorites: "Expect great things from God." "And you think it's HOT here."

I was nervous when I started off that morning; I would be at the highest point in Virginia that afternoon at Mt. Rogers. At the moment, however, I was riding along Bridle Creek on Highway 58. I stopped at a little roadside store and three guys in a county work truck came over to ask some questions. I gave them abbreviated answers, still thinking about the ride ahead, when the light bulb turned on. They were from the highway department, so I began asking *them* questions. They told me I didn't want to go over the pass to Konnarock. They said semi-trucks weren't allowed over that pass because it was so steep! They told me to turn off on Highway 16 at Volney and go through Trout Dale. They were some good ol' boys and I really appreciated the information. They were freaking out that I had ridden a bicycle over 9,000 miles and had been living on the road for nine months. But what they really wanted to know was how I was able to retire at 44 years of age—planning and good luck.

At Volney I stopped for some pancakes. Bobbie Lee was sitting at the table next to me and began asking questions about my bike and trailer. She was 5' tall, had firm young body, and a smile to die for. She was in her mid 20s and told me she was "100 percent country." As I was explaining The Journey to her, my waitress, Jackie got involved in the conversation. Before I left, they both gave me cards like my friends had back home, telling me to be safe. They asked if I would send them a postcard to let them know I was OK. They also confirmed that I should take Highway 16. I asked Bobby Lee to marry me so I could quit The Journey but her Mom, the owner of the restaurant, didn't think too much of that idea.

It was a steady climb to Trout Dale, but nothing serious. From there I turned west on Highway 603, an old, curvy, back road. The ride that afternoon, coupled with my morning encounters, made that one of the best days of cycling on the whole trip. There were very few cars and the road went in and out of forests and meadows that were loaded with various species of birds. I enjoyed the ride so much and I couldn't say enough about the people of Virginia. If I had to move anywhere east of Colorado, I'd move to Virginia.

CHAPTER 26

▼

REDNECKS AND SOUTHERN HOSPITALITY

Tennessee, "The Volunteer State," state #36. I found it quite interesting to notice the changes when crossing over a state-line; asphalt, as well as attitudes. My royal treatment in Virginia quickly disappeared in Tennessee. No one ever threw anything at me, but they were constantly going by and yelling insults. And it always seemed to be three guys in a truck. What they were saying wasn't always clear. It may have been the southern drawl or maybe it was the chew in their mouths, but I knew they weren't words of encouragement.

Originally I was going to ride into Kentucky from Virginia, but after looking at the map and talking with some locals, I decided to approach Kentucky from Tennessee to avoid as many passes as possible. I hated leaving the good people of Virginia, but my body was dictating that I find the path of least resistance to finish this trip. I still felt strong, but I had chronic pain in my right elbow, my back, both knees, and now both feet.

The wear and tear was beginning to take a toll on my feet. By the end of each day they were throbbing with pain. It hurt to pedal or walk. I was taking Anacin and Ibuprofen at noon to help get through the afternoon. The new ailment was added to the growing list attributed to long-distance cycling.

I rented a motel room that night with the intention of leaving the trailer there the next day and riding up to Kentucky through the Cumberland Gap. It would be another 100-mile day and I didn't need to be dragging *B.O.B.* the whole way.

It was mid-September and the days were getting shorter, so I was ready to go at sunrise. Thank God I didn't have any extra weight with me. It was as hot as any day that summer and I was riding five miles up Thorn Hill to Veteran Overlook. At the top there was a rest area and a tribute to Veterans of Foreign Wars. There was only one other person there and he came over to see what I was doing. He was on a Harley Davidson and was waiting for some friends to join him on a ride. While we were talking he said, "Your angel is crooked." I reached for the angel on my jersey and discovered the back clasp was missing—I was about to lose my angel. He said, "That's no problem, I've got some extra clasps on me." His vest was covered with pins, including an angel, and sure enough he had an extra clasp. It sort of blew me away. I'm on top of a mountain in Tennessee, I'm about to lose my angel, and some guy on a Harley not only notices my angel, but also has the piece I need to fix it.

That encounter put me in a good mood and I rode up to the Cumberland Gap ignoring the rednecks and concentrating on his kindness. At the tunnel leading into Kentucky I saw a familiar sign "No Pedestrians, Bicycles..." I stood there for a minute and considered my options; it was 1 p.m., 92 degrees outside, and I had already ridden 50 miles. About then I noticed someone in the security shack. I introduced myself and asked if it was OK to ride my bike through the tunnel. He said, "No sir!" I told him what I was doing and that I needed to touch all 48 lower states...

He said, "Ya ain't rid'en thawt bicycle thru thawt tunnel!"

He told me how I could back track and find a road that went *over* "The Gap." I told him I had already pedaled 50 miles that day and still had another 50 to go, any additional miles were not a favorable option—they could be fatal. Then I noticed his truck and asked if he could take me through the tunnel.

He said, "No sir!"

I asked, "Is it against the law to hitch-hike?"

He said, "Naw it ain't agnst the law ta hitch-hike, yawll just can't ride thawt bicycle thru the tunnel."

So I went over to the edge of the shoulder and stuck out my thumb. I was trying to remain positive and not think about the redneck in the shack. In a matter of minutes, a big white truck pulled a U-turn and headed right for me. Jacob "Bill" Davis was a tall, good-looking man and didn't look close to being 71 years old. He said he used to ride bicycles and was willing to go out of his way to give me a ride through the tunnel. He was wearing a pair of coveralls that he had picked up at a flea market that had the name "Bill" on them. I was taken aback when he introduced him-self as Jacob and we had a good laugh about the mix-up. Jacob was telling me about some of the history of the area and that his great, great grandfa-ther used to hang out with Robert E. Lee. When he dropped me off, he pulled out his atlas and had me circle where I was from in Colorado and write down my name and address. My Mom told me that she prays every-day for angels to take care of me. I knew Jacob was one of those angels.

This was southern hospitality at its finest. Jacob and his wife went out of their way to help me. They were coming through the tunnel heading south and made a U-turn to take me into Kentucky. All afternoon I rode with the thought of his kindness and didn't even notice the rednecks. What I did notice was the same sensation I experienced in Virginia. It was at the end of the day and I knew I was going uphill because I had coasted down the same stretch that morning. This time I shifted into a higher gear and accelerated pedaling uphill. I couldn't make sense of it, but I tried not to analyze it and just let it happen. I was hot and tired and anything that helped me return more quickly, I wasn't going to question. I rode 105 miles that day and decided that would be my last century. My body was too worn down to be putting that much stress on it, especially in this heat. Earlier that day I stopped at a roadside stop and some lady came over to find out what I was doing. She kept putting her hands on me exclaiming, "I can't believe you are riding a bicycle in this heat." I couldn't either!

The next day I was on Highway 25E heading toward North Carolina, and summer had returned with a vengeance. I was just outside of Newport, Tenn., at a convenience store taking a break, when I noticed something was wrong. I wasn't sure what was going on, but all of the people had cloudy auras around them—fuzzy—and I couldn't understand what they were saying or doing. It was like they were talking in slow motion. I was on a bad trip, but I didn't know where I was going to go to get out of it. The building was air conditioned, but I had to get away from the people. I opened the door to go outside and it was like walking into an oven. I walked over to the side of the building where my "stuff" was, sat up against the wall and passed out.

When I came to, sometime later, I knew I was in trouble. Maybe I over extended myself the day before doing the century, or perhaps I dehydrated or had eaten some bad food. I sat there drinking some fluids until I could make a rational decision. I found a motel and spent the rest of the day eating, drinking and resting. All of this time on the road and I never had a problem with exhaustion, dehydration, sunstroke or food poisoning. I didn't know what happened, but I knew it wasn't right and was thankful I wasn't out in the middle of nowhere.

I was paranoid as hell the next morning when I took off. I felt OK, but I was riding over the Appalachians to get to North Carolina. The morning ride was perfect; riding along the French Broad River, in the shade of the trees, with very little traffic. I stopped a couple of times to ask people how far it was until I started climbing the pass, but no one knew. I thought that was odd and then wondered if I was still sick, since no one was making any sense. I crossed into North Carolina, state #37, "First in Flight," and I wished I had an airplane. My knees hurt, the bicycle wasn't working properly, and it was hot.

In Hot Springs, N.C., I stopped for my morning breakfast fix. There were a few locals in the café, but I didn't pay much attention to them, nor they to me. As I was paying the bill, an attractive young lady sitting in a booth asked me where I was heading. I told her and asked if there was a big pass to go over. She told me there was and wanted to know if I would like a ride up the pass. I didn't even have to think about it. After what I experienced the previous day, and the condition of the bike and the weather—it was a no-brainer. Genia Hayes and her father, Bobby, helped me load the bike and trailer into her little truck. Ernst, a friend of Bobby's, came along for the ride, so I rode in the back with my "stuff." We headed out of town and began to climb. The longer we climbed, the better I felt about my decision. We made it to the top and started down the other side. In minutes we were climbing another pass, and another pass, and another…28 miles later they pulled over and helped me out. Yahoo! Of all the days to run into these people, this was the day I really needed it. Some more angels taking care of me. God bless them!

It was only 10 miles to Ashville and almost all downhill. I was in town by early afternoon so I took the bike in for a much-needed tune-up and to troubleshoot the clicking from the rear derailleur. I found a great little bike shop and Wayne really got *B.O.P.* in tip-top shape. I upgraded the rear derailleur. The rear gear-cluster was now seven gears (the one I bought in Washington, D.C.) instead of five, and the old derailleur wasn't handling the stretch of two more gears. Later I found a beer garden and treated myself to a beer, while catching up on writing some postcards.

I checked into the Wolfe Den Hostel at 5 p.m. The hostel is part of Gary Wolfe's home. He lives upstairs with his family and the hostel uses the ground floor, with a shared kitchen. There was a big carved statue of a wolf in the front yard and a spacious fenced-in backyard with a deck. It was September 15 and summer vacations were over, so there was only one other person staying there and I never saw him. Gary was a young, short, dark-haired man with a dark goatee that gave him a sinister look. I quickly found out the look suited him. Another control freak with signs all over the place, he let me know right away that this was his house and he was in charge.

First I asked him if I could bring my bike inside.

"No way! You can lock it to the fence out front."

"How about locking it to the deck in the back?" There was already a bike chained to the deck, so I didn't think adding another one would be a problem.

He said, "That's my bike and I don't want to attract any attention to the backyard by letting you bring your bike around back. And I can't allow you to bring it inside because then I'd have to allow everyone to bring their bike inside."

WHAT? I couldn't believe what I was hearing. I thought I must still have some heat exhaustion because he wasn't making any sense to me. No one else was there with a bicycle and I wasn't going to be telling people he let me bring mine in (although I am telling people he didn't let me bring it in). I decided to try one more time. Very calmly I explained to him that my life was contained on that bike and trailer. He had a sign up by the front door that read, "If it can be sold, they will steal it. Don't leave anything lying around." Thus my concern with leaving my bicycle locked in the front yard. He asked me if I had a good lock and I told him I did.

He said, "Then your bike should be fine, locked to the fence!"

I knew there was no sense attempting to reason with him; like the little cop in Connecticut, he had a complex and he really wanted to make sure I knew he was in charge.

Looking back on it, I should have ridden off and gone to a motel or camped out. Instead, I completely unloaded the bike and trailer and hauled everything inside—more of an ordeal than it might sound. I locked *B.O.P.* and *B.O.B.* to the fence and sat on the front porch; looking at my bike, eating peanuts, and trying to figure out why this guy was running a hostel. Of all the hostels I'd been in on the trip, this one and its owner were the most bizarre.

That night I walked around the place reading some of the signs to see if I could better understand this guy. All over the kitchen were signs about not touching this and not using that. But the sign that really got to me was the one in the bathroom exclaiming when "to and not to" flush the toilet. Maybe there was a reason only one other person was at the hostel. I was wondering what it said in the hostel book about the place.

I decided there wasn't anything I could do about Gary, but I wasn't going to let his negative energy bother me. There was a stack of dirty dishes in the sink, so I washed them. The standing rule in hostels is to clean up after oneself, so maybe these were the owner's. Later, when I was doing my laundry I found the dryer full of towels and sheets. I folded them and put them on the stairs. I thought maybe no one had ever done anything nice for this guy. He saw the clean dishes and the folded laundry, but he never said a word.

My rig was loaded and I was gone the next morning before anyone else was up. I found Highway 225 heading south toward South Carolina. What a great ride I had all day; no traffic and the trees were so big they created a canopy that allowed me to ride in the shade. I eventually was riding in the Greenville Watershed Area. It ranked right up there with one of the best rides of The Journey.

No longer wondering if I was going to be able to finish The Journey, I was questioning my ability to write a book about it. I couldn't truly convey the beauty of the ride, the beauty of Nature. I could not articulate my true feelings and thoughts. I was reading William Least Heat Moon's book "*Blue Highways*," a classic on traveling and searching. In fact, we had a few things in common; we lost our jobs, were divorced, and traveled around America. Now if I could only write a fraction as well as he did. I was impressed with how he captured the moments of his journey and the way he expressed his thoughts and feelings. I had some thoughts in my head the other day, but was unable to put them down on paper in the same context. I'm a good preacher in my head, but I'm not a good enough actor, artist or writer to make the transfer.

Once again there were warnings about doing activities outside. The air temperature was 92 degrees and the humidity was 97 percent, which put the heat index somewhere around 112. I only rode 60 miles that day and took a lot of breaks. The next day was much the same and I continued to make frequent stops to eat and drink. Just outside of Clemson, S.C., a young man came over to see what I was doing. The one thing he warned me about was to be on the lookout for fire ants. He lifted up his pant leg and showed me where they had attacked his ankles. I thanked him for the warning.

That afternoon I rode into Georgia, state #40, where the sign read, "We're glad Georgia's on your mind," printed over a picture of a peach. I was hot and tired with only eight more states remaining, so I treated myself to a motel with a pool. When I walked into the lobby of the Shoney Inn in Toccoa, Ga., I asked the lady behind the counter what kind of deal she had for bicycle riders. She chuckled and looked at the man standing at the end of the counter. While she was looking at him she said, "I guess I can give him a corporate rate?" He called her over and whispered something to her. She came over to me and said, "We're go'na give ya the old corporate rate, *with* an AARP discount!" There was that good ol' "Southern Hospitality" again. Johnny Picket ran the motel and I was glad he was standing there when I checked in. He showed me around a little and even introduced me to his brother. He seemed pretty impressed with what I was doing. He told me it was 97 degrees outside with 97 percent humidity. All of a sudden, I was impressed with what I was doing. I went to the pool and swam laps until I was completely exhausted.

Something that is very prevalent on a cross-country bike ride, and especially in the summer, is the smell of death. Every day I would see a variety of dead animals and birds along the roadway—and if I didn't see them, I'd smell them. A smell I never got accustomed to, but one I will never forget, either. I was on Highway 23 heading toward Atlanta and I continued to smell this strange odor; it was death, but it was different. Death didn't have this smell in any of the other states and it was bothering me. Later that day I pulled into a truck stop and there was that smell. It was a truck carrying chickens, and it was the grossest thing I have ever seen or smelled. Chickens crammed into tiny cages; some dead, some alive, some with broken legs, some defecating on the chickens below them—it was enough to make me throw up. I didn't know if it was from the sight, smell, or conditions, but it made me ill.

I was on my way to see my good friend Thom Hostetter in Atlanta. Thom was another friend from Summit County. We had stayed in touch after he left Colorado and, in fact, a few of us came down to Atlanta when Thom and Anne married a couple of years earlier.

It was a little after noon when I stopped to eat a grapefruit and a little pickup pulled over. The driver, Wayne, got out and asked me where I was headed. I told him and he said he was going to go home, empty his truck, and come back to give me a ride. He said it was too dangerous for me to be traveling on that highway. I was on Highway 369, which was a two-lane road with a good shoulder. In fact, it was the best road I'd been on all day, but I didn't tell him that. It was still hot and humid, I'd already pedaled 50 miles, and he wanted to give me a ride the last 30 miles. I wasn't going to argue. While I was sitting there waiting for him to return, I realized that my hair and beard didn't seem to bother the southerners as much as the rest of the country.

Wayne was an interesting character. He was about a foot shorter than I was and about 10 years younger. He wore his baseball cap backwards and he had some sporty sunglasses. He was working at a grocery store, but we had to stop at his old job at the lumberyard to pick up his final check. He told me what a good driver he was as he downed shifted and took the corners way too fast. He also let me know that his true ambition was to become a state trooper in Texas—he liked the Dallas Cowboy cheerleaders! He had a picture of Jesus hanging from his rear view mirror and he told me we were "Brothers." Apparently, we weren't all brothers, however.

When a car with New York license plates was going too slow, the driver was a "damn Yankee." And when a black man almost stepped in front of him, he was a "nigger." I appreciated the fact that Wayne had enough compassion to help me, but I didn't appreciate his selective indignation. I looked at the picture of Jesus and then looked at Wayne; I couldn't put the two together. I told him we were close enough to where I was going and he could let me out at the convenience store. As I was unloading my rig, Wayne asked me if that was the friend I was looking for. I looked over and said, "No." Then I did a double take—there was Mad Dog.

CHAPTER 27

▼

MAD DOG, THOM AND JANET ANNE

Mad Dog had been attending a conference in Atlanta and was spending the weekend with Thom before heading home. Here I was at a convenience store in a suburb of a city with millions of people and there is Mad Dog.

Mad Dog came by his name honestly. When I met him he had a full head of curly, brown hair, a full beard, and he liked to party. He looked like a mountain man and late at night he often turned into a mad dog; not mean or destructive, just out of control. In fact, for all the years I've known Mad Dog I have never seen him in a fight. And the only person I ever saw him strike was me, but that is a story for another time. We always knew when Mad Dog was about to lose control because he would start speaking "Swedish." From there he could easily become a one-man show and frequently did. He was one of the shortest guys in the group, but he had some girth and always used to brag, "When you have a big tool, you need a big tool shed!" He was a good-looking guy, with steel blue eyes and the ability to turn on the charm. He was also a good athlete; point guard on the basketball team, arguably the best catcher to ever play softball in Summit County, and no one could vaddle down a ski slope like Mad Dog. He's a tamer Dog now, but stories about him will live forever in the Old Dillon Inn in Summit County.

I thanked Wayne for the lift and Mad Dog and I went to have a beer while we waited for Thom to finish up at work. Thom was one of the Texans that helped christen the house that Richard and I bought. Thom and I had experienced some wild times in Colorado together, but had actually grown closer since we settled down. Thom was a voracious reader and we liked to share with each other the new and exciting ideas we discovered in books. When I first met Thom, he had one goal in life—to have fun! Like Nancy in Chicago, Thom laughed a lot, but unlike Nancy, he had a deep baritone laugh that shook buildings when he let loose. Thom was still having fun, but now it was with his work and new family. He was a successful businessman and a good husband and father to Anne, Jamie and Lauren.

Mad Dog, Thom and I had a nice reunion through the weekend. We talked about old times, new times and times to come. Mad Dog left for home on Sunday and Anne left for a conference in Utah on Monday. The girls were busy with school, work and boyfriends. And Thom had a full schedule at work. I was just hanging out, so I borrowed Anne's car and made arrangements to meet Janet Anne in St. Augustine, Fla. It would be about a seven to eight hour drive for both of us, as she would be coming up from the Florida Keys.

Jan and I were married by Dillon Reservoir in 1982 and soon moved to New Zealand for a year. When we returned to the United States, we settled back in Summit County and spent the next 10 years there. We did everything together; skiing, biking, hiking—we had a very active lifestyle. We traveled all around Europe and on Jan's 40th birthday, we went back and bicycled around France. We could have lived our whole lives together, but at some time in the 90s, we decided to quit communicating with and caring for one another. Now we communicate with each other better than ever before and we care for each other tremendously. Divorce was not easy, but we both accepted it and moved on with no blame or ill will towards each other.

Jan looked good; she was tan and fit. We met at the Saint Augustine Hostel and spent a couple of days touring the oldest city in the U.S. and strolling the beaches. Unfortunately, Hurricane George was approaching the Keys and was dominating Jan's attention—to the point where we moved out of the quaint and charming hostel into a dumpy motel to be near a TV. I tried to take her mind off the hurricane for at least a few hours by going to a movie. Wouldn't you know it, there was a hurricane scene in the movie. As George continued to bear down on the Keys, Jan became more obsessed with the weather channel. She wanted to be down there to take care of her stuff. Jan is the type of person who would have ignored the evacuation warnings. Sure enough, the hurricane went directly over Big Pine Key. I was glad we had made arrangements to meet in St. Augustine and that she was not home.

We both cried the day we said good-bye. Although we no longer had a physical relationship, our bond had grown stronger through our recent spiritual developments. I really missed sharing life with her.

I made it back to Atlanta and Thom and I went to a Braves game. We enjoyed hanging out with each other and as with Jan, Thom and I had grown closer to each other through our spiritual paths.

I felt lucky and blessed to have these relationships in my life, especially now.

CHAPTER 28

▼

THE DEEP SOUTH

Thom gave me a ride to the southwest side of Atlanta so I could miss the city traffic on my way to Alabama. It was threatening rain and I wasn't into beginning The Journey again. I had a nice 10-day reprieve and I knew I was close to being done. I also knew that I needed to stay focused and persevere. As I prepared to leave, Thom handed me the gloves, headband and water bottle that I had left in the van. I made a comment about being a loser and Thom reminded me that baseball players get paid millions of dollars for succeeding 30 percent of the time. He said I had a much higher average than that and told me I was a winner. I really appreciated his positive attitude. We hugged each other, wished each other well, and I was on the road again.

It didn't rain, but what was the difference. I guess that means the humidity was only 99 percent. My whole plan was to be in the southern states in the fall/winter and the northern states in the spring/summer. Well, I was in Alabama, not just the South but "The Heart of Dixie," and it was fall, September 28. Unfortunately, because of El Nino or La Nina,

this was the hottest autumn on record. It was still over 90 degrees on a
daily basis and I was just going to have to deal with it. After my experiences in the East, I knew I could do it, but this certainly wasn't what I was
expecting.

When I crossed the state line into Alabama I stopped at a little convenience store. I was sitting outside eating a snack when three black men
came over to see what I was doing. We were standing there talking and we
all watched this white woman come out of the store and slide into her car.
Nothing out of the ordinary, a normal male activity, watching women.
One of the men told me he would be hung if he were caught with her. I
thought he meant by his wife, but he told me by the Klu Klux Klan. I told
him I didn't know that kind of activity still went on. They let me know
that certain things had changed with the Klan, like having to keep their
face exposed when they wore their robes, but that the old attitudes were
still there.

At noon, I stopped at the post office in Five Points, Ala., and sat in the
shade eating my lunch. A man approached me and asked me about my
journey. He also cautioned me about the weather. Apparently, Hurricane
George had gone out into the Gulf of Mexico from the Keys and was
coming back on shore in Alabama. I thanked him for the information,
finished my lunch, and continued south on Highway 431. I was heading
south because I still needed to ride into Florida, even though I had just
spent a week there. Otherwise I would have headed straight west to
Mississippi and missed the storm.

Just south of town there was the young man from the post office. As I
approached his house, an older woman walked down the driveway and
asked me if I would like a soda. Ann Hasslebach was a pleasant woman
and I appreciated her offer. Apparently, Adrian, her son, came home and
told her about meeting me at the post office, so she was prepared when I
came by. I enjoyed talking with them and especially enjoyed their southern hospitality.

That evening I was trying to decide if I should camp out or find a motel. This thought came to me, "A stronger man would fight through the adversity of the weather and camp out, but a lesser man wouldn't even had made The Journey." I decided I better secure a room and find out about the hurricane.

Just before reaching town, two men sitting off the road called out to me. I went over to talk to them and they invited me to stay with them. The sort of offer I loved on this journey, but I turned them down. They were so drunk they could barely enunciate their words, speaking "Swedish" as it were. I thanked them for their offer, then rode into Opelika, Ala., and found a Motel 6.

The hurricane was hitting Louisiana, Mississippi, Alabama and Florida with a purpose. It started raining that night and it was still raining the next morning. Only this was rain like I had never experienced before in my life. I always marvel at the force of Nature and I just sat in my room and was hypnotized by the magnitude of the storm. I weathered my first tornado in Sioux City, Neb., and now was preparing to do the same with my first hurricane. I went down to rent the room for another night and saw they were fighting a battle to keep the water from coming in the front door of the office. I could tell it would not be long until they were going to be losing the battle.

I spent three days waiting out the hurricane and its aftermath. Needless to say it was very humid, but I thought the temperature might drop after the storm passed—no such luck. I was still going to be riding in the summer-like heat. There was standing water everywhere and some detours were encountered because of washed out bridges.

I encountered something else in Alabama, more dogs than in any other state. I had a procedure when dogs came after me. I would yell at them as loud and stern as possible, "NO!" They would almost always hesitate for a minute, giving me enough time to escape a confrontation. If they weren't barking or if they were wagging their tail, I would talk to them like I knew them. On one particular occasion, I spotted two dogs up ahead, big dogs.

As I approached them, I noticed the bigger of the two was wagging his tail. I took that as a good sign and went into my good dog routine. What I took as a sign of friendship was actually him saying, "All right, some fresh meat." I quickly switched to my bad dog routine, "NO!" which had absolutely no effect on him. He was a German Shepherd and he was on me in a second. One thing about riding a loaded bicycle, it is hard to pick up the pace. So once a dog is upon you, it is very difficult to pull away. I was lucky in that most of the dogs that chased me almost always went for the trailer. It was down on their level so they would always end up a couple of feet behind me. But he was big enough to come right at me and he was inches from my ankle. The trailer did bother him, however, because he kept looking back at it to see if it was gaining ground. I didn't know if I should try to outrun him or stop and fight. He never tried to bite me; he just kept running alongside me showing his teeth and growling the whole time. I couldn't figure out if he was happy I came along and gave him something to chase, or if he was truly pissed that I was there and wanted a piece of me. He was the fiercest dog I encountered on the entire trip and he pursued me for a long time, but fortunately he eventually gave up.

With the help of some locals, I stayed on county roads heading down to Florida; county roads 223, 21 and some roads that didn't even have numbers. The asphalt was a little chopped up, but there was very little traffic to deal with and numerous species of birds to watch and listen to. The biggest drawback was finding drinking water.

One morning I had stopped around 10 a.m. on the side of the road for my mid-morning snack and made a mental note to myself that I was going to need water shortly. It was very hot and I had been working very hard in the hills of southern Alabama. With all of the standing water, a new hatch of bugs had come out so I didn't rest too long. A half-mile down the road there was someone sitting on the porch of a little cabin. He spotted me and jumped off the porch asking me where I was headed. I told him to Florida and asked if he might have some water. He said, "Sure!" And invited me to join him on the porch.

Jack Grochet was 52 years old, a retired newspaperman from Pittsburgh, and was traveling around the United States. He was on a journey to travel through all 48 states—on a horse. He left Pennsylvania two years ago and was in his 10th state. In fact, he had two horses, two dogs, a cart, and he was relegated to traveling the back roads. He was held up in this cabin courtesy of Auburn University while the highway department repaired a bridge that had been washed out by the hurricane. The distance I had traveled that morning on the bike had taken him three weeks. But he was in no hurry. Jack took me out into the pasture and introduced me to both of his horses, after I had met both of the dogs. We returned to the porch and began telling traveling stories. Some were quite similar and some were very different. After a while I looked around at his "stuff," the dogs and the horses and said, "Jack, I couldn't do what you are doing!"

He looked over my "stuff," the bike and the trailer and said, "Well, I couldn't do what you are doing, either!"

I realized that we both thought the other guy was crazy! But we also had respect for what the other guy was doing. Later Jack told me, "This is the hardest thing I have ever done in my life, but it is also the most rewarding." A sentiment I had shared with a lot of people along the way, and I knew Jack and I had a bond stronger than just traveling through the lower 48 states. We both understood the trials and tribulations the other was experiencing, but we also recognized the freedom each had achieved. When I told Jack he looked like he was 42 years old he told me he felt like he was 22.

While I was there, a family from down the road stopped by with some food for Jack. I was glad to see he had some angels watching out for him as well. We shared some food, water and conversation. But more importantly we shared a spirit; a spirit to break free, to change, to be different—and not for the sake of being different, but because to stay the same was wrong. Of all the people I met on The Journey, I didn't feel more connected with anyone, as far as what I was doing and why, than I did with Jack.

Jack told me this was rural Alabama, which was very desolate, and because of all the water I needed to be on the lookout for Water Moccasins and Timber Rattlers. I couldn't imagine anything being more desolate than western Texas or eastern Montana and I've never been afraid of snakes, but I thanked him for the advice and headed off on Highway 29. Unlike Jack, I could continue. He was confined to back roads whose washed-out bridges would be the last ones fixed. As I said, he wasn't in a hurry and he had a nice little set-up in the cabin.

I made it into Brewton, Ala., in the early afternoon and rented a motel room. There wasn't any dry ground anywhere for camping and even the motel had been flooded during the storm. The carpet was still damp in the room but I didn't care. I just wanted to drop the trailer off and ride into Florida to mail a postcard to Janae, much like I did in Kentucky and West Virginia. It was a pleasant ride without all my gear, but there was devastation all around. It looked like "The Bayou" or "The Land of 10,000 Lakes," but it wasn't supposed to.

As I was riding back into Alabama from Florida, I realized that all of the roads I would be on from then on would be heading north or west. I also had crossed over to the Central Time Zone, so I was getting closer to my home. Yahoo!

I was heading home and I couldn't get there fast enough. My entire body was falling apart. I had encountered different kinds of pain along The Journey, but the one thing that impressed me was how my body was able to rejuvenate every night. I would go to sleep at night thinking this was the end and wake up in the morning ready to go. But now I was waking up with the same pains I went to bed with. My body was no longer responding to the rest. I wasn't tired, but I was still sore. And the two places I noticed it most were in my hands and my feet. My hands were so sore that by the end of the day I couldn't find any position on the handlebars that didn't cause me pain. And my feet were even worse. Not only was it painful to pedal, even walking at the end of the day was excruciating.

One morning while massaging my feet before starting out, I noticed they had become deformed. I had knots sticking out on the outside of my feet, just before the little toe. I soon learned I had bunions, the cause of most of my pain. The constant pressure from pushing on the pedals every day had caused the bones in my feet to rearrange. The fact that the bones were moving was reason enough for pain, but because they were constantly being pushed against the inside of my shoes on every pedal and every step, it was driving me insane.

To add to my misery, my knees were shot. I had no idea there were so many hills in Alabama and Mississippi, but all day long it was up and down. And even the down was bothering me. As I would get into a tuck position to go downhill, my right knee would lock up on me. It eventually reached a point where I could only coast with my right leg forward. I would usually alternate which leg went forward, as the rear leg always had more stress on it. Now I was worried about what I was doing to my left leg.

I needed this trip to end soon, but it wasn't just because of the pain. Everything I owned that was being exposed to the elements was either falling apart or rotting away, especially my panniers and clothes. My life was being held together by bungee cords and duct tape. I had only six more states to go, but it seemed like I might receive more pain and damage in finishing those states than in the previous 42.

The air was so thick in Alabama I had to pedal downhill. It was still over 90 degrees everyday and it was early October. I made it into Mississippi and the humidity dropped to 97 percent—Yahoo! But now I had wicked logging trucks to contend with. What made them wicked was the way in which they were loaded. The logging trucks out West were always filled with trees that had been topped and limbed. The trucks in Mississippi had the whole tree. As a result, the tops and branches sometimes extended beyond the sides of the truck. So even though the *truck* missed me, there was still a chance the *tree* would clobber me.

Consequently, every time they blew their horn I bailed off the six-inch shoulder into the gravel.

That night I looked at the map to see if there was another way across the state so I could avoid some of the truck traffic. The next day I turned off Highway 84 onto little Highway 28. I soon discovered that not only did I still have the truck traffic, but also the smaller highway accentuated the problem.

I also figured out that people could drive better if they kept both hands on the wheel instead of honking at me or flipping me off. When they honked it just caused me to swerve and become more of a hindrance. Oh well, part of The Journey. Some ladies in Laurel, Miss., made me feel better when they pulled up next to me at a light and started flirting. One lady asked, "Is there any room on there for me?" I told her, "Sure, hop on!" We both smiled as they drove away.

Halfway across the state I was caught in some bad weather and spent an extra day in Magee, Miss. I had a day off so I decided to sleep in. I didn't get up until 5:10 a.m. I've been an early riser my whole life, so the term "sleep in" doesn't really work for me. Anyway, I was watching TV in the motel room and saw they had a big drug bust in Magee the night before. They had 13 people in custody with a possible 30 more arrests. They told people to be "wary" of their neighbor and then I began thinking about my appearance; long hair, a beard and wrap-around sunglasses. No wonder everyone was staring at me more than usual in the grocery store.

The storm was a blessing in disguise, behind it came cooler temperatures. Finally autumn was here. Of course, I was getting ready to ride through the Ozarks, but I didn't care. I was so tired of the heat and humidity. I'd take the cold weather in the mountains. Speaking of the Ozarks, I stopped in Georgetown, Miss., for some lunch and ended up sharing a table with a Wal-Mart truck driver, Jimmy. He was giving me some good information about some upcoming roads. When I asked him, "What's the best way to get across Arkansas?" He replied with a grin, "There ain't no good way to get across Arkansas on a bicycle!" I decided I made it across the Rockies, the Sierra Nevadas, the Cascades, the Appalachians and upstate New York, so even as banged up as the bike and I were, we could get across the damn Ozarks—somehow.

The next morning I received directions from T. Brooks Miller on some back-roads that helped me all the way to the Louisiana state line. I rode on so many back-roads in Mississippi—the one thing I always would remember about the "Magnolia State" was the abundance of birds. The quantity and variety of species were awesome and I enjoyed their company through the deserted countryside roads.

Before I left Mississippi I stopped at a little country store out in the middle of nowhere for some water. One of the good ol' boys in the store wanted to know what I was doing. When I told him I was biking through all 48 lower states and this was number 43, he became excited. He kept telling me over and over, "Don't give up what you're doing." I didn't bother telling him that I only had five states left and there was no way I was going to give up now.

He said, "I'm gunna go home an get ma bicycle ana rope."

I asked, "What's the rope for?"

He said, "To hook onta yawll to pull me."

We laughed and I went out on the porch to eat some lunch. Pretty soon he came outside and told me I had a lot of nerve. I never had anyone put it quite like that so I just looked at him. He had been drinking and, in fact, I observed a few good ol' boys drinking as they pulled up to the store. It was Friday afternoon, so I assumed they were getting an early start on the weekend. Then he told me, "Someone could just come up along side y'all and shoot ya." I immediately had a vision of "*Easy Rider*" and the fact that these guys were drinking wasn't making me feel any better. I hopped on the bike and just kept pedaling until I reached the Mississippi River, fortunately there were no encounters.

Even with the bizarre weather, the chronic pain and the chance encounters, I was still sleeping soundly every night. In fact, I looked forward to going to bed at night. As soon as I would close my eyes, the movie would begin. I would have these images that were crystal clear—usually images of faces. I didn't know who the people were, but their faces always were very detailed. Sleeping, and especially dreaming, was never more enjoyable than what I experienced on The Journey. That night I dreamt I was leaving the Deep South.

CHAPTER 29

▼

MONKEY

The next morning I crossed the Mississippi River into the "Pelican Sate," Louisiana, on Interstate 20 because the bridge on Highway 80 was closed. No problem, but the asphalt was a mess. Later on Highway 80, I realized these were the worst roads I'd been on since Michigan. Ironically enough, that afternoon, Highway 65 was the best road of the entire trip; eight-foot wide shoulders and brand new asphalt—it couldn't have been any smoother. Louisiana was a breakthrough state for me. It was the first time since Ohio that I was not riding my bike through a forest. I could actually see the horizon. I looked out on the cotton fields and I felt things opening up. All of a sudden it seemed like I had been in a tunnel the last three months. I savored the moment; wide-open spaces, and the temperature was cooling off.

In Transylvania, La., they told me about a guy who had been in town and was paddling a canoe from Yellowstone down to New Orleans. I said that sounded crazy and that I would never do something like that. One cowboy reminded me that I was doing something equally crazy. He said he couldn't ride a bicycle to his neighbor's house and he couldn't understand how or why I was doing this. I just said, "Forrest Gump" and everyone laughed.

That evening as I was preparing to stop for the night, I met a young man in the grocery store who called himself "Popcorn." He also had a story about a canoeist and for a moment I thought he was going to ask me to spend the night at his place. He didn't, so I headed out of town by the lake for a place to camp. As I was walking around I discovered something was wrong. My ankles were covered with fire ants. I remembered the young man in South Carolina warning me about them, but this was my first encounter. I quickly moved away, removed my shoes and socks, and brushed the ants off. But the damage was done—they had devoured my ankles. Instead of camping, I stayed at a motel and doctored the bites.

The next morning I crossed into Arkansas, "The Home of William Jefferson Clinton," as the sign that welcomed me to "The Natural State" reminded me. More important to me was the fact that it was state #45.

When I was riding through Ohio, I discovered a funny phenomenon. No one seemed to know the name of the next little town down the road. I was on back-roads like Highway 303 and I'd stop in a little town like Hudson to ask about Shalerville or Freedom; they would tell me they had never heard of those towns that were just a few short miles away. And it happened more than once, which is why I noted it in my journal. But it only happened in Ohio. It reminded me of when I was in Zimbabwe and a native told me that a tribesman could spend his whole life living on the Zambezi River and never meet anyone from the tribe down river. Well in Arkansas, it was just a little different. They knew about or had heard about the neighboring towns, but no one seemed to know the mileage, and even truck drivers were giving me numbers way off the mark. It happened more than once and, to this degree, it was unique to Arkansas.

One day I was preparing for an 80-mile ride. After 15 miles I stopped for a snack and came upon some locals sitting around a Formica table smoking cigarettes. I asked them how far it was to my destination. They came to a consensus that it was 80 miles away. I was pretty sure that was-n't correct so when I went outside I asked a truck driver who was standing there. He told me 120 miles. It was like the Twilight Zone. The more I asked, the further away the town was. It made me think back to Ohio and I got a smile on my face wondering what kind of force field had hold of the two states.

I was on Highway 425 heading north to Pine Bluff, Ark., when I saw a highway patrolman up ahead with a van pulled over. The shoulder of the highway was gravel, so I had been riding in the highway as close to the white line as possible. Whenever anyone honked or if there was a semi-truck coming, I would bail off the highway onto the gravel shoulder. I could maneuver the bike and trailer to ride in the gravel for a few seconds, but then I'd steer back onto the highway. There was no way I would be able to continually ride on the shoulder. When I passed the patrolman he said to me with no expression, "Keep off the highway with that thing." I didn't bother to stop and tell him this was a road bike and that I couldn't ride it through gravel. I just said, "OK," and tried to get on the right side of the white line while still staying on the pavement. I looked in my mir-ror and could see he was standing there staring at me.

A few miles down the road the van that had been stopped pulled over in front of me. A lady got out and started walking toward me. She said rather agitatedly, "That cop is in a foul mood and he is coming after you! He just gave me a ticket for ninety F_____ dollars! This state SUCKS!" After her release, she calmed down a bit and we talked. She was from Arkansas, but when she found out what I was doing she reiterated her opinion of the state and told me, "Don't stop! This state is so backward, don't even stop to eat or sleep. Just keep pedaling until you are out of the state." I knew she was in an excited state so I didn't take her literally, but I was concerned about the cop.

The patrolman never showed up but it was still a tough day for me; no shoulder, battling the traffic and 77 miles. Earlier I had decided that I shouldn't ride more than 50 to 60 miles a day because of the condition of my body. By the time I had ridden 50 miles everything ached and to ride further was masochistic. Now here I was riding 80 miles and I couldn't believe I was riding more than 100 miles a day just a few months ago.

It was October 13 and I was about to begin my tenth month on the road. More importantly, I had forgotten my mother's birthday the previous day. I was so consumed with myself, with finishing the trip, that I didn't even take the time to call my mother to wish her a happy birthday. I instantly became depressed. I thought about how tired I was of missing everything back home; family gatherings, holidays with my friends, sleeping in my own bed. I wanted The Journey to be over. I was a mess physically and mentally and just wanted to be home. I called my Mom and couldn't apologize enough. Being a Mom, she let me know that it wasn't "that big a deal." She just wanted me to be safe and get home. She was ready for The Journey to be over as well. I knew this trip had been a strain on my family at times; worrying about me biking on the road all-day and sleeping somewhere different every night. My mother's voice really had a tone of concern that night.

My emotions were right on the surface the next couple of days. I missed my family and friends, my body was disintegrating and the Ozarks loomed ahead. At a country store in Mayflower, Ark., I met a young truck driver, Doug, who was into biking. He began asking questions about where I had been and where I was going. He got a puzzled look on his face though when I told him I was preparing to ride up Highways 65 and 62.

"Why are you going that way?" he asked.

I explained that I needed to get over to the west end of Arkansas so I could ride into Oklahoma before heading up to Kansas City. "Yeah, but is there a particular reason you're using that highway to get there? Are you flexible at all on your route?" he asked with some concern. I told him I was very flexible and he suggested I take Highway 64 over to the Oklahoma state line. We had a couple of different maps spread out in the store and he showed me how it followed a valley all the way to Ft. Smith, Ark. He told me Highways 65 and 62 were terrible roads to be riding a bicycle on. I couldn't thank him enough for his valuable input.

Later that day I met some guys who wanted to know, "How come you haven't been on TV?" I shrugged my shoulders. And at Conway, Ark., I just missed the "Toad Suck Festival." Apparently, in the old days when traders would bring their goods to sell down the Arkansas River, they would stop in Conway and sit by the river "sucking on beers until they swelled up like a toad." Heather, at the local Chamber of Commerce, gave me a t-shirt commemorating the event.

Everyone I met that day seemed to help bring me out of my funk. I have to mention Eugene Jones, the 80-year-old man I met on a modified bicycle just outside of Dyer, Ark. His bicycle actually had been turned into a tricycle with a big basket behind the seat in which he collected aluminum cans. He received a little cash and some exercise, and I thanked him for helping to save the Earth.

The cooler weather also was helping to lift my spirits. It was the first time since the previous winter that I was riding with my long-fingered gloves on. And even though it was cool now, the long summer had kept the leaves green. I'm sure I was missing a color sensation, but I wasn't going to wait around for it.

Just outside of Ft. Smith, after another 77-mile day, I stopped at a motel to rest up for my assault on Boston Pass the next day. I even asked the lady working at the motel which road would be better to bicycle over, Highway 71 or 59. She told me they were both dangerous highways and that I probably shouldn't be on either one of them with a bicycle. When I returned from dinner, she called my room and asked if I could come see her. I walked in and she told me that there was a man staying at the motel who would give me a ride over the pass in the morning if I was interested. I said I was and she gave me his room number.

Clarence "Monkey" Beard was a big man and had been driving a semi-truck most of his life. He greeted me without a shirt on and I could see some serious scars on his chest and shoulders. He said he had room to strap my rig on his flatbed if I wanted to meet him for breakfast at 5:30 a.m.

Well the time wasn't a problem, but when I walked into the café and sat at the booth with "Monkey," I had to wonder what all the other truckers were thinking watching him have breakfast with a longhaired guy in Spandex. He didn't seem to think twice about it. In fact, over the next few hours he talked to me like he had known me forever. Monkey told me about his family and about the wreck he was involved in last year on the very pass we were going over. It wasn't his fault, but he sustained considerable injuries, thus all the scars.

Looking out the window at the poor condition of the asphalt and the grade of the climb, I was thankful to be in the truck. I could have made it on the bike, but it would not have been easy. God bless Monkey!

After Monkey dropped me off just outside of Fayetteville, I rode straight west for 21 miles on Highway 412 to the Oklahoma state line. I biked into Oklahoma, mailed Janae a postcard, and biked back into Arkansas. I picked up Highway 59 and headed north to Missouri. I stopped at a convenience store in Gravette, Ark., and Judy and Suzi wanted to know all about my journey. They also asked me if they could be in my book. I said sure but, again, I couldn't put everyone in the book that had been nice to me. Outside, I noticed I was running out of lip balm and went back in the store to purchase some. The ladies donated some to The Journey, which secured their names in the book.

Later that day I was in Missouri, state #47, the "Show Me State." I rode eighty-seven miles. I really needed to quit doing that to myself. I actually gave myself some grief for not riding another 13 miles and doing another century—I had a sick mind.

CHAPTER 30

▼

THE LAST STATE

Today I would make it into state #48, Kansas—or at least I was hoping to. I woke up to overcast skies and packed up everything preparing for rain. As I rode that morning, the sky grew darker. By the time I made it to Joplin, Mo., it was raining and before I left Webb City it was pouring. It wasn't safe for me to be on the road with all the rain and the darkness, so I looked for a place to wait out the storm. I saw a building off the road that looked abandoned, so I headed down the drive. It was a church and I pulled in under an overhang. I was standing there watching the storm and eating a snack when someone called out to me. It was the janitor and he told me I could wait inside. He didn't have time to talk to me, but he said I could stay as long as necessary. I wrote a couple of postcards and then laid down on the floor to take a nap. When I woke up it was just drizzling outside, so I thanked the janitor for his hospitality and took off.

After a while it quit raining, but it was still very dark outside. I was on Highway 171 with no shoulder, but very little traffic as well. I was rounding a bend and there was a sign with big yellow letters on a blue background—Welcome to KANSAS! It was the most beautiful sign I had ever seen. I never thought I could be so happy to be in Kansas. I crossed over the state line, stopped and patted my bike, and told *B.O.P.*, "We did it!" I saw an image in my mind of the map of the United States and the route we had taken to ride through the lower 48 states and the District of Columbia, and I began crying like I had never cried before. I was sobbing and I couldn't quit. Arriving in Kansas was a tremendous release for me and I just let my emotions drain.

A few minutes later, God began crying and His tears were pounding down on me. I pulled myself together and began riding toward Pittsburg, Kan. It was the hardest rainstorm I had ridden in the entire trip, but I didn't care because I was in state #48. All that was left was to visit some friends and then ride across Kansas. It was October 17 and I should be home by the first week in November.

For a brief moment I considered continuing on from Pittsburg, but safety was an issue with a storm of that magnitude. So I searched for a motel instead. Watching reports on TV, I realized I made a wise decision. The area was surrounded by severe thunderstorms and flood warnings.

The next couple of days I wore long underwear while I was riding. The high temperature was only 41 degrees, but the sky was clear and everything looked so beautiful. The leaves were finally changing colors and everywhere there were beautiful reds and yellows. The crisp weather reminded me of home. I felt as if I rode west for a few miles I'd be able to see the Rocky Mountains. I could feel the tug of Colorado and I was anxious to let it bring me home, just as soon as I finished visiting a few friends.

First were Tom and Wilma Arbogast in Spring Hill, Kan. Tom had been the pastor at the First Baptist Church in Pueblo, Colo., in the late 60s and the 70s. I didn't get much out of Tom's sermons back then when I was a teenager and pretty much knew everything there was to know. But now, I received new enlightenment whenever I talked with him. Tom was one of the few Christians I could talk to about my spirituality who didn't have to bring Jesus into every conversation. Tom talked to me about a place in me that needed to be filled with the Spirit of God. Of course, he hoped that filling that place with the Spirit of God would lead to my acceptance of Jesus Christ as my savior, but he allowed me just to be filled with Spirit at the moment. Tom had turned me onto books from C.S. Lewis, who had struggled with his own spirituality at one time and Henri Nowan, who had written letters to his nephew about spirituality. While I was there, Tom gave me "Tuesdays with Morrie" by Mitch Albom, a very moving book about the bond between a student and his mentor. Maybe I would have that bond with Tom someday. Tom and Wilma are loving people and my time with them was very healing. They helped me fill that place in me with the Love of God.

On Tuesday morning, Tom took me with him to the weekly Rotary Club meeting. They decided to forego their normal meeting and allowed me to talk about my 10-month odyssey. I felt very comfortable standing in front of these strangers and telling my stories. Which was something I had always dreaded before, public speaking. A few weeks earlier I had been thinking that nothing had changed in me during the trip, but now I knew that I had been wrong. I was more confident in myself, more patient, more compassionate, more understanding and less judgmental, and I was happy. I was content with who I was and what I had accomplished in my life; not just riding my bicycle around America, but having the courage to ask myself questions and trying to make myself a better person. So many times those questions led to answers that I didn't want to acknowledge. I knew that these improvements in my life would require a life-long maintenance program to hold on to them, but recognizing them was a good start.

I left the Arbogast's that afternoon and had one of the shortest rides of the trip. I biked 13 miles to Olathe, Kan., to see my good friends Buck and Sherri Arnhold.

Buck is one of the coolest guys I know. If it were 1960, Buck would be a beatnik. Unfortunately, it was 1998 and he seemed like a lost soul at times. He is a liberal thinker with a conservative appearance. In fact, most people think he looks like either Sylvester Stallone or Al Pacino. He is very good looking and has a tremendous God-given talent as an artist, with an unbelievable eye for detail. He does all of the official banners at Arrowhead Stadium for the Kansas City Chiefs promoting charities. He works as an artist and relaxes as an artist. He has a good life. I was trying to get him to grow his hair long, grow a goatee and wear torn clothes, to have that artist look. But he said he had to maintain a certain appearance for social occasions with his wife. And if the truth were known, that was why I really liked Buck, because he married Sherri.

Sherri is the most beautiful person I know—and not just physically, although she comes by her good looks honestly. Her mother, Shirley, was a beauty queen from Colorado Springs and her father, Earl, was a star athlete from Pueblo. But Sherri's beauty goes much deeper than her looks. She is so kind and compassionate. She always has a smile on her face and is always helping someone. Sherri teaches 4th graders at Heatherstone Elementary and they were having parent/teacher conferences while I was there. All of the parents, according to Sherri's colleagues and principal, just rave about her. And having spent time in her classroom, I could tell her students had a true affection for her, as well. Sherri had arranged for me to come to school the next day and talk to the 4th, 5th and 6th graders about The Journey.

I've known Sherri since early childhood. Our parents attended high school together and started families as neighbors', so all the kids grew up together. Sherri's brother was Jeff Hobbs, the young man whose funeral I attended just before leaving on my trip, whose angel I wore on my jersey everyday. As I mentioned before, Ataxia had devastated Sherri's family and I admired her strength for what she had endured. I asked Sherri if I could talk about Jeff to the students, because he was a big inspiration to me along The Journey. She said it was OK and asked if I also would write to the Ataxia Foundation to let them know what I did in Jeff's memory. We talked a bit more about what I would say and I went to bed that night with some apprehension and much excitement.

The next morning I showed up at the school around 10 a.m. I was a bit nervous. Talking to a group of businesspeople at the Rotary Club was one thing. I knew their limits and attention span, but talking to a group of kids…

The kids were great! We were in an auditorium with several hundred people and they were as quiet and polite as could be. But what really impressed me were the questions they asked after I finished. Not "Were you scared?" or "Were you tired?" They asked questions like: "What was your motivation for the journey?" or "How did you handle riding through big cities?" The assembly could not have gone any better. Afterwards, Mhari Doyle from The Kansas City Star interviewed me for an article in the paper. I ended up having lunch with the kids in the cafeteria and spending some time with them at recess. Sherri also invited me back to her classroom and her students read to me what they had written in their journals that morning about the challenges of riding a bicycle around America. They wrote before the assembly so that what I had to say wouldn't influence their thinking. Hearing them talk about food, water, hills, going to the bathroom and getting lonely—everything I had encountered, provided some good laughs.

As I rode away from the school that afternoon I knew this was the highlight of my trip. Then I thought, "This is one of the highlights of my *life!*" These children were so open and honest, with so much energy. They were like a sponge absorbing my stories and then a waterfall flowing with questions. It was so refreshing. I wondered, "When do we lose that absorbing and flowing? When do we begin to shut down being open and honest? Can we ever get back to being that way, so innocent and free?"

Besides all of Sherri's great attributes, she is also one hell of a cook. She fattened me up for several nights, but Buck and I gave her a break when she was working on the student evaluations for parent/teacher conferences. We went out for some Kansas City barbecue and the blues. We found both at BB's Lawnside BBQ. The absolute best, barbecued ribs I have ever had in my life, with the sounds of John Paul and The Flying Circus. It was a special night with Buck; sucking those bones clean and enjoying the blues.

On my last day with the Arnholds, we went downtown to meet up with Eric Peterson, his wife, Shannon, and their new little boy, Evin. Eric used to work for me at Keystone and now owned The Delaware Market Cafe in Kansas City. A few years earlier I had one of the best ski days of my life with Eric in Alta, Utah. There were 36 inches of new snow in three days and we skied every shoot in bounds at Alta, and a few that weren't. It was good seeing Eric again and especially good seeing him working hard with his new business and family.

The next morning was one of the toughest mornings of The Journey. It felt similar to the very first morning when I began in Texas. I absolutely did not want to get on that bicycle and I did not want to leave the Arnholds. They made me feel so comfortable. I wanted to be around Buck. We enjoyed a lot of the same things (except the wagon pull at the Stock Show) and he was so easy to talk with. Sherri was just a joy to be around and I was going to miss her energy. They came outside while I loaded up the bike and trailer. We talked, took pictures, and just kidded around with each other. We said our good-byes while I got on the bike, and then I rode away in pain. It wasn't located anywhere, it was like the feeling you have with a fender bender in your first car; you're not injured, but you wished it hadn't happened. I didn't want to leave my friends, but I had to get back to Colorado. I turned around one last time, threw them the peace sign, and rode away hurting.

The past few days had been some of the best of the entire trip. The Arbogasts, the Arnholds, the Petersons, the kids and staff at Heatherstone Elementary had all made me feel so special. Unfortunately, it had a feeling of wrapping up The Journey and now I was having a hard time gearing up to ride my bicycle another 800 miles. To make matters worse, there was a

wind coming straight out of the south and I was heading southwest coming out of Olathe.

The wind continued out of the south for the next four days, picking up
in intensity each day. I've talked about the strain of holding up the bike in
the wind, but at this point in The Journey, everything was magnified. It
felt as though I had exposed nerves in my hands and feet at the end of the
day and the wind was requiring that I hold on to the bicycle with both
hands. I just had to keep telling myself; 10 more days, nine more days,
eight more days,…

On the fifth day, I woke up to something different; the wind was coming out of the north. But it wasn't blowing that day, it was howling. I
couldn't believe it! This couldn't be happening! I was heading north that
day on Highway 183 to visit some good friends in Hays, Kan. I now knew
that "biking gods" did exist and they were intent on making this final leg
of The Journey a real challenge.

My biggest challenge that day, however, wasn't the wind or traffic or
pain, it was finding a place to relieve myself. I had diarrhea and I was in
the middle of nowhere. Trying to get out-of-sight on the plains of Kansas
is the ultimate test. I was flunking the test, but I gave myself an A for
effort.

It was 4 p.m. on October 29. There were only 15 miles to go to Hays,
but at 8 mph, it would take another two hours. The sun was setting
around 6 p.m., so I was just going to make it. As I was rolling through
Liebenthal, Kan., a spoke popped on the rear wheel, non-drive side. I
pulled over next to a fence surrounding the church in town and replaced
the spoke. But before the wheel was back on, the tire went flat. This was
the second time that had happened. The tape that goes around the wheel
to protect the tube from the spoke nipples was completely worn out. I had
to tear off ¼-inch strips of duct tape to line the wheel. After fixing the flat
I headed out of town knowing I might be arriving in Hays after dark.

Just a couple miles out of town, I heard a strange noise coming from
the trailer. At first I thought it was the wind rattling something around,

but then I noticed the trailer wasn't tracking correctly. Upon stopping, I found out the tire on the trailer was flat. I fixed the flat and prepared to ride when I discovered the front tire on the bike was flat. Unbelievable, I must have ridden through a sticker patch back in Liebenthal. I didn't curse or cry, even though I felt like it. I just grinned and had a conversation with the "biking gods." I wasn't looking for favors, but I didn't need this aggravation either. Looking down at the angel on my jersey, I felt Jeff, Steve and Shirley smiling at me. In fact, they were laughing at me because I was ONLY dealing with a flat tire!

As I was repairing the flat, a Kansas state trooper drove by. I jumped up and flagged her down in the rear view mirror. I was surprised she didn't initially stop, but was glad she saw me waving. She gave me some kind of lame excuse that she thought I looked "OK" on the side of the road. I think she was on her way home for dinner! Anyway, she let me use her phone and I called my friend Greg Hobbs to come pick me up. I was done, through, defeated. I gave up. I could have taken more, but I didn't want to. The road, weather and "biking gods" had won. I lost and I accepted my defeat. I didn't care. I was tired, very tired.

When I first made it to Kansas, my mother suggested I could fly home from Kansas City. I had made it through all 48 states, so I was done. I politely refused because I wanted to BIKE home. Now, at that moment, I was looking for an airport. But here came my friend, Greg, to the rescue.

Greg is Sherri's younger brother. He too had been through a lot in his life dealing with the deaths of his grandmother, mother and two older brothers. Like Sherri, Greg was good looking and had a contagious laugh. Greg reminded me so much of his Dad. He was a good athlete and he loved to fish. When I was a kid, I remember being at a lake fishing with Earl, Greg's Dad. No one else was catching any fish, but every once in a while you would hear this giggle down the bank, and Earl was hauling in another fish. I never saw a better fisherman in my life, but I was thinking Greg could probably give him a pretty good run.

I spent three days in Hays. It rained most of the time I was there, which was fine with me. I had a roof over my head and I got to spend Halloween with the Hobbs. I noticed the kids had inherited their father's athletic ability. I watched Dustin play basketball, Brook play volleyball, and Summer bounce off the walls at home. Chris, Greg's beautiful wife, took me to church, fed me tons of food, and generally made me feel comfortable. Chris and Greg were the perfect hosts and I enjoyed my time there.

It had been almost one year since I had been in Hays for Jeff's funeral. I took one afternoon to go visit his gravesite. While I was there, I placed my mojo, a good luck charm, I had been carrying on my bicycle next to Jeff's headstone. I said a little prayer and thanked him for accompanying me on The Journey. I thought about everything I had experienced the past nine months. As a tear began running down my cheek, I heard Jeff, clear as a bell laughing out loud.

When I woke up Monday morning it was dark and dreary outside. Sheets of rain were coming down and I could not get psyched up to begin riding. Chris offered to have Greg give me a ride to Scott City, Kan., that night when he got off work. They were reluctant to ask because they thought it might offend me. At that point I would have taken a ride home.

It was still raining that evening when we loaded up *B.O.P.* and *B.O.B.* into the truck and headed off for Scott City. Greg and I were able to spend a couple of quality hours together talking about life. We were both a lot more spiritual than when we hung out together as kids and I really enjoyed being able to talk with him on a different level from in the past. This time with my friends helped fuel me for the next and final leg of The Journey.

The next morning was cold, gray and dry—my kind of weather. I went down the street to have breakfast at the local café before I took off. Because of all the wet weather the past four days, the café was full of local farmers. The ground was too wet to farm, so they were all just hanging out. I'm not the normal sight a farmer in Kansas is expecting to see in

November, especially first thing in the morning. When I walked in, everyone looked at me, but no one said anything. I sat down at the counter and, a moment later, was joined by the last farmer to meet with the group. They were a rowdy bunch and everything was funny to them, especially stories about President Clinton. Pretty soon, Tom Graham, the farmer next to me, began asking me questions about what I was doing. He was the only one who had seen my bike and trailer, as he was the last to arrive at the café. When I told him I had just biked through all the lower 48 states and the District of Columbia, he seemed impressed. He began yelling at the rest of the group to go outside and look at my bike. They began asking all kinds of questions and giving me leftover food off their plates. I thought how easy it would have been for them to make fun of me and instead, they were feeding me and offering me encouragement and congratulations. What a great way to start the day.It was more fuel for my journey home.

I was no longer wearing my long-fingered biking gloves while riding; I had pulled out my ski gloves and ski hat. The high temperature that day was 39 degrees, but I didn't care, I thought it felt great. I was in the flat lands of Kansas and loving it. I stopped in Leoti, Kan., for a huge buffet lunch. I was only riding 46 miles that day, but eating like I was going twice that distance. Actually, I was treating myself because I had entered the Mountain Time Zone—Yahoo!

I didn't know if I was numb from the cold or because I was almost home.

CHAPTER 31

▼

HOME

I spent my last night in Kansas at the Thunderbird Motel in Tribune. The owner, Ann, was very kind to me. She had dealt with plenty of bikers over the last 22 years, as Highway 96 was part of the Bi-Centennial bike tour and people still used that route when crossing the continent. She told me, however, she had never had someone ride through in November!

The next morning I went to the local V.F.W. and had some pancakes before I took off for Colorado, 16 miles away. My good friends, Chuey and Lupe', were supposed to meet me somewhere along the road either that day or the next. I hadn't talked to them in the last few days, so I wasn't crystal clear on the plan, but I was hoping they might be at the state line.

The weather was the same as the day before, so I began pedaling to generate some body heat. Before I knew it, I was at the Colorado state line. I stopped and stared at the sign welcoming me to "Colorful Colorado." My emotions were not comparable to when I made it into Kansas. I was just proud of myself for actually doing this. Riding through 48 states and

Washington, D.C., I was always proud to tell people I was from Colorado and now I was happy to be back. I kissed the ground and headed for home.

Three miles inside the state line is the town of Towner, Colo. I thought my friends might be waiting for me there in a little café. I figured it was too cold to be waiting outside and that was why they weren't at the state line. But there was no sign of them at Towner either, so I kept pedaling.

Out of nowhere, a pickup pulled in front of me and there were Chuey, Lupe' and Lupe's wife, Sally. I dropped my bike to the ground and began hugging all three of them. I tried to tell them how much I missed them and how very glad I was to see them, but nothing came out. My eyes were full of tears and it felt as though those cotton fields in Louisiana were growing in my mouth. So I just kept hugging them.

Their plan was to ride with me that day to Eads, the next day to Ordway, and Chuey would ride the final day with me into Pueblo. Lupe' and Sally had previous plans for the last day. They would take turns riding, while someone drove the truck and I took the opportunity to unhitch the trailer and put it in the truck, as well.

There was almost no traffic, so we were able to ride three abreast and catch up on 10 months' worth of news. Lupe' was 47 years old and had just retired, something he had threatened to do for the past couple of years. He had run a water-engineering firm in Denver for over 20 years. He was joining the ranks of the retired, with Chuey and me. Chuey had retired the year before, moving back to Colorado after working in Africa for several years. Neither one of them had done much riding this year, which shocked me, but they were both big-time cyclists and had done cross-country trips, so I wasn't worried. In fact, I appreciated having them along because they would understand some of the events I had experienced over the past year. We talked so much I was surprised when we rolled into Eads in the early afternoon.

We secured a motel room, took a shower, and went across the street to have a beer and celebrate our reunion. We were sitting around telling stories when the entire bar became quiet at 4 p.m. The television set was on and everyone, including old-timers and the bartender, watched Northern Exposure. I hadn't been in many bars recently, but I couldn't ever recall witnessing something like this in the past. Maybe this was something new or maybe they just did this in Eads, Colo. When in Rome…—we watched right along with them. All of a sudden it seemed the program had been turned on for my benefit. Chris, the philosophical disc jockey on the show, was preparing a winter light show for the entire town. He talked to everyone about how important it was to pay attention to the voice inside, the Spirit that guides us. He told them to follow their dreams, to set their goals high and to reach for the stars. He then proceeded to light up the dark Alaskan sky, while the town stood there contemplating the Universe and their place or purpose in it. I was sure that Chris was talking directly to me, that he was welcoming me home and congratulating me for accomplishing my goal. I looked around the bar half expecting to see clocks on the walls bending over because the whole scene was so surreal. I thought maybe I was in a Salvador Dali painting.

The clocks remained fastened to the walls and everyone went back to what they were doing before the show started. I accepted that I wasn't in a Dali painting, but I wasn't so sure I wasn't in a dream. And if I wasn't dreaming, reality was going to be more of an adjustment than expected.

We went out for some Mexican food that night, but it still didn't meet my expectations. I couldn't wait to get back to Pueblo for some chili rellenos at The Mill Stop. Vicky had turned me on to their food before I left on The Journey and I had yet to find any Mexican food that compared, and I had been all the way around America. That would have to be a top priority after I made it home.

We woke up to some serious fog, so we took our time getting ready and eating breakfast. We only had 61 miles to ride, so there was no big hurry to get started. Sixty-one miles, without pulling a trailer and while riding with friends, was a piece of cake. I enjoyed every single mile of the ride;

the sun came out, we saw flocks of Canadian geese, Snow geese, and sand-hill cranes, and we told lots of stories. We made it to the Ordway Hotel by 3 p.m. and Marilyn, the owner, welcomed us with open arms. We asked her if there were televisions in our rooms because we wanted to get cleaned up and watch Northern Exposure.

That night we went out to dinner to celebrate Lupe's and Sally's wedding anniversary—plus, my parents, my sister, Vicky, and my grandmother, Helen Merrell all drove down from Pueblo to have dinner with us. For some reason I wasn't very emotional when they showed up at the restaurant, but I sure did enjoy sitting at the table watching and listening to my family and good friends.

Later that night, my uncle, J.W. and his wife, Alex, showed up at the hotel. They were going to ride part of the way with Chuey and me the next day. We all got together for breakfast and then were joined by Duane and Jeanette Flory, the couple I stayed with in Tucson. Duane was going to ride the final 50-mile day with us, while Jeanette drove the sag wagon.

This was it! My final day of loading up the bike and trailer, of fighting the wind, asphalt, and traffic, of blood, sweat and tears. But it was also the final day of meeting new people, seeing new places, and spending my days with the birds, wildlife and Nature. I had a lot of mixed feelings.

It was an absolutely beautiful morning, with white snow geese con-trasted against the blue Colorado sky. Nothing against Carolina Blue, but Colorado Blue is deep, dark and absorbing. And I was absorbing every-thing that was going on around me on my final day. One thing I noticed was that everyone seemed a bit nervous preparing to leave, while I was extremely calm. I found out later they were intimidated to be riding with me, concerned with keeping up. Weren't they paying attention? I had 100 pounds of "stuff" in tow.

We took off into a building wind out of the northwest and we were rid-ing due west. I wouldn't have had it any other way. Thirty miles down the road we were riding into Boone, Colo. There was a girl I liked in high school that used to live in Boone and for some reason I was hoping she was going to be out by the road welcoming me home—I was delusional. Instead, there was my sister's pickup with Sherri, Buck and their son, Paul. They had driven out from Olathe, Kan., to welcome me home and Buck and Paul where going to ride the last 20 miles on bicycles. It was so good to see them again and it really warmed my heart.

Another 12 miles and we were pulling into the parking lot of Fujita's Restaurant. The restaurant had been run for years by the parents of Hideo, my old college roommate, but now was owned and operated by his sister, Paula. She was outside along with some more of my family and friends to welcome me back to Pueblo. This would be my final staging area before making it home. I stopped and talked with everyone and picked up two more riders; Sonny and Janae were going to ride the last eight miles.

All of a sudden everything changed: the wind was now at our backs, I had absolutely no pain anywhere on my body, and I was the only one looking nervous. A mile from town we stopped. Chuey suggested that I wait a minute while the rest of them rode into town so I could make a grand entrance.

They all took off and I stood there over my bicycle watching them leave me, while the moment surrounded me. I also was surrounded by the most beautiful scenery anywhere on earth; the majestic Pikes Peak was to the north, the Green Mountain Range was in front of me, the mysterious Spanish Peaks were to the south, and the prairie lands were behind me. What a panoramic view!

I had just spent the last 10 months riding my bike 11,800 miles. I still didn't know how I did it, but I had. What an unbelievable journey. I tried to imagine how I was going to feel in a few moments when I saw everyone again. What were my emotions going to be? Would I laugh or cry? I finally decided to quit trying to figure it out and just experience it.

Everyone was waiting in the parking lot at my sister's chiropractic office. As I was coming up the hill I saw a photographer from the newspaper snapping pictures of me. At the top of the hill, I saw my family and friends. I had a huge smile on my face and flashed them all the peace sign.

I was at a major intersection and had to pay attention to the traffic. I thought how awful to go all this way and then...

I turned into the parking lot and the only voice I heard was my mother's. I dropped my rig to the ground and ran over to hug her. We were both crying and I told her, "How appropriate this is to end The Journey the same way it began, with tears."

I was home!

Afterword

The parking lot was full of family and friends. Buck had created a couple of posters welcoming me home. Dusty and Melva presented me with the largest can of cashews I've ever seen. And there were a couple of bottles of champagne.

Gayle Perez, from the Pueblo Chieftain, was there to interview me for an article in Sunday's paper. I told her how happy I was to be home, about some of the highlights of The Journey, and about seven things I was looking forward to.

First, I wanted to eat some of my mother's home cooking and then watch a Broncos' game with my father. I wanted to ride my bike on Monday without all my "stuff" on it and go to The Mill Stop for the best chili rellenos in America.

I told her I had plans to write a book, build a house, and then hike the Continental Divide from Mexico to Canada.

We all went back to my parents' house to celebrate. Besides my family and close friends, there were friends I hadn't seen in a long time and people I didn't even know—all congratulating me on my accomplishment.

I was experiencing my 15 minutes of fame. I knew it was fleeting, so I was trying to soak it all in. But there was a strange disconnection associated with the moment. I remember watching athletes being interviewed after winning a big championship and saying, "It really hasn't sunk in yet." I always thought, "What are you talking about, it hasn't sunk in yet? You've just won a world championship!" But now I knew the feeling and I couldn't explain it to anyone.

I knew what it felt like to hit the game winning homerun in the bottom of the ninth inning in the seventh game of the World Series, to make the winning basket in the seventh game of the NBA Finals, or to score the winning touchdown in the Super Bowl.

I had won!

ABOUT THE AUTHOR

Monte is currently living at 9,900 feet in a little cabin in the old mining town of Fairplay, Colorado where he is finishing up work on a children's book with artist, Buck Arnhold, called Spanky and the Pork 'n' Bean Can.

He is also working on plans to hike the Continental Divide from Mexico to Canada, currently scheduled for his 50th birthday…in two years. But presently, he is spending time with his family and friends and hanging out with his cat, Adrienne. He has cut his bike riding down to 200—300 miles per week.

If you are ever touring through Fairplay (it's on the '76 Bi-centennial bike route), be sure to give Monte a call. He always has some beer and nuts on hand, plenty of room to spend the night, and a few tales to share about touring. (719-836-4523) or *bike48@msn.com*